Promise of Spring

T.K. Conklin

Promise of Spring

© 2019 by T. K. Conklin

Cover design by Melody Simmons

Butterfly Shadow Publishing

PO Box 182 Buffalo, Wyoming 82834

First Printing: December 2019

ISBN: 978-0-9986983-5-9

Published in the United States of America

FOR ED
THANK YOU FOR YOUR ENCOURAGEMENT
SO MANY YEARS AGO AND PUSHING ME TO
CHASE MY DREAMS.

Chapter One

Wyoming Territory, 1839

True Tucker stood on the hard-packed dirt before a log building that served as the trading post. She glanced at her travel trunk that sat in the dust beside her and clutched the handle of her carpet bag tightly in her hands before she lifted her dark eyes to watch the wagon train pass by. She waved at the many friends she had made on her journey this far and wished them prosperity. Weeks of travel with them had proved they were a determined group of people and she knew they'd make it to Oregon, weather permitting as winter was close.

The cool wind plucked fussily at her blond hair where it had come loose of the long braid hanging down her back and she brushed strands from her face as she looked around the tiny settlement. The farther west she went the more primitive things had become. She was almost afraid to see what Rimrock, her final destination, was going to be like. And though she knew it would be far different than Charlotte, her hometown, she wasn't prepared for or expecting such isolation. This part of the country was unsettled and untamed, but the reality of it shocked her. She hadn't been in such uncivilized country since she had been a ten-year-old waif. Now at twenty, she lived in a beautiful city with every luxury she could want.

"Life certainly does change," she muttered to herself as she looked around.

The few buildings were little more than shacks, and several canvas tents were set up. People here wore simple clothes, with most of the men covered in furs and buckskins. Many stopped to stare at her and the burgundy dress she wore, which was the latest fashion, as was her fine coat. She soon felt like a sideshow attraction.

True thought of the reason for her trip to the untamed land and a small smile tugged her mouth. For the past year she had been receiving letters from her two sisters, neither of which she had seen in over four years, and the news that she would soon be an aunt had made her long to be with her family again. She would spend the winter with Joanna and Shyfawn before returning to Charlotte and to their Aunt Molly's in the spring.

This was the final leg of her journey, all she had to do was meet a man with a freight wagon heading to Rimrock and she would be on her way again. She sighed as she looked around. *Where do I find him?* She looked at her trunk, she didn't want to leave it while she went into the trading post to ask where to look for a freight wagon but she wasn't strong enough to lift it and take it along.

Minutes passed as she contemplated her

dilemma when a man emerged from the trading post and walked toward her. He wore dirty buckskins, a fur hat and his build was lean. A thick beard covered his face, but he appeared to be in his early thirties. Her fingers tightened on the handle of her carpet bag as she held it close and waited.

"Good morning, ma'am," he said as he stepped up to her and removed his hat to reveal shaggy blond hair. "Are you Miss Tucker?"

True nodded "Yes, I am. Are you Toby?"

He smiled at her, showing tobacco-stained teeth, and nodded. "I sure am. I'm here to fetch you to Rimrock."

"It's nice to meet you, Toby," True said with a forced smile and offering her hand. *Just what kind of man had her sisters sent to get her?*

Toby hesitantly took her hand, gave it an awkward shake, then released it and put his hat back on. "I'm ready to leave now, if you are," he said, as he scratched at his beard with dirty fingernails.

She nodded. "Yes, I'm ready."

"Follow me." He stooped to pick up the trunk beside her, grunting at the weight but easily carrying it around to the back of the trading post.

True followed a pace behind, and rounding the log building, saw a wagon loaded down with supplies and six mules harnessed to it. Without a word, Toby hoisted her trunk into the back of the wagon, then held a hand out for her carpet bag, which also was tossed into the wagon.

Waving her toward the seat, Toby waited while she gathered her skirts and put one foot on the wheel axle, ready to hoist herself up onto the seat.

Suddenly, Toby's hands were on her waist helping her up. True sat to the far left of the wooden bench seat as Toby climbed up and sat beside her. Then, taking up the reins, he slapped them on the mule's backs and the wagon lurched forward.

True let out a long breath as the last leg of her journey began, letting her mind slowly fill with her sister's letters of how happy they were and how much they loved their new lives and husbands. Husbands that loved them for who they were, and not because of social standing or bloodlines.

She thought of her fiancé, Steven, who she knew loved her, but did he love her enough to accept who she really was? Did she trust Steven enough to tell him the truth? He was a good man and could provide all the extravagances of the life she was accustomed to. Extravagances she would never find out west. She had lived in poverty once and vowed never to do so again.

Heaving a deep sigh, True shifted on the seat and closed her eyes, letting the cool breeze wash over her face. She returned to thoughts of her life and of her sisters, and how much they would have to talk about. She planned to spend all winter with her family and knew it would break her heart to go back to Charlotte in the spring. She shifted again to ease her aching bottom, almost wincing. She thought of the weeks of traveling by train, then wagon, and now by freight wagon. She wasn't looking forward to the long trip back.

***

The next two days passed quickly, as the wagon raddled down the rutted path Toby called a road. She found her traveling companion to be somewhat uncivilized, but he treated her with respect and was very thoughtful. Obviously, her sisters trusted the man or they never would have allowed him to be alone with her, especially Joanna. Steven would be horrified if he knew she had spent two nights alone with Toby.

Steven...

True sighed, he had proposed months ago, and it had been quite a shock. She had never thought of marriage, never even wanted to get married. But Aunt Molly had pushed her to accept, wanting to see her niece married to a man of position and from a good family. True had always heard that bloodlines were very important in high society, it gave a person power and respect.

Bloodlines. True almost laughed out loud. What a joke. What would Steven and his family say if they found out about her *real* bloodlines?

Aunt Molly had been passing off True and her sister, Shyfawn, as the daughters of an English Duchess. Molly claimed True's mother had married a wealthy Duke from England, but the couple had been killed in a terrible accident when True and Shyfawn were young. This tragedy brought the two girls to Molly, who insisted on raising them in Charlotte. She also told everyone that their older sister, Joanna, had gone to study abroad in Europe. A bald-faced lie. But for the past ten years, nobody in Molly's circle of society friends in Charlotte had questioned the story.

So far, the masquerade had held as truth, but what would Steven do if he ever found out where

True and her family had come from? Or the special gifts the women of the Tucker family possessed. No doubt he would cast her aside and look for a new bride. She sighed and tried to get the familiar tension to leave her mind and body.

All the more reason to leave Charlotte and head west to visit her sisters, she needed time to relax and be with her family. They were both happily married and living in Rimrock. Maybe she would like the little town and decide to stay. Even as the thought surfaced, she pushed it down. She couldn't leave everything she knew for the unknown. Yet she desperately longed to be with her sisters again.

True looked forward to sleeping in a soft bed again and getting rid of the aching kinks in her back sleeping on the cold lumpy ground had caused. She also longed for female conversation. Though Toby could be interesting and she enjoyed his stories, no matter how exaggerated they might be, she wanted the comfort of a soft sofa and a fragrantly steaming cup of tea while chatting with her sisters. Toby had offered the whisky he took a pull from a few times a day to ease her aches and pains, but she chose to decline. The brown liquid smelled rank and burned her nose whenever she got a good whiff of it.

Her journey west had been filled with hardships far more uncomfortable than she had been expecting. She was no stranger to the unpleasantries of life, but the past ten years had been easy for her. Those years of being pampered and waited on had made her forget the hardships of surviving in the frontier. And she definitely preferred city life.

So, no matter what she had endured or might

endure, she would spend the winter with her sisters in their small frontier town, and then return to Charlotte and the life she loved.

"We'll make camp soon," Toby assured her when he saw her shift uncomfortably on the seat.

She gave him a smile of appreciation and said thank you, then pulled her coat tighter. "Is it always like this in October?"

He shrugged. "Sometimes. Usually the snow comes later, but this year we got a couple early storms."

She let out a long breath. "I should have come earlier in the year."

Toby nodded in agreement before he spit a stream of tobacco onto the ground. "Might have been a more pleasant journey for you."

True smiled and let her eyes move over the land around her. They had gone from open windswept plains and were now among the trees at the base of the mountains. It was colder here and large patches of snow covered the ground. Her eyes lifted to the sky, she hoped there would be no more snow until she made it safely to Rimrock. The overcast sky and chilled air dashed her hopes.

True fell back into silence as thoughts of the past months crowded into her mind. She had told Steven of her plan to visit her sisters; and though he hadn't been too pleased with the idea, he hadn't forbidden it. He had, however, come up with many reasons to postpone her trip with business dinners, social functions, and their engagement party.

When it came time for her to leave, she had no trouble until St. Joe. Finding a wagon train to travel with had been a little difficult because it was so late in the travel season, but she had managed. After that, she had found Toby and her journey had continued.

"I just hope going back in the spring will be easier and warmer."

Toby chuckled. "It'll be wet. Spring rain in this country comes hard and fast most of the time. And it's a cold rain."

True groaned but smiled at the humor in his voice. "Something to look forward to."

They talked idly for the next few hours before he pulled the team to a stop at the edge of the trees. She was glad for the day's travel to be over, her body hurt, and she needed to stretch her legs. Toby helped her down and it took her a moment to get her stiff muscles to cooperate. She didn't miss Toby's soft chuckle at her hobbling efforts and shot him a frown, but it was wasted, as he was busy unhitching the mules.

"I'll be right back, Toby." She didn't wait to see if he had heard her and walked into the trees and snow to find a place to relieve herself. When she was finished, she took a walk through the trees, enjoying the peace and quiet. It had been so long since she had been in untamed country. It brought back old memories – memories she would rather forget.

When she and Shyfawn had arrived at their aunt's in Charlotte, they were about as backward and uncivilized as anyone could be. Molly had hired tutors to educate them in the proper ways of society before introducing them to her circle of wealthy friends.

"Molly taught us a lot," she said softly to the trees as she walked through them.

The peace was suddenly broken by a gunshot. True cried out in alarm. It had come from the direction of the freight wagon.

She ran back the way she had come and when the wagon came into sight, True hunkered down behind a tree.

Two men stood by the fire with Toby. They held their guns on him as he held his arms out from his sides. Two horses, saddled and bridled, were tied with the mules a small distance away from the freight wagon.

"Just take what you want and go," Toby ordered sharply.

One laughed. "We will," he said, and pulled the trigger of his pistol.

True slapped a hand to her mouth to hold in her scream as she watched Toby fall backward, blood splashing across the nearby snow as he fell onto the ground. He lay still.

Jesus, they killed Toby.

She watched in horror as the two men casually sat at the fire and ate the meal Toby had prepared.

Who are these heartless bastards?

True tried to calm her rising panic. Toby was dead and she had to get away before those men found her and killed her, too. She wouldn't make it far on foot.

I have to get to their horses.

Taking a deep breath, she watched the men finish their meal. They tossed down the plates and went to the wagon and began rummaging through the freight. They were distracted. Now was her chance to get to the horses.

Very quietly, True eased her way through the trees and toward where the mules and horses were tied. Carefully stepping over a log and walking up to the animals, she spoke softly to them as she gathered the reins in her hands. Mounting one horse and leading the other, she prayed they would stay quiet as she moved them away from the camp.

"Hey, stop!" a man shouted.

True kicked the horse into a gallop, away from the camp. She hadn't been on a horse in years and held on for dear life as she turned the animal into the trees for cover. She heard gunfire and waited for a bullet to strike her but, much to her relief, none did. As the sound the two horses hooves pounded through the trees, the shouts and gunfire soon stopped, and she knew she was out of danger – for now. The mules weren't broke to ride, and the men couldn't catch her on foot.

When True felt she was a safe distance away from the camp, she slowed her horse to a walk and tried to think. She had no idea which way to go. She didn't know this country and the darkness of night was creeping in on her, so she couldn't pinpoint any landmarks to ride toward. With a sigh, she gave the horse his head and let him guide the way.

"It's up to you, boy," she told him quietly. "Take me someplace good."

True looked up at the sky. Tiny snowflakes were falling.

I made it across the country and within a day of

reaching my sisters only to be lost in the forest and likely freeze to death. Steven was right. She should have stayed in Charlotte where she was safe.

"I should have listened to him," she told the horse, who only blew through his nose and tossed his head. "I was foolish to think I could come this far on my own." She felt tears fill her eyes and blinked them back. Then, she took a deep breath and straightened her spine. Feeling sorry for herself wasn't going to help. The women in her family were fighters, and by God, she was going to get through this. She would find help and she would find her sisters no matter how long it took.

Tears overflowed as she thought of Toby, the image of him lying bloody in the snow filled her mind. Toby had been a kind man and she considered him a friend, now he was dead. *Why didn't I see it? Why didn't I have a vision?* Her *gift* had once again failed her and Toby had paid the ultimate price.

"Joanna was right, we don't have gifts. We are cursed," she told the horses, her voice trembling with emotion. "I'm cursed with visions I don't want to see. Visions of what I can't change."

True sniffed and wiped at her cheeks, crying wasn't going to help her any and she had to keep strong. She would silently grieve for Toby and once she arrived in Rimrock, she would be sure that someone went back for Toby's body. He deserved a proper burial.

"What's that?" She pulled the horse to a stop and listened. "Running water."

Urging her horse toward the sound, True found

a swiftly-flowing creek. She smiled and headed her horse along the creek bank. Where there was water, there was usually civilization. She would follow the creek until she found help.

Things were looking up.

The snow began to fall steadily, and the wind picked up. She shivered and pulled the horse to a halt. She urged the horse she was leading closer, remembering seeing a coat strapped to the back of the saddle with the bedroll. Somehow, she managed to get her cold fingers to work the ties free. She slid the big coat on and buttoned it. It was made for cold weather and she was glad to have it, even if it did smell like something had died in it recently.

Chapter Two

By sunrise, True was barely able to keep herself in the saddle. The air was cold and the snow was growing heavier. She had stopped shivering long ago and she wasn't sure if that was a good sign or not. She was drifting in and out of sleep as she rode and when she woke, she was thankful that the horse was still following the creek. Her heart jumped then, as she realized her mistake, she had been riding upstream, not downstream. She was going up into the mountains.

"Maybe somebody lives around here," she said to her horse, needing to share a hopeful thought. Then added wearily, "We better keep looking."

She had no doubt her horse was just as exhausted as she was. She knew she should have changed mounts hours ago and given him a rest, but she was afraid if she dismounted, she would never be able to mount again. Her muscles were stiff and she could hardly move for the cold that penetrated her. She must find help soon and get warm again. If she didn't, she would die.

True closed her eyes and let the steady sway of the horse rock her. She refused to die out here in the middle of nowhere, where nobody would find her. And she was damned if she'd let the wolves eat her.

She shuddered at the thought and tried to get her cold fingers to tighten on the reins, but she could no longer feel them. She tried to wiggle her toes, but she had lost feeling in them long ago. *Do I even still have toes? What if they snapped off my foot and are just rolling around in my boots?* She tried not to think about that.

She let out a surprised cry as lights burst behind her eyes and images rushed into her mind. The unexpected sound startled her horse and she instinctively tightened her muscles as he jerked beneath her. Pain shot through her cold body at the movement. The images in her mind were clear. She saw snowflakes, big fluffy snowflakes. There was a little girl dressed in furs with her head tipped back, trying to catch the snowflakes on her tongue. A black dog was running around her, barking happily. Then a snowball hit her in the stomach, knocking her on her rear. She got up and made a snowball, as best she could, and threw it at a tall man also dressed in fur. Another man, similar to the first, joined in the play. The two men bombarded each other with snowballs, then began to wrestle. The dog leapt around them, barking at the excitement.

The little girl played happily by the creek, where she began throwing snow into the open water, watching it melt and disappear as the water swirled it away. She reached down to get more snow and her foot slipped, and she fell into the ice cold water. Her head went under as the current swept her away, her head came up once, then disappeared again and didn't come back up.

True's head jerked up and she gasped for

breath. Her sudden movement startled her horse and she nearly fell from the saddle. She did her best to calm him as her tired eyes scanned the creek bank. She didn't see a girl, dog, or men anywhere. Was she so cold that her visions were scrambled? Was she on the verge of death and was seeing the deaths of others? She tried to calm her racing heart and urged her horse to keep moving. If she was having a vision, it meant people were close and she had to find them before she froze to death.

"Steven was right, I never should have come here," she told the horse and felt tears burn her eyes. "I'll never see him again."

True let her mind drift back to Charlotte and her fiancé, Steven Edwards Jr., a fine man from a good family with a successful business. He was charming and handsome with his bright blue eyes and blond hair, and he always dressed in the latest fashion. He was wealthy and had promised to provide her everything she could ever want when they were married. He had been courting her for the last two years and had finally asked her to marry him a few months ago. He hadn't been pleased at her announcement of spending the winter with her sisters.

"I wish you'd reconsider," Steven said, as he sat beside her on the sofa in her Aunt Molly's lavishly decorated parlor. "It's such a long way to travel."

True gave him a reassuring smile. "Steven, I'll be fine. I know it's a long way, but I want to see my sisters. I haven't seen them in years."

"I don't like it," he told her. "You shouldn't go

alone; it could be dangerous."

"Don't worry about me. I'll stay with Aunt Molly's friends along the way," she said, trying to ease his mind. "My sister Shyfawn has a friend in St. Louis that will meet me at the train station while I'm there. I won't always be alone."

"Maybe I should go with you," he offered.

True sighed. "Steven you can't be away from your business for that long. I'll be gone for months." Truth was, she needed time away from him and time to think about what she really wanted.

He took a calming breath. "I don't like the idea of you spending the winter there. It will be cold."

She gave him a smile. "And I'll be warm and snug in my sister's house the entire time."

"But you'll be there all winter," he protested.

"Shyfawn is going to have her baby soon and I want to be there," she said, unable to hide her growing irritation with Steven. "She'll need help after the birth and I want to be there to help."

"She has a husband to help," he practically snapped at her. "She'll be fine without you."

She gave him a hard look. "I'm going and nothing you say will change my mind."

"We are to be married next summer and I don't like the idea of my future wife running off to Indian country to play nursemaid," he said and got to his feet.

"We're not married yet and I'll do as I please," she informed him. "Your family lives here and you see them all the time. Mine lives half-way across the country and I haven't seen them in years. I'm going, married or not."

Steven took a deep breath and turned to her. "I'm sorry, True. I'm just worried something might happen to you." He sat beside her again and took her hand in his. "I love you and I want you safe."

She gave him a small smile. "I'll be fine, Steven. I'll be back before you know it."

"It's going to feel like years instead of months," he said, patting her hand. "You can't get back soon enough. While you're gone, I will make arrangements for the wedding. You will be back in May and we'll marry in June."

True managed a smile, but the idea of getting married so soon after her return was a little overwhelming. "Can you wait until I get back? I'd like to be a part of the planning," she said, knowing it was only an excuse to put the wedding off a little longer. She was still adjusting to the idea of it.

He brought her hand to his lips and kissed her knuckles lightly. "Of course. I will try to be patient."

"Thank you." She heard the relief in her voice.

"In the meantime, I want to spend as much time as I can with you before you go."

"I'd like that," she said, gazing down at their joined hands.

They had spent their time going to parties when he wasn't too occupied with his family's business. She wouldn't have to worry about Steven being able to provide for her. She would live in a nice home and never want for anything.

But right now, she was riding a stolen horse through the snow and slowly freezing. She would give anything for a fire, something hot to drink, and a warm blanket.

True took a deep breath of cold air. She had to find someone before she froze to death. For all she knew, she already had died and was in limbo, her mind wandering aimlessly. Yet, she was breathing and cold, a good indication she wasn't dead yet.

She closed her eyes and concentrated on the sounds around her to keep her mind occupied as she tried to ignore the cold. She could hear the creek rush by, the sound of the horses as they made their way through the snow, wind whistling through the trees, men laughing, and a dog barking.

True's eyes flew open and she looked around. Ahead of her, at a bend of the creek, she could see two men and a dog wrestling in the snow. Relief flowed over her. She knew they would help her, and she would be warm again.

Then she gasped. Her vision was being played out before her eyes. The men wrestling, the happy dog, and the small child near the creek.

She forced her frozen hands to release the horse she was leading, then she managed to kick her horse into a faster pace. It hurt her cold body as he loped along, needles of pain stabbing her at every move. She had to reach the child before she fell into the creek. She hadn't been able to save Toby, but there was a chance she could save this little girl. Seconds later she saw that it was too late. She watched as the girl tumbled into the frigid water.

One of the men shouted, though True couldn't make out his words but easily heard the fear in his voice. She reached the bank of the creek, her eyes probing the water for the girl. She stopped her horse next to a swirling pool and slid to the ground. Her legs wouldn't hold and she went down into the snow. She heard the men running toward her and the dog barking, low and protective. Somehow, she got her feet under her and moved to the creek bank.

Looking down, she saw the small body sinking toward the bottom.

Stripping off her coats, True jumped into the icy creek. She came back up in an instant, gasping from the shock of the cold water, chest deep on her. Stretching her arms out, her hands connected with the girl's fur coat. True pulled the girl up to the surface and held her close as she moved back to the creek bank. True's muscles were weak and her soaked petticoats made her progress slow. Her breath was coming in great gasps as she managed to pull the child up to the bank of the creek.

The girl coughed and gasped desperately for air; her dark eyes wide with fear. When she had enough air in her lungs, she started to cry. True tried to drag herself up onto the creek bank but didn't have the strength. She pushed the child up onto more solid ground and was slipping back into an icy grave when strong hands pulled her up and away from the creek. True lay on her back, gasping for air as the cold seeped into her already-frozen body.

Hearing a low growl, she looked up into a pair of brown eyes and a set of snarling teeth. True glared at the big black dog. Suddenly, the dog was shoved out of the way and a man leaned over her. One of the men in her vision. He helped her sit up and she looked around for the little girl. The taller man had her in his arms and was hurrying away.

She imagined it was to someplace warm. True desperately wanted to go with them.

True struggled to her numb feet with the help of the man beside her. She did a mental check of her body; everything was cold and numb. Not much change from before only now she was soaking wet. She looked at the man in fur – he was an Indian! She felt a surge of fear but was so cold she couldn't act on her fear and run. The man in front of her began to blur as dark spots danced before her eyes. She swayed and started to fall, but the Indian caught her, then carried her in the direction the other man had gone. True didn't care where she was going, as long as it was warm.

A brief thought of the Indian scalping her flitted by just before blackness engulfed her.

Chapter Three

Sam ran through the snow with his daughter in his arms until he reached the tiny cabin. Rushing inside, he had Marie out of her wet clothes and into her warm little bed by the fireplace in record time. She was shivering and her teeth were chattering, but she had stopped crying.

"I'm cold, Daddy…"

"I know, honey." He added more wood to the fire, and then pulled her bed closer to the blaze. "You stay in bed and we'll get you warmed up."

Raven entered the cabin carrying the woman, kicking the door closed behind him as the black dog darted in. "She is almost frozen."

"Put her on my bed," Sam ordered.

Raven did as he was told, gently laying her down. Sam joined him and the two men began stripping off her wet clothes. Sam struggled with the layers of her heavy dress. Who was she and how had she gotten so far from civilization? Answers would have to come later. For now, he was concerned about getting her warm.

Once shed of her clothes, they lay her on the soft bed and covered her with blankets and furs.

Sam then went back to his daughter. "Are you getting warm?" He tucked the covers around her neck.

Marie nodded. "Daddy, help the pretty lady."

"I'm doing what I can for her. She's much colder than you are." Sam motioned the dog to the bed. "Cody will lay with you and keep you warm."

Sam signaled for the dog to jump on the bed. At the impact of the animal, the small bed shook and Marie giggled. She pulled her arms out from under the furs and hugged the dog around his big neck.

"You stay with Cody." Sam tucked her arms back under the covers, then added her rag doll. "I have to take care of the lady."

"Okay." Marie nodded and snuggled against the dog.

Sam smiled. She loved that ugly dog more than anything. Then his smile faded. What if he had lost Marie? He shook the question from his head and turned his attention to the woman in his bed. Raven leaned over her to feel her face.

"How is she?" Sam stood by his friend.

"She is still out." Raven straightened. "I would like to stay and help you, but I must go. It's snowing again and I must return to the village." Raven took the few paces to the door. "I will find the horses she had and put them in your corral before I go."

Sam nodded. "I'd hoped to leave tomorrow and head back to town, before Marie and I got snowed in up here." Sam glanced at the woman. "But it looks like we'll be stuck here…"

"I will return soon. Maybe I will bring Snow with me. I'm sure the woman will appreciate another female around after being cooped up with you." Raven chuckled.

"Very funny." Sam laughed. "I'll see you soon then."

"Bye, Raven," Marie called from her bed.

"Bye, Chipmunk," he told her before he opened the door and left the tiny cabin.

Sam's attention returned to the woman. He hoped she would wake up soon. He needed to find out why she was out here in the first place. Sam shook his head. It didn't matter why she was here. He was just glad that she had been there to save Marie.

How could he have been so careless? He had turned his attention from her for only a moment and had nearly lost her.

The woman was shivering uncontrollably. Sam would have to warm her fast.

Stripping down to his long underwear, Sam pulled back the covers and lay down next to her. Her body responded to the heat of his and she moved closer to him. It was a long time before her shivering subsided and her body temperature rose to normal levels.

Sam slept the night with the woman, only leaving long enough to place more wood on the fire and check on Marie. When he got back in bed, she snuggled up against him. Sam placed an arm around her and held her close.

It was like she was meant to be there. It was the most natural thing in the world for him to hold her.

With a sigh, Sam tried to sleep. An act that proved difficult with the woman pressed up against him. He hadn't lain with a woman like this for years. Piper had been gone so long that he had almost forgotten what it was like to hold a woman at night. A sudden longing he had never felt before shot through him with great force. The feeling startled him, and he tried to force it away, but it lingered throughout the night.

***

True awoke with a groan. Her body hurt all over as she shifted on the bed. She tried to retrieve from her foggy mind what had happened, Slowly, the memory surfaced. She had been on her way to Rimrock on the freight wagon. *But why am I hearing a crackling fire and a child's voice?* Her eyes were heavy and she had difficulty getting them to open. After a moment, she was successful and began to look around.

She saw a man standing next to a table, stirring something that smelled very good. Her tummy rumbled with hunger, reminding her how long it had been since she had last eaten.

Where am I? Memories returned in a jumble. Bandits shooting Toby. Her escape from them. Riding for a very long time, her body slowly freezing. She caught her breath. Saving a child from drowning. And after that, everything had gone black.

Looking around, she saw that she was in a small cabin, sparsely furnished with a table and two chairs. A small bed sat across the room from where True lay in a larger bed, covered with blankets and furs. A fireplace was between the two beds and lining the wall next to the table were a few shelves with cans and pots on them.

Her eyes suddenly hurt from the strain of looking around the room, and she closed her eyes against the pain.

"Look." The child's voice filled the cabin. "The pretty lady woke up."

True forced her eyes open again and saw the small girl she had rescued standing next to the bed. Her hair was long and black, and her dark eyes were bright. True tried to smile but it took more effort than she could muster.

"Hi…" she managed to whisper.

"'Ellow, I'm Marie. Who are you?" the girl asked happily.

"Marie, don't bother her." True looked for the source of the deep voice. The man was very tall and strongly built, with eyes as dark as Marie's, sandy brown hair, and a short beard. He had a bowl in his big hand and came to sit on the bed facing her, holding a steaming bowl of stew.

"Here, you need to eat," he told her.

True tried to sit up, but she was too weak and her body ached terribly. She had to lay back down. "I'm not sure I can get up."

"Let me help you." He set the bowl aside and stood.

True tried to sit up again and when she couldn't, he put an arm around her shoulders and helped her up. She sat with her eyes squeezed shut against the pain of her head and aching muscles. *Why is my back cold?* Opening her eyes, she looked down and realized the blanket had slid down, almost exposing her breasts. *My God! I'm naked!* She pulled the blanket up over herself and looked at the man.

"Where are my clothes?" she demanded.

"They were wet. We had to take them off," he explained.

"We?"

"Raven and I," he told her simply.

True stared at him, horrified at the thought of being undressed by two strange men. *What on earth would Steven think?* She could never tell him. He would be scandalized.

"We had to. You were unconscious. If we would have waited for you to wake, you would be frozen and probably would have gotten sick with fever."

True knew he was right, but that didn't ease the horror of them seeing her naked. She remembered being cold, and also of snuggling up against something very warm. It had been him! This man she didn't know had lain in bed with her while she was naked!

Steven would never understand. She must keep this secret from him forever.

Sam looked at her with concern. "Are you all right?"

She stared open mouthed at him. "You slept with me last night."

He nodded. "Had to. You were so cold. Had to get you warmed up as soon as possible."

"But I had no clothes on…" she informed him.

"I know," he said simply.

"Did you have clothes on?" she demanded.

He gave her a slight grin, apparently enjoying her horrified expression. "Yes, I had my long johns on. You were perfectly safe."

"It wasn't proper," she protested.

"I wasn't thinking proper at the time. I was trying to save your life." He picked up the bowl of stew and handed it to her before he once again sat on the bed.

He was right. She would have frozen to death if he had not warmed her. She took the bowl, letting the warmth of it heat up her hands. Her hands hurt and her fingers were red and swollen, so she had a hard time holding the spoon. Then the man picked up a blanket and draped it around her shoulders.

"Thank you." She sipped the stew. "This is good."

"Daddy's a good cook." Marie leaned against the bed looking at True. "What's yer name?"

"My name is True," she said, taking another sip.

"What happened to you?"

"Marie, it's not polite to ask so many questions. Now go sit at the table and eat your stew." He shooed her away. "Sorry, she doesn't know any better," he told True as he watched the girl sit at the table and pick up her spoon.

"That's all right. I'd like to know who you are as well," True said between bites.

He looked at her. "Sam Barkley. And that's my daughter, Marie," he said, as he looked over at Marie, who waved at them, spoon in hand, then happily went back to eating.

"Where is your friend?" True asked, remembering the Indian.

"Raven. He had to go back to his village. He

didn't want to get stuck in the cabin with us when it started to snow."

True handed the bowl back to him when she was finished. "That was good. Thank you."

"Would you like more?" Sam asked.

"Maybe later." The stew made her feel better, but she was still so tired.

Sam continued to sit on the edge of the bed and held the bowl in his big hands. "Thank you for saving Marie."

"I'm glad I was there to help," she said, knowing she couldn't tell him about her vision. "Is she all right?"

Sam nodded. "She had a scare, but is fine."

"Good," True said with relief.

"What are you doing this far from civilization and alone?" Sam asked flatly.

"I was on the freight wagon headed west, when two men came. I was in the trees and they didn't see me." Tears stung her eyes. "They shot Toby, and then went through the wagon looking for things to steal."

"Toby?" His brow furrowed as worry lined his features. "Did they kill him?"

"You know Toby?" He nodded. "I think so. He wasn't moving and there was a lot of blood."

"Damn…" he grumbled, with a sad shake of his head.

"Daddy!" Marie snapped. "Language."

"Sorry," he said absently. "How did you manage to get away from them?"

"They were so focused on taking things from the wagon, I was able to get to their horses," she told him as she thought back. "They saw me, but by then I was mounted and riding away. They shot at me, but luckily, they missed. I didn't know where to go, so I just headed away from them. When I got to the creek, I followed it, hoping I'd find a house."

"I'm glad you came along." His dark eyes went to Marie. "I could have lost her."

"I didn't even think," she said honestly. "I just went in after her."

"She would have drowned by the time I got to her." He met True's eyes again. "I owe you."

She only nodded and looked at her hands as she flexed her red, swollen fingers. At least they were still attached to her hands. She wiggled her toes and winced in pain.

"My toes." She looked at him. "Do I still have all of them?"

He nodded. "Yes, you do have a touch of frostbite, but you won't lose any of them."

She let out a sigh of relief and almost laughed at the thought of her considering her toes rolling around in her boot. "Good. I was worried."

"True, you said you were on the freight wagon," he said and waited for her to nod. "Where were you heading?"

"To Rimrock, to visit my sisters."

He studied her for a moment. "Are you True Tucker?"

She blinked, and then nodded. "How did you know?"

He smiled at her, and it was a smile that would make any woman go weak at the knees. He was a very handsome man and she suddenly wondered just who he was. Her eyes flicked to Marie. She was also interested to know if he was married.

She quickly shook those thoughts away. She was engaged and had no business thinking like that.

"I know your sisters," he told her. "I've worked for both Shyfawn and Jo's husbands over the years."

"Shyfawn's gonna have a baby," Marie stated, then scooped up a spoonful of stew.

True couldn't help but smile. "I know. That's why I'm here. I came to help her take care of the baby after it's born."

"She'll be glad when you get there, she's been looking forward to your visit for months," Sam told her.

True nodded. "I've been looking forward to the visit as well. It's been years since we've all been together. However, I wasn't expecting the trip to be so long or so dangerous."

"It can be hazardous around here," he admitted.

She bit her lip a moment before she spoke again. "If you don't mind, I'd like to get dressed now."

He nodded, then took the bowl to the table before going to a trunk in the corner of the room. He picked up a pile of garments on top of it, then lay her dress and petticoats onto the bed before going back to the table. She watched as he turned Marie's chair so her back was to True, Marie giggling as the chair moved. Sam turned the other chair around and also sat with his back to True.

"There's no dressing room, so this is all the privacy I can offer."

True smiled as she pushed the blankets back and stood, wincing at the pain in her feet. She watched the two seated across the room carefully, making sure Sam didn't try to peek. Her fingers fumbled with the buttons and laces as she dressed. She would be glad when the swelling went down and her fingers were once again nimble. Her feet hurt, but she was thankful to have all her toes.

"I'm finished," she said, once she was dressed.

Marie turned and her eyes went wide. She jumped from her chair to rush to True. "It's so pretty!" she exclaimed, reaching out to touch the lush fabric of True's burgundy dress.

True looked down at her dress, thinking it one of her plainer dresses. Marie would probably ooh and ahh over one of True's party dresses.

"Thank you," she said and looked at Sam's back. "And thank you, Sam, for helping me ... but I think I should head for Rimrock. If you'll point the way for me."

He turned in the chair to look at her. "Not until your fingers and toes are fully healed. Besides, it's been snowing since yesterday and there's no way you could make it down the mountain. Marie, you better finish eating."

Marie scampered back to her chair, clambered onto it and dug into her stew bowl again.

True stared at Sam. "I can't leave?"

He shook his head as he got to his feet. "Nope, I'm afraid you're stuck here with us for a while."

True wasn't sure what to say as irritation, panic, and frustration warred within her. She didn't want to be trapped in this tiny cabin with Sam and his daughter. Marie appeared sweet, but True didn't know anything about children and had never been around many. Sam was a different worry all together. Being trapped in the cabin with a man, a mountain man, who probably hadn't seen a woman in a long time. She knew what those kinds of men were like and she wanted no part of it.

"I'd rather leave," she informed him.

"I'm afraid you don't have a choice," he told her flatly. "You're in no condition to travel and the snow will have the pass blocked by morning."

She pulled in an angry breath. "Mr. Barkley, I intend to leave today."

"And you'll be dead in two hours," he snapped. "You don't know the way and the snow will bury you."

She wanted to argue, but knew he was right. "You are a stubborn and bossy man."

His brows descended into a scowl. "I just don't intend to let a snobby city woman get herself killed because of her own foolishness."

True stared at him. "Snobby!"

"You don't have a clue what's out there." Sam gestured to the door. "You can't walk, and you'll exhaust a horse forcing him through that snow. The wolves or bears will find you and you don't stand a chance against them."

She felt her anger growing. "Are you trying to scare me?"

"It's all right, True," Marie said happily from the table. "Daddy's not as scary as he looks."

"Thank you, Marie," Sam said dryly.

"You bet, Daddy," she told him proudly, as if

she had just solved a great dilemma.

True couldn't stop the bubble of laughter that escaped seeing the indignant look he shot Marie. A small rumble of laughter left him as he looked at True once again, his smile so very charming. She supposed that when he was shaved and cleaned up, he would be turning every woman's head.

"I love her brutal logic," he said and met True's eyes evenly, his face more serious. "I understand you not wanting to be here with me, but I assure you that I won't do what you're thinking."

She felt her face heat. "I meant no disrespect, but it's just not proper."

"Around here, we can't always do proper," he told her simply. "But … you can trust me."

She looked at him for a long time before nodding. "Okay," she said softly, and deep down, she believed him.

***

The day passed quickly and though she was mostly confined to the bed, she found herself enjoying the company of the mountain man and his daughter. She wanted to be up and moving around but her feet hurt when she tried to walk. She hated to admit that Sam was right, she wouldn't be able to leave the cabin until her feet were healed.

It was late into the evening when Marie yawned and Sam shooed her off to bed. True watched as he tucked her in and the dog jumped up onto the bed. When Sam turned to look at True, she had a sudden thought.

True cleared her throat. "Um, about sleeping…"

"What about it?"

"Where will you be sleeping?" she asked flatly.

"In my bed," he told her. His face wore a quizzical expression, as if he wasn't entirely sure what she was getting at.

She stared at him for a moment. "Where will *I* be sleeping?"

He shrugged casually. "In my bed, too."

She gaped at him and struggled to her feet to argue properly with him. "I can't do that! It is extremely unacceptable."

A small smile tugged at his lips. "You're right, it is."

Her eyes narrowed. *He's enjoying this!* "Then what other arrangements would you suggest?"

He chuckled. "I could suggest one of us sleep in Marie's bed, but it is far too small for either of us. I don't see any other choice than to share my bed."

She shook her head. "I will not," she said firmly.

"You already have," he said with a grin.

True wanted to shriek with outrage but held off, gritting her teeth and clenching her fists as she glared at him. Then, without a word, she grabbed the fur from the bed and dragged it in front of the fireplace. Mincing back to the bed, she snatched up a blanket and then dropped it on the fur. She turned to face him, hands on her hips.

"You can sleep here." She pointed to the blanket before the fire.

Sam no longer looked amused. "You think so?"

"Yes," she snapped.

"I'm not sleeping on the damn floor!"

"Daddy, language!" Marie instantly bellowed.

Sam looked up at the ceiling and muttered something under his breath. True fought to keep her grim look in place and not laugh. At least she could count on Marie to keep Sam in line. When he looked at her again, she could tell his fight was against losing his temper.

"Fine," he growled through clenched teeth. "I'll sleep on the floor."

She smiled sweetly. "Of course, you will." And as she stepped around him, she gave his chest a pat, and then caught her breath as her heart lurched into a pounding rhythm. That one brief touch confirmed that he was very solid and muscular, something she had already assumed by observing him, but touching him had sent her heart racing.

I must be sure not to touch him again.

Chapter Four

Sam woke with an aggravated groan as he tried to get his sore body to move. He had been uncomfortable as hell all night. Sleeping on the hard dirt floor put kinks in his back he would have to suffer through all day. He rolled to glare at the bed where True slept peacefully.

After a long time, Sam stood and stretched before pulling on his clothes. Cody jumped from Marie's bed and walked to the door, stretching and waiting for Sam to let him outside. Sam's eyes went to his daughter's bed and his heart jumped in his chest. She was gone! His eyes darted around the cabin and he saw her curled up in bed with True.

Stepping up to the bed Sam watched them sleep. Why would Marie want to sleep with her? Realization struck him, True had saved Marie and the girl wanted to be close to her. It was possible that Marie had had a bad dream about falling into the creek and had sought out True for comfort. Fear made his stomach tight as he thought of how close he had come to losing his daughter.

Cody whined from the door and Sam pulled his eyes from Marie and walked to the door to let the dog out. Standing in the open door, Sam stared at the falling snow and heaved a great sigh. Damn weather was going to trap him in the cabin, for longer than he cared, with that woman.

Sam went about getting breakfast together and as he worked, his eyes kept straying to the woman sleeping in his bed. She looked beautiful and peaceful. He tried not to think of the night before, when he had held her to warm her. He had been secretly hoping to hold her again last night, but she had put a halt to that.

He heard Marie stir and smiled.

"Morning, Chipmunk," he said, glancing over at her.

"Good morning, Daddy," she said sleepily as she yawned and slid from the bed

He watched her pad to the table with her ragdoll and scramble up onto her chair. He filled a bowl with stew and placed it before her, then kissed the top of her head. Then, dishing out another bowl of stew for himself, he sat next to her. She chattered away about nothing in particular while he listened patiently, smiling and nodding. His daughter viewed every day as a new adventure and though she could be exhausting at times, he loved her dearly.

Watching her, he was amazed, as always, at her resemblance to her mother. He felt the old, familiar pain in his chest as he thought of his wife, Piper. She had been so small, and Marie's birth had been difficult for her. At least she had held Marie for a while before she passed away. He had never felt such gut wrenching pain as that day he held his wife's hand and watched her die. And not being able to do a damn thing to help her.

Marie halted her chatter to look at him, a frown creasing her brow. "Daddy, you look sad."

He gave her a small smile. Marie never missed a thing. "I was just thinking, honey. Are you finished?" he asked, diverting any questions she might have asked.

"Yes," she said and pushed her bowl across the table to him before she slid from the chair with her doll to go to her bed and dress.

True rolled over and sat up in bed, drawing Sam's attention to her. She brushed her tangled hair from her face to look over at him. He picked up Marie's bowl and filled it before walking to the bed.

"Sleep well?" he asked dryly.

She gave him a sweet smile and reached to take the bowl from him. "Very well, thank you. How did *you* sleep?"

He scowled at her and turned to head for the door. She made a noise of disgust, which caused him to turn around. She was eyeing the stew as she stirred the contents.

"What on earth is this?" she asked, wrinkling her nose.

"Food." Sam said before taking a calming breath. This woman was wearing on his nerves and she had only been there a day. He jerked his hat and coat from the pegs by the door.

"Where are you going?"

"I have to go hunting." He slipped into his coat. "With all this snow, we'll be here longer than I expected, and with an extra mouth to feed, we'll be running low on meat soon." He went to the door.

"What am I supposed to do?" True protested.

Sam turned and looked at the blond woman in his bed. He had spent several years in Boston and he now remembered what city people had been like. It was selfish, self-absorbed women like her that made his stay unpleasant. "Could you look after Marie? I won't be gone long."

She stared at him. "But—"

"Thanks." Before she could protest any further, he turned and left.

True stared at the closed door. He was the rudest man she had ever met. Leaving her alone in this God forsaken cabin with his daughter. She had never taken care of a child before and she certainly had no idea how to entertain one.

True held her bowl and looked at the contents. She wrinkled her nose again and mumbled, "What is this stuff?"

"Houp." Marie said, sitting on her bed happily playing with her doll.

"Soup?" She stirred it, picking at the contents. It was the stew from last night, watered down, with a few other things thrown in.

"It looks awful. Is it good?" She kept stirring.

Marie hopped off her bed, leaving her doll behind, and walked to True's bed. "Not really." She looked up at True. "But ya won't starve."

True couldn't help but smile, she appreciated Marie's honesty. "Would you like to help me eat it?"

Without answering, Marie ran and got another spoon, then climbed up and sat next to True, her feet hanging off the bed. True held the bowl so both of them could eat. Marie had been right, it wasn't the best tasting concoction, but it would keep her from starving out here in the middle of nowhere.

True watched Marie for a moment. She had been startled in the night when the little girl had climbed into bed with her. She had tears on her cheeks and cried softly as she curled up against True. True had held her small body close and did her best to sooth the child. She murmured about being afraid of the creek in her dream and True didn't need to ask to know she'd had a nightmare.

"Are you okay this morning?" she asked gently.

Marie nodded. "It was just a bad dream. Daddy says bad dreams can't hurt anyone."

"He's right." She absently brushed Marie's hair back. "But if you get scared again, you can sleep with me."

Marie smiled happily at her before going back to eating. "Okay."

True wasn't entirely sure how much longer she would be in the cabin with Marie and Sam, but she wanted to ease the girl's fear of her ordeal at the creek while she could. True herself had been afraid as she went into the water after the girl. She couldn't let Marie drown but she also knew she was so cold and weak, there was little chance she could save herself. Thankfully Raven had pulled her from the water and Sam had cared for her.

"Marie, how far is it to town?" True asked as she thought.

"It took me and Daddy two days," she said with a mouthful of food. "But he says you can make it in one long day."

True nodded and took another spoonful of the soup. One long day. She was looking forward to that day, she would go stir crazy locked up in this tiny cabin. She had no doubt her sisters knew something had gone wrong by now and would be worried sick about her.

"Marie," she said as a thought struck her. "Why are you and your father in this cabin?"

"We went to Raven's village," she told True simply. "We stay here when Daddy checks on the Indians."

True wasn't entirely sure what to make of that statement. "Are they nice." Maybe Sam was checking to see if they were going to make trouble. She had heard stories of the Indians in the west and some of them were terrifying.

"Yep."

True waited for Marie to elaborate but she was content with digging her spoon in the soup until she found a chunk of meat. She plunked it into her mouth and chewed happily. True didn't know how long Sam intended to stay and *check on the Indians*, but True was ready to leave. She flexed her feet and knew she wouldn't be able to walk far, but didn't think riding would be a problem. Her hands were still a little tender, but she was sure she could hold reins. There shouldn't be any reason why she couldn't go to Rimrock soon. All Sam had to do was point her in the right direction and she could make it on her own.

***

Several days had passed and True had adjusted to Sam and Marie's routine tolerably well. She enjoyed Marie's company, but Sam tested her patience. He didn't want her there, that was clear, but he wouldn't let her leave either. Her fingers were back to normal and her feet no longer hurt. She didn't see why she couldn't leave and he could get back to doing whatever it was he did.

True watched Sam in the light of dawn drifting through the windows as he squatted before the fire to add more wood. She had more than once caught herself looking at him in a way that wasn't appropriate for an engaged woman. He was a handsome man, with his dark eyes and that smile. The last couple days they had even had several pleasant conversations and she found she liked the sound of his voice. He hadn't called her snobby again, which was an improvement in his manners.

"Sam, my feet are fine now, I think I'm ready to leave," she said, glad her voice was confident.

He looked at her for a moment before answering. "I'm glad you're feeling better, but you can't leave."

"What?" True stared at him as he picked up the poker to adjust the burning wood. "You have to be joking."

"No. It has snowed for the past four days and the valley will be impassable," Sam explained as he set the poker aside.

"Isn't there another way out?" she asked hopefully.

Sam stood and looked at her for a long time. "Yes."

Hope flared inside her. "Then we can leave, right?"

"No," he said shortly.

"What do you mean, no? You just said that

there was another way."

"No offence lady, but there is no way I can travel the mountain trail with a little kid and a woman and get us all there alive." Sam walked past her and sat in the chair at the table.

True wasn't going to give up so easily. "But there has to be a way. What about the way I came?"

"You rode that in the dark," he informed her. "If it had been light, you would have seen the two miles of cliff trail. You're damn lucky you didn't fall."

"Daddy…" Marie scolded from her bed, rubbing at one eye with her fist. "Language."

"Sorry," he grumbled. "And now the trail will be slick with snow and ice. There's no way we can make it down that way."

True couldn't keep the small smile from tugging her mouth at the interaction between Sam and Marie. "How long before the pass clears?"

"Hard to say," he told her honestly. "Depends on how many snowstorms blow in."

She let out a frustrated breath and folded her arms. "Can you venture a guess?"

"No, I can't. If I had my way, I would take you down today, but that's not going to happen." His voice was harsh. "I don't like this any more than you do, but we're stuck here and you're just going to have to deal with it."

"I don't want to deal with it. Being stuck in this primitive little cabin is very unpleasant. It smells, it's cold, and the food—"

"This isn't Charlotte," he snapped. "You're not going to be pampered or waited on. There are no maids, cooks, or butlers here."

True felt her anger rising and had to control the sudden urge to slap him. "I'm well aware of that."

"Neither of us want you here, but there isn't anything we can do about that right now. If you can refrain from acting like a spoiled princess, this stay will be more tolerable for the both of us."

Marie slid from her bed and went to stand beside Sam, reaching up to take his big hand, her little fingers tightly gripping two of his. Sam's body stiffened and he looked down at his daughter. Her dark eyes held his for a long time, before he took a deep breath and let it out slowly.

"That's better," she told him. "Now, be nice."

With that, Marie turned to go back to her bed to dress and Sam's gaze followed her.

True took a moment to study Sam. Apparently, a touch from Marie would calm him. True would remember that for any future arguments between them. She would make sure Marie was always close to keep Sam in line.

Sam muttered under his breath before looking at True. "I apologize, Miss Tucker. This situation is beyond our control and we'll just have to do our best to tolerate each other until we can get you to town."

She let out a long breath, and though she was frustrated with the situation, she knew he was right. "I'll do my best to be patient."

"Please do." He tried to keep the irritation from his voice but failed. "I'll need to go hunting again today." He went to the door and pulled on his coat and gloves. "I'll be back."

True watched as he picked up his rifle and went out the door, Cody eagerly following him. He was still irritated with her and apparently wanted to get away from her for now. She didn't mind, she would be glad to have time free of his rude remarks and backward ways. *Mountain men...* She rolled her eyes. Sam may be attractive and even pleasant at times, but he was a far cry from the men in Charlotte. And she liked that.

Chapter Five

True paced the cabin restlessly as she waited for Sam to return from hunting. She had to get out of there and get to her sisters, the sooner the better. How bad could it really be out there? She had made it this far in the snow, she was sure she could make it to town from here. She would just go out and see how possible it was for her to leave.

Grabbing her coat, she headed for the door. "I'll be back," she told Marie as she went outside.

She buttoned her coat as she stood looking around at the snowy ground. The sun was shining and the air was warm. Snow melted and icicles dripped. That was a good sign. She looked toward the shed and corral, where the three horses were. She would take a horse, get a few supplies from the cabin, and get the hell out of there. She would walk to the corral and see just how deep the snow really was. Because in the morning she intended to leave.

Summoning her courage, True stepped off the small porch and went knee deep in snow.

"Damn it," she grumbled as she gathered her dress and trudged her way toward the corral.

She made it halfway and realized it was hopeless. She had fallen three times and her legs were cold and her dress was getting soaked. Letting out a frustrated growl she turned and went back to the cabin, shaking off as much snow as she could before she went back inside.

The warmth washed over her as she entered the tiny space and she let out a thankful sigh.

Marie looked up from playing with her doll before the fire. "You okay?"

True fought tears of frustration and nodded. "Yes, I'm fine."

She removed her coat and wet shoes before going to the trunk to find something dry to wear. She rummaged around and found a shirt she was sure belonged to Sam. It would have to do. She stripped out of her wet dress and put on the shirt, quickly buttoning it up before Marie saw too much. Thankfully, the girl was intent on her doll. True draped her clothes over the chairs to dry, then she sat down by the fire with Marie.

A deep sigh flowed from her. She would have to face the fact that Sam was right.

She couldn't leave.

***

It was late in the evening when Sam returned to the cabin and saw the trail through the snow toward the shed. Anger went through him. That damn woman had tried to leave. Not only would she have left his daughter alone, but he would have had to go out and save the woman's behind before she got herself killed.

He flung open the door and stepped into the cabin, then closed the door with a bang, almost catching the tail of the dog as he shot inside.

True met his hard look with one of her own as she stood on the other side of the table. He didn't have to say anything. It was obvious that he knew she had tried to leave when he took in all the clothes drying before the fire. His gaze swung back to hers. One gloved hand tightly clenched a rope at his side, at the end of it hung three lifeless rabbits, skinned and gutted, and the other hand held the rifle.

She didn't say anything and neither did he. They stood glaring at each other while Marie played on the rug before the fire. She squealed happily as Cody greeted her, both oblivious to Sam and True and the angry tension in the room.

Finally, Sam moved. He took a few steps toward the table. He had no doubt he looked mad as hell and she braced herself for a fight. He had to give her credit; she wasn't intimidated by him at all.

When Sam stepped around the table, he could see True's full length. She was wearing his shirt and it only came mid-thigh on her. Her legs were bare and she stood, feet slightly apart, waiting for the argument to come. Her long golden hair hung freely down around her shoulders and down her back. Damn it, she was beautiful. All he could do was stare at her. He almost forgot he was furious with her. Almost.

"You would have left Marie here alone?" He ground the words out.

"No, I just wanted to see how deep the snow was. I was going to leave in the morning."

"You can't leave until the pass is clear." He shifted his grip on the rifle. "And while you're here, you'll do what I tell you."

"Or what, Mr. Barkley?" She folded her arms and shifted her weight to one leg, hip a-kilter.

Sam tried not to notice the way her arms framed her breasts or the way the hem of the shirt had worked up slightly.

"Or something bad could happen to you, Miss Tucker." *Outside or in here*, he added silently.

"Don't you dare threaten me," she snapped.

Sam lifted the rope to drop the three dead rabbits on the table. Her look of disgust gave him slight satisfaction. "Now, I have things to do outside, so make yourself useful and cook those." He nodded toward the rabbits, ignoring the hurt and anger in her eyes, turned, and stomped to the door. He leaned the rifle against the wall by the door before he went outside, closing the door with a bang.

Sam went back to the deer he had killed and drug it to the shed. He was glad to be busy. It would let his temper cool. Damn that woman. She was stubborn, intolerable, aggravating, beautiful – and looked good in his shirt. He was taken completely by surprise at her standing there wearing nothing but his shirt. He had no doubt her legs would feel like silk.

With a shake of his shoulders, he changed the direction of his thoughts and focused on the deer.

When he was finally finished skinning the animal, then cutting and storing the meat in the shed, the sun had set and it was starting to snow again. He looked up at the sky and muttered a curse.

At this rate, he would never get off the mountain. He and Marie would be stuck here even longer – with that woman. The thought of True staring at the dead rabbits on the table triggered a smile. City girls were accustomed to having every meal already prepared for them. He had no doubt that True came from a house full of servants. Shyfawn had often talked of their Aunt Molly and the fine house she had in Charlotte.

His stomach rumbled, reminding him he hadn't eaten since breakfast. Well, he was just going to have to wait until he got the rabbits cooked. Sam walked to the cabin door, forcing himself to remain calm. After stomping most of the snow off his boots, he entered.

The aroma of cooking filled his nostrils. He stood staring at the table and the pot of steaming stew. True, still wearing his shirt, stood next to the table with a slight smile on her lips. Sam thought how much he would like to come home to this sight every night. The only thing missing was her in his bed. He remembered holding her the first night and remembered how good it felt. He wondered how soft her long legs were, and how they would feel wrapped around him.

"Sam?" True's voice snapped him back to reality. "Are you trying to heat the outside?"

"Oh!" Sam quickly shut the door behind him. Taking off his coat and boots he turned back to her. "I must say I'm surprised." Sam sat at the table and she filled a bowl for him. Marie climbed up on his knee and he adjusted her to sit comfortably.

"I haven't always lived in Charlotte, you know." True dished food into Marie's bowl and placed it in front of the girl before she served herself. She took her seat and smiled at Sam. "I know a few things that would surprise you."

"Such as?" Sam asked, glad that they were finally having a nice conversation.

"Well, for one thing, I know how to cook, I can skin and cut up an animal, I can snare rabbits, and a few other useful things."

"Can you shoot a gun?" Marie asked, her eyes filled with excitement.

True nodded. "Yes, I know how to shoot, but it's been a very long time."

"Daddy can shoot a gun, too." She looked happily at her father. "I can't because I'm too little, but I wanna learn."

"It's a useful skill," True agreed.

"Daddy says I'm too noisy to take hunting," Marie said casually. "But when I learn how to shoot, and be quiet, he'll take me with him."

True smiled at Sam, who shrugged and gave her a grin.

They set into an easy stream of conversation. The atmosphere in the cabin was far different than when he had first arrived. True was pretty sure he had wanted to choke her, but not in front of Marie. Now, he was quite pleasant and even laughed as they talked. She liked his laugh. There was a lot about Sam she liked, and that could be a problem.

They continued to sit at the table talking after they had finished their meal. Marie scampered off to play with her doll and Cody before the fire. When she yawned and rubbed at her eyes, Sam stood and put her to bed. She protested only a moment before she settled down with Cody at her side. She was asleep in moments.

Sam returned to the table and sat. "I don't

know about you, but I'm tired, too."

True nodded. "Yes, I am, too."

"Probably from trudging through the snow," he said, his tone carefully devoid of irritation.

True let out a long breath and met his eyes evenly. "Sam, I just needed to see for myself that I couldn't leave. I wouldn't have left Marie alone. I may not want to be here, but I would never risk Marie by leaving her alone."

"Are you now satisfied that I've been telling you the truth?"

"Yes."

"Good. Just don't ever try that again," he told her firmly.

"I won't."

"You've already tried to freeze to death and drown," he said seriously. "Let's not add more to that. Jo will kill me if I don't get you to Rimrock in one – unfrozen – piece."

True smiled and nodded as she looked over at her wet clothes. Somehow, she was glad that they weren't dry yet. She liked wearing Sam's shirt, and she liked the way he looked at her. It had sent an unexpected heat through her body. It was very improper for a man to see her like this, especially a man she wasn't married to. There had been something in his dark eyes that told her he wanted to see all her skin, not just her legs.

With the thought of Sam looking at her bare legs she felt slightly guilty. What would Steven think? She would never have paraded around in nothing but a shirt in front of him. He would have gotten embarrassed and been such a gentleman. She liked what she saw in Sam's eyes, and wasn't that part of the reason she came west? To get away from all the properness and smugness of Charlotte. To try to find out what she really wanted. To find out who she really was.

The letters she had received from her sisters came to mind. They were filled with happiness and love. Growing up, all she had heard about was how terrible the West was and how nothing good could come of going there. Her sisters had gone West and they were happy.

Maybe True was meant to be in the West with her sisters. After being separated for so many years, was it fate that they were living in the same town, and now True was going there? Were they all meant to be together after all? To have her family be whole again?

Family. Was Marie Sam's only family?

"Sam, where is Marie's mother?" True finally asked the question that had been on her mind a lot lately. "Doesn't she object to you bringing Marie here?"

He said nothing for a long time, then bent to unlace his boots. "She's dead."

"Oh. I'm sorry." She felt bad about bringing up the subject. "I shouldn't have asked."

He kicked off his boots and slouched down in the chair. Fingering the tin cup on the table, he added, "I doubt she would have objected, but if she were alive, Marie wouldn't be here with me. She'd be in town with her mother." His voice was hollow, his eyes focused on the tin cup.

True wasn't sure what to say now, so she kept

quiet. She had a few more questions she wanted to ask, but knew the details of his wife's death were none of her business. Being a widower might explain the way he had looked at her tonight, maybe he hadn't been with a woman since his wife had died. True somehow doubted that logic. Sam was very much a man and she was sure he visited the local whore house from time to time.

"You should get some sleep."

True felt that meant all conversation was over. "Goodnight, then." She got to her feet and walked to the bed. After climbing in and pulling the covers to her chin, she settled in comfortably.

She watched Sam for a long time as he sat at the table, his eyes focused on Marie, hand absently fidgeting with the cup. She never should have asked about Marie's mother; she had no doubt he was now thinking of the day she died.

Closing her eyes, True forced herself to relax. She guessed nobody really had a perfect life. She and her sisters had grown up with a father that scared the hell out of them. After they had escaped him, they had lived the lie of being of good breeding. All the while keeping their special gifts a secret from being discovered.

But life had a way of changing, and she hoped that Sam would find happiness once again.

Chapter Six

True stood in the field overlooking the old house she had spent most of her childhood in, and was once again a little girl. The sun was unusually bright that day and there was a slight breeze that tossed her tangled hair around her shoulders. She walked toward the house, picking the wildflowers as she went. She knew there were pretty blue flowers next to the barn. Mama would really like them in a jar on the table.

True hummed a little tune as she approached the barn, picking the blue flowers. She was on her way back to the house when she heard a sound. Something told True to walk past the barn door and go to the house, but she ignored it. Peeking through the barn door she saw nothing, then the sound came again, along with a muffled cry. Pushing the door open, she went in, rounded the corner, and stopped dead in her tracks. The flowers fell to the ground and she covered her mouth with her hands to hold in a fear-filled cry.

Joanna was hanging by her wrists from a nail on the wall. She had been stripped naked and her back was bloody. A man stood behind her with a whip in his hands, which he swung up in the air. As he did so, his body half turned to her and she gasped. It was her father. He struck Joanna, then threw the whip down and walked up behind her. He was speaking to Joanna, but True couldn't make out what he was saying. Then he pulled Joanna's body up against him and fumbled with the front of his trousers.

True turned and fled from the barn, she knew what was happening and she didn't want to see it. Not again. Their father had abused Joanna so often. Her heart jumped when she heard footsteps behind her. True turned and looked, her father was coming after her, whip in hand.

This had never happened in the dream before. Wake up! Wake up! Suddenly she was thrown to the ground, looking up she saw her father. She screamed in terror.

Hands grabbed her, tearing at her clothes. She was going to end up like Joanna, but if she was lucky, he would kill her. True fought with all her strength, but suddenly she didn't seem to have any, she couldn't move. True opened her mouth and screamed as she was grabbed again and shaken roughly.

"True!"

The voice came from far away and she fought. "Let me go! Don't touch me!"

"True, damn it! Wake up!"

She was being shaken vigorously. Her eyes popped open to see a man leaning over her, his hands gripping her shoulders. She really was being attacked! True fought for all she was worth.

"Get away from me!" she screeched. She pushed at the man, but he was too big, she couldn't get away.

"True, it's Sam! Stop it, you're all right."

True stopped fighting, her breath coming in great gasps. The face in front of her suddenly came into focus. It was Sam, his face clouded with worry.

"Sam." True's eyes filled with tears and she choked back a sob

Sam pulled her into a sitting position and put his arms around her to hold her close. He could feel the wet tears on his bare chest as she cried. Great sobs racked her body as he held her. Sam smoothed True's hair back and kissed her forehead. She was still trembling, her breath ragged.

"True, it was just a dream," Sam said softly, trying to sooth her as he held her.

"Daddy?" Marie's frightened voice drifted to him.

He looked up to see her sitting up in bed staring wide eyed at him. "Everything is fine, honey. True just had a bad dream. Go back to sleep." She reluctantly lay back down and hugged Cody as she closed her eyes. After a few moments, she was again asleep, breathing evenly.

Sam held True in his arms for a long time before she stopped crying and pulled away from him to wipe her face with the sleeve of her shirt. Sam lowered his arms and leaned back, feeling a loss from no longer holding her.

"I'm sorry, I always have this dream. Only this time it was different." True brought her knees up and rested her chin on them.

"You want to tell me about it?" Sam coaxed.

She sniffed. "I suppose it would make me feel better." True looked into the dying flames of the fire. "It might take a while. Could you put more wood in the fire?"

Sam did so and sat next to her again, facing her. Waiting for her to begin.

True told him about the dream, about the man that they had called father and the terrible things he had done to Jo. She stared into the fire the entire time she was telling him, as if he wasn't even there. The sound of her voice sent shivers down Sam's spine; it was like she was in some sort of trance.

"Usually I just go back into the house and play with Shyfawn, but I could still hear Jo's cries. This time the dream ended so differently." She closed her eyes and took a shuddering breath, then continued to stare into the fire.

"I should have stopped him, but I was so little and so afraid. I was afraid that if he knew that I had seen him that he would do that to me, too." Tears filled her eyes again. "I never even told my sister that I saw what happened, and that it wasn't the first time. I saw him do a lot of other horrible things to her, but I never told her. I was afraid that she would be angry with me if she found out I knew."

Sam sat disbelieving. It wasn't just a dream. It had actually happened and she was reliving the events from her childhood in her sleep. True was carrying around guilt for what had happened, blaming herself for not stopping her father from raping her sister.

"Our father tried to touch me one night." Anger filled her eyes. "But I kicked him between the legs and he never touched me or Jo again. After that, Jo tried to take us away from him, but he caught up with us. She killed him and we went to live in Charlotte with our Aunt. She was the only family we had." She went silent.

Sam nodded in understanding and took one of her hands in both of his. He waited for her to get her emotions under control and thought of the few times he had heard Shyfawn and Jo talk about their childhood. It had been bad and they never said much about their parents. The stories were of when they were children playing. He had learned some of the sisters history from Jo's husband, Jack. At least True and Shyfawn had been spared the abuse Jo took on, trying to keep her sisters safe. The man wasn't their real father. They didn't know who their fathers were, as the man had sold their mothers body to drifters passing through.

"I'm sorry," she said and wiped at her cheeks with her free hand. "I don't mean to cry."

"Don't worry about it," he told her and reached up to tuck her hair behind her ear. "You had it rough growing up – at least you had the chance to get out and have a good life."

She gave him a small smile. "Yes. Aunt Molly is an amazing woman, and life in Charlotte was like a fairytale."

Sam chuckled and continued to hold her hand. "I can imagine it felt that way to you."

"The parties and the beautiful dresses made me feel like a princess."

Sam glanced over at Marie. "She'd love to have a fancy dress." He looked at True again. "But fancy dresses aren't very practical living in Rimrock."

"I don't suppose they are." She looked over at

Marie. "She'd love some of the dresses that Steven has given me."

Sam felt his heart jump and his stomach tighten. "Your fiancé," he muttered and released her hand. How could he forget something like that? True hadn't told him about Steven, but he was there when Shyfawn had gotten True's letter telling of her engagement. "I imagine he can give you everything you could ever want."

She met his eyes for a long time before nodding. "Yes…he can…" she said and lowered her eyes to fidget with her fingers.

Sam hadn't missed the undercurrent of doubt in her voice. "But…"

She shook her head and looked at him. "Nothing."

True looked like she wanted to tell him so much more, but she kept silent. Maybe she was having second thoughts about her dashing prince. He could always hope. He was starting to like her far more than he should. Her fiery stubbornness and her sweet innocence were a combination that called to him. She was an engaged woman though and that was something he would have to keep reminding himself.

"Try to go back to sleep," he told her and stood.

"Wait." Her hand caught his. "Will you sit with me until I fall asleep?" Her voice was pleading.

"Okay," he said gently and she kept hold of his hand as she lay back down.

Sam used his free hand to pull the covers up over her shoulders before he reached to brush her hair back from her face. He let his fingers drift through it, savoring the feel of the silky strands. She closed her dark eyes and he just sat there, gazing down at her.

True was very beautiful and her figure was perfect, as far as he was concerned. The sight of her bare legs had stirred a desperate need inside him, and he spent a couple hours before sleep came to him, indulging in fantasies about her. Of course, she would be horrified if she knew what he had been thinking, but she would never find out. It had been a long time since he had been with a woman and remembering the feel of holding her that first night was never far from his mind. He had a feeling the sooner he got her to Rimrock, the better off they would both be.

When she sniffed and he saw tears leak from her closed eyes, Sam tightened his hold on her hand. "True, what's wrong?"

She shook her head and he knew whatever she was thinking, she intended to keep it to herself. He let out a long breath and released her hand to stand, she made a noise of protest and looked at him, her dark eyes shining with tears. He pulled back the covers and slid into bed with her, surprisingly she didn't object as she moved over to make room for him. He put his arms around her and pulled her close.

"Everything will be all right," he told her, and hoped he was telling her the truth.

He brushed her hair from her forehead and placed a gentle kiss there, she let out a soft whimper and nestled into him. Sam knew he shouldn't be laying with her like this, but she was upset and needed comfort. He would hold her for the rest of the night. Tomorrow night, he would go back to sleeping on the damn floor.

***

True woke and blinked her eyes open to look at the ceiling, a smile playing on her lips. She was alone in bed, but clearly remembered last night and the way Sam had held her. It had felt so good. Sam was big and his arms were strong as he held her close. She had replayed his kiss on her forehead over and over most of the night. She hadn't gotten much sleep, enjoying the new feelings he was creating in her.

A frown formed as she thought of those feelings. Would Steven make her feel like this? Steven was so much different than Sam. Would Steven hold her all night like Sam had? How would it feel? Steven was much smaller and not nearly as strong. Steven's quick kisses never made her feel the way Sam's lingering kiss on her forehead had.

True knew she could never tell Steven about her time here with Sam. He wouldn't understand. Yet another secret she would have to keep from him. So many secrets. Her true parentage, her visions, and now Sam.

True sat up in bed and took a deep breath, smelling meat frying and coffee. She could hear Marie chattering nonstop. True yawned and rubbed her eyes as she tried to wake up. She blinked until her eyes found Sam at the fireplace. Marie sat on the floor beside him playing with her doll.

"How many slices of salt pork do you want?"

he asked Marie when there was a lull in her chatter.

"Two would be fine," she said, as she scooted close to his leg.

True smiled as Marie sat on his foot and wrapped her arms around his leg. She held onto his leg as he moved from the fireplace to the table and back. He dragged her back and forth and True suspected Marie did this often.

She watched as Sam set the table and placed the food on it. He moved to a chair and with an exaggerated groan he lifted his leg to place his foot on the chair. Marie giggled and scooted off his foot to sit in the chair. He laughed and pushed her chair to the table. He placed a kiss on the top of her head before he turned to pour himself a cup of coffee.

True couldn't help but smile as she got to her feet. "Good morning," she said cheerfully.

Marie turned and smiled at True. "Morning. Thought you was never gonna wake up."

"Marie," Sam said firmly, though he tried not to laugh.

True did laugh. "I thought about sleeping all day." She pushed strands of hair from her face. "But your dad's cooking smelled good, so I thought I'd get up."

She grinned. "It tastes good, too."

True smiled at Sam. "I'm sure it does."

Sam's eyes moved over her in a way that made her stomach tighten. She still wore his extra shirt and his gaze locked onto her legs for a long moment. Her steps faltered but she managed to get herself to the table and seated in a chair. Steven had never looked at her like that and she had a feeling he never would. There was something in Sam's eyes she couldn't identify when he met her gaze. Whatever it was, it sent her stomach fluttering.

"Granny Milly showed him how to cook and she's the best cook in town," Marie said with great enthusiasm.

Sam poured True a cup of coffee. "I won't argue with that."

"She taught you well," True said as she lifted her cup to her mouth.

Marie nodded. "She taught Mama how to cook too, but I never got to taste it before she went to Heaven. Bet she was good at it."

True's eyes went to Sam and she noticed the way his body tensed as memories seemed to wash over him. He let out a breath and stroked Marie on the head before lifting her from the chair to sit on his lap. She continued eating, and an old pain flickered across his face before he hid it away.

"She was a great cook," he told Marie softly.

She grinned at him. "Maybe someday I'll cook just as good."

He gave her a smile. "I bet you will."

"I bet Daddy can teach you to be a good cook," Marie told True.

"I think I'd like that," True said with a smile, her gaze going to Sam, only to find him watching her closely. She couldn't tell what he was thinking and wasn't sure she wanted to know. Something had changed between them last night and she had a feeling it was a change neither of them were ready for.

Chapter Seven

Sam woke at the sound of the door closing. He raised up and looked around the cabin. Marie lay sound asleep. Cody looked at the door for a moment before lowering his head again. Sam looked to True's bed and found it empty. He swore softly as he got to his feet. What the hell was she doing wandering off at this hour? She was going to get lost and he didn't intend to spend all night searching the mountain for her.

He jerked on his boots and pulled on his coat before he opened the door and went out. He pulled the door shut just as he saw her standing out in front of the cabin. She stood wrapped in her long coat, looking out across the meadow. He pulled his coat closed over his bare chest and stepped up to her.

"You all right?" he asked her.

"Yes," she said with a nod. "It's so pretty," she told him quietly. "The full moon shining on the snow and the trees like that."

Sam looked out over the meadow. The moon cast light over the snow-covered landscape. "It is pretty," he agreed.

"And so quiet," she said and hugged her arms round her middle. "It's never this peaceful in Charlotte."

Sam nodded. "I know what you mean." He

thought of the time he spent in Boston.

True shivered and let out a sigh. "Aunt Molly said I was foolish for wanting to spend the winter here."

Without thinking, Sam stepped up behind her and wrapped his arms around her shoulders to pull her back against his chest. He tensed when he realized what he had done and waited for her to protest. She didn't and he fully intended to take advantage of the moment.

"I can understand how your aunt might think like that," he told her, glad that his voice was even.

True laughed softly and leaned back into the warmth he offered. "Maybe so, but I'm glad I came. Even if the trip hasn't turned out as I had planned."

Sam laughed and brushed his cheek against her hair. "So, running from bandits and being trapped in a tiny cabin with a charming stranger and his lovely daughter wasn't what you had in mind?"

"Not exactly," True admitted with a laugh. "Even though you're right. She is lovely."

"And you don't find me charming?" he teased.

She thought for a moment. "Not always. Not when you're bossy, callous, rude, cranky—"

"I get the point." He laughed. "I guess I have been a little hard on you."

"Maybe a little." She leaned her head back against his shoulder and looked up at the stars. "I haven't exactly always made things easy for you. I'm sorry for that."

Sam tightened his arms around her. "You've been through a lot. To tell you the truth, I think you've adjusted quite well."

"I really didn't have much choice," she said simply. "But it hasn't been all bad."

"Look," Sam said quietly and pointed across the meadow. "Out there."

True looked in the direction he indicated. She saw several large animal shapes moving across the meadow. "What are they?" She looked hard and smiled. "Elk?"

He chuckled. "Very good, you'll make a mountain man yet."

She elbowed him gently in the ribs. "It's been years since I've seen elk."

"They're making their way down the mountain for winter," he told her. "The snow gets too deep up here for them to graze."

True leaned back into him and watched the herd of about thirty head of elk move across the meadow. They leisurely grazed on the patches of grass. Her trip west had taken a giant detour and for that she was glad. She was beginning to enjoy her time in the mountains. She had lived in the city for so long she had almost forgotten what it was like in the vast wilderness.

"We better go in," Sam said against her ear. "You're shivering."

"Not yet," she whispered.

True was cold but she was enjoying the night. She was enjoying watching the elk, and the moon on the snow made it all so beautiful. She mostly enjoyed Sam holding her. His body curved along hers, his arms held her tight and she liked his warmth against her. She wanted to stay like this as long as she could.

"Come on." Sam turned her in his arms. "We better go in and get some hot coffee down you."

True looked up at him and Sam felt his heart squeeze. She was so beautiful standing in the moonlight. Her dark eyes shone and her pale skin nearly glowed. He couldn't keep his hand from coming up to touch her face. He let his fingers brush her soft skin before he cupped her cheek. He ran his thumb over her full lips and couldn't stop himself from lowering his mouth to hers.

True held her breath as she watched him move closer to softly brush his lips to hers. Her stomach tightened as his mouth teased over hers. She let her breath out in a soft sigh and leaned into him. Sam pressed his mouth firmly to hers and traced the seam of her lips with his tongue, coaxing her mouth to open to his. She did so and he kissed her deeply, his tongue exploring as he put his arms around her and pulled her close.

Her body melted into his and her arms went around his neck to pull his mouth harder to hers. She tentatively touched her tongue to his and he let out a low groan. His arms tightened and the kiss deepened. True's body went to liquid fire. She had never been kissed like this before and she wanted more.

Sam couldn't stop the groan that escaped him. She felt damn good in his arms and she tasted so sweet. His body stirred in a way it hadn't in years and he wanted her, wanted her with every fiber of his being. He held her body tightly, so tight he was afraid she might not be able to breathe. He eased his hold slightly and devoured her mouth.

Sam opened her coat and pushed his hands under it to wrap his arms around her again. His own coat fell open and he felt the cold air on his skin. He pulled her close, her breasts pressed to his chest, only the thin shirt separating them. His body warmed and heat settled in his groin.

He kissed her until they were both breathless, then his mouth drifted kisses over her face to her neck. His mouth tasted and nipped her tender skin and a soft sound escaped her, sending a surge of heat through him. She lowered her arms and her hands splayed across his chest.

Sam's breath hissed out and he jerked back. "Damn, your hands are cold." He was silently thankful for the cold jolt back to reality. At the same time, he was mad as hell.

True gathered her scattered wits. "Sorry," she managed to say, though she found it hard to breathe.

"We better go in before we freeze to death," he told her and moved her toward the door.

True cast one last look at the beautiful moonlit meadow and the grazing elk before she went inside. The warmth from the cabin was a blessing on her skin. She hadn't realized just how cold she was. Sam helped her out of her long coat as she kicked off her shoes.

"Is that all you had on?" he asked as he stared at her. She wore only her sleeping shirt.

She nodded. "I wasn't planning on being out long."

Sam could only stare at her as he somehow managed to take off his coat and boots. Her long bare legs beckoned to him and her nipples peaked and strained against the shirt.

"*You* don't have a shirt on," she pointed out. Her eyes drifted over his solid chest and arms.

When he only stared at her, she followed his gaze to her breasts to find her nipples straining against the material. She let out a cry and covered them with her arms as she turned her back to him. She shot him a glare over her shoulder when he laughed.

"Go sit by the fire and I'll get the coffee going," he told her. "It's only a couple hours to sunup, no point in going back to sleep now."

True nodded and sat down on Sam's sleeping pallet. She didn't argue, there would be no sleeping for her now. The memory of his kiss was too fresh in her mind. She could still feel his mouth on hers and the taste of him. She pulled a blanket up over her legs and clutched it to her chest.

It didn't take long for the coffee to heat and Sam handed her a cup of the hot liquid and sat beside her. She looked at him when he chuckled.

"What's so funny?" she asked.

He smiled at her, his dark eyes twinkling with amusement. "I bet you never thought you'd be stuck in the middle of nowhere sitting by a fire with a half-naked man and you wearing his shirt."

Her mouth dropped open and she stared at him. She saw the humor in his eyes and smiled. "Can't say that it crossed my mind."

"What would the proper ladies back east think?" he teased.

She let her eyes trail over his chest as he took a drink of coffee. "That I'm very lucky and they don't know what they're missing."

Sam coughed and choked on the coffee. True laughed and slapped him on the back several times. He looked at her in shock and she couldn't help but laugh at him.

"I think you're blushing," she said and laughed.

He smiled at her. "I guess you turned the tables on me."

"Daddy?" Came Marie's sleepy voice.

They looked to see the little girl sitting up in bed. She rubbed her eye with her fist.

"I'm sorry, honey," Sam told her. "We didn't mean to wake you."

Marie said nothing as she hopped from the small bed and moved to her father. She yawned and sat down in his crossed legs to curl up, using his knee as a pillow and was asleep again in seconds.

Sam leaned and stretched to grab a blanket on Marie's bed. True watched him as he moved. The muscles in his chest and arms rippled as he tried to pull a blanket from the bed. Cody growled and bit at the blanket as it moved beneath him. Sam swore at the dog and jerked the blanket and dog from the bed. He covered Marie and Cody came around to lay beside True. She absently reached down to stroke his head.

Sam tucked the blanket around Marie. "There you go," he told her even though she was asleep.

"Sam," True said after a while. "I hope you don't mind me asking and you don't have to answer. How long has your wife been gone?"

He looked at her for a moment before looking at Marie. He stroked her dark hair back from her face. "There are days it feels like a lifetime," he said quietly. "She died the night Marie was born. There were complications and she lost too much blood."

True felt her eyes burn at the emotion in his voice. "I'm sorry, I shouldn't have asked."

"It's all right," he told her as he stroked Marie's cheek. "It's natural for you to be curious."

True watched as his big hand lovingly caressed his daughters face. She couldn't imagine what it would have been like for him, to lose his wife, and then care for a child all alone.

"What does Marie think of living in a cabin?" she asked hoping to direct the conversation to more pleasant things. "I imagine she's adjusted better than I have."

A smile crept over Sam's lips. "That she did." He let out a long breath. "She adapts well and views everything as an adventure."

"She'll have to teach me how to do that," she said with a chuckle.

Sam looked at her. "I think you're doing fine. It's not every proper city woman that can escape bandits, nearly freeze to death, and be trapped in a cabin in the space of a few days."

"Ah, but I had an advantage, I haven't always been a proper city woman," she said with little humor, thinking of her hellish childhood.

"Maybe so." He gave her a grin. "But I'd say you're having a hell of an adventure."

She smiled at him. "Yes, I believe I am."

***

Two more days passed and two more nights of True thinking about the night Sam had held her.

Each day they went about their daily routine, which didn't consist of much given the weather and the small space in the tiny cabin. Each night after Marie went to sleep, Sam and True would stay up and talk for hours, she was thankful they no longer argued. True had grown content with her time with Sam and Marie.

They had finished their breakfast when True looked up to see Sam putting on his coat. "Going someplace?"

"Hunting," he told her simply as he put on his hat and gloves before picking up his rifle. "I'll be back in a few hours."

Before True could say anything, Sam was through the door and had it closed behind him. Sam had been unusually quiet all morning, something was certainly weighing on his mind.

"True?"

She turned to Marie to see the girl coming toward her with her doll in her hand. "Yes?"

"Can you sing pretty like Shyfawn?" she asked as she crawled up onto the table to sit before True.

A soft laugh left her. "No, I can't sing as pretty as Shyfawn, but I'm not terrible."

"Good, she taught me a song. We should sing it."

"I'll do my best."

Marie told True the song and it brought burning tears to her eyes. It was an old song that the sisters would sing together when they were young. They may not have had much growing up, but they had each other.

Shyfawn was the singer in the family, her voice

was beautiful and mesmerizing. It had saved her life all those years ago. She had been kidnapped along with several other women and taken to a saloon to be sold for pleasure. The cruel man that had taken Shyfawn had heard her singing and decided to use her voice to draw in customers. She struck a bargain with the man that she would sing only if he didn't sell her as a whore. He billed her as the singing virgin and had raked in a fortune.

Thankfully, Joanna had found Shyfawn and helped her escape. That was when Shyfawn had met Matthew, and though they had butted heads more than once, they had fallen in love and were now going to have a family. Shyfawn was in love. Joanna was in love. Was True in love? She suddenly wasn't so sure.

"Let's sing it again!" Marie squealed.

True laughed and they sang the song again. Then True taught her a few new songs. She enjoyed Marie's company and was glad they had become friends right away. When Cody started to howl from his place by the fire, True decided they had done enough singing. Marie laughed and scrambled from the table to sit by Cody and sing to him. He would howl and she would giggle hysterically.

The day passed swiftly. Sam still wasn't back and she was starting to worry. She paced restlessly for a long time, listening to Marie as she told Cody a fairytale. Sam should have been back by now. *Where is he?*

True smiled at her question. She could find out. Going to the table, she sat down, closed her eyes, and concentrated on Sam.

Lights flashed behind her eyes and pain stabbed her head as she forced the vision, then she saw him. Riding his horse through the snow, he stopped to overlook the pass. There would be no way of getting through it yet. He turned and headed back toward the cabin through the big snowflakes that started to fall.

True sighed and opened her eyes. He would be back in a few hours. She would keep the stew she had made warm and wait for him. She stood and went to the trunk, where she remembered seeing a deck of cards. She could entertain herself for a while with a few card games.

Chapter Eight

It was well past dark when Sam reached the cabin. He had thought the long ride would help clear his head. He had been wrong. True had filled his mind all day and his feelings for her were growing. He had used going hunting as an excuse to get some distance between them and give him time to think. It had done little good, he had thought of True and nothing else.

He fed and stabled the horse, put his gear in the shed and headed for the cabin. He hoped they could get down the mountain soon, with the two extra horses to feed the hay supply was getting low.

He stomped the snow from his boots before entering. He stepped inside to see Marie and Cody asleep and True sitting at the table playing with his deck of cards. She was wearing his shirt again and he wished she would stand up so he could look at her legs.

She paused long enough to glance up at him. "Come in and warm up. I kept the stew hot for you." She flipped another card over.

He had expected her to be irritated with him for being so late, but she sat there quite content. He shrugged and slipped off his gloves, stuffing them into the pockets of his coat. Taking off his coat and hat, he hung them on the pegs by the door.

"I was never any good at this game," she muttered, flipping over another card.

"What game?" Sam stepped up to the table.

"Solitaire." She glanced at him. "I seldom ever win."

He shrugged. "Cheat."

"I can't do that; it would take the fun out of it."

"I don't know what kind of games they teach you in Charlotte, but solitaire isn't one of the fun ones." Sam dished up a bowl of stew and sat across from her.

"What kind of games do they teach around here?" she asked, tossing down the cards.

"Poker."

"Poker?"

He shrugged. "It's a good pastime. We'd play it in the bunkhouse most evenings. Have you ever played before?"

"No, but I would watch the men play when my Aunt gave parties."

"Good. I'll teach you." He pushed his bowl of stew aside and picked up the cards.

After shuffling them, he dealt each of them five cards. He quickly explained the object of the game and the various winning hands. True caught on fast, occasionally she had to show him her cards and ask if she was winning or not.

"Are you ready to lose some money now?" Sam asked as he stood.

"I don't have any money," she told him as she watched him get the small tin match box from the shelf.

"Neither do I, so we'll have to play for

matches." He sat down again and dumped the box of matches out onto the table. He divided them evenly into two piles.

They played several hands of poker, each winning and losing, and now and then Sam would take a bite of his stew. Soon True had most of the matches and Sam had bet his last three.

"I'm out of matches."

"Give up?" True asked giving him a big smile.

"Never!" Sam said dramatically.

True laughed at him. "Then you can bet Marie."

Sam glanced over at his sleeping daughter. "I would rather bet the shirt off my back."

"I'll take it then," she said tilting her chin in a challenge.

Sam studied her. "Fine." He laid his cards face down and slipped his shirt off over his head and tossed it on the table along with the matches. "I call."

True stared at him. She had only been bluffing.

He sat across from her, chest bare and wearing that grin she liked so much. He was magnificent. Her mouth went dry and she couldn't take her eyes off him. She had seen him without his shirt before and it still sent her heart racing. Memories of being held against that strong chest filled her mind. She doubted that Steven would even come close to looking this good without his clothing on.

"True?"

She gave a start and quickly pulled her eyes from him to focus on her cards. "What?"

"What are your cards? I have three kings." Sam

couldn't help but enjoy the reaction she had to him taking off his shirt.

She swallowed hard. "I-I have three jacks and two sevens." She laid her cards down. "That's good, right?"

Sam chuckled. "Yeah, that's good."

True whooped with delight. "I won again." She gathered the matches, and his shirt, toward her and added them to her pile.

"Looks like you wiped me out." He quirked an eyebrow at her. "That is unless you would like to play for my boots and pants."

True's hands stopped organizing her matches and she gaped at him, her eyes wide. "Sam!" she said, her voice full of shock.

Sam threw back his head and laughed. It was a hearty laugh that came from his toes and True liked the sound of it. Realizing that he was only joking, she laughed along with him.

"I was just kidding," he said, trying to catch his breath.

"I should hope so." She leaned back in her chair and smiled at him with amusement. She looked at his bowl of food that he had only half eaten. "You better eat some more before you starve to death. You probably worked up an appetite going all the way to the pass today."

Sam stood with his bowl and went to the pot that still hung over the fireplace. He stopped, and then turned to her. "How did you know I went to the pass today?" He hadn't told her where he had gone.

True's heart leaped, she had slipped. "Where else would you have been. You didn't bring home any meat and you got home so late tonight. And since you haven't told me I can leave yet, I'm assuming that it's still closed." True held her breath, hoping that he would believe her.

He shrugged. "Makes sense." He filled the rest of his bowl with hot stew and went back to the table and began to eat. "And yes, it's still closed."

True watched him, the firelight and lamplight casting shadows over his muscular chest and arms. He was so big and strong; she was sure that he could snap her like a twig if he wanted. But there was also something very tender and caring about him. When he held her close, he had been so gentle with her. His jaw was strong, too, and she wondered what he would look like without his short beard. Some stew was on his lip and his tongue flicked out to get it. True's stomach muscles tightened and her heartbeat fluttered faster.

"I'd better move the pot." She cursed her voice for sounding breathless.

Sam watched her abruptly stand and go to the fire. Her movements were hurried and jerky, she used a rag to protect her hands from the heat and lifted the pot from the hook above the fireplace, then set it on the wooden stand in the corner. She tossed a rag over it and went to the fire, doing her best not to look at him.

Sam frowned, what was wrong with her? She poked around at the fire, then added another log. Her long gold hair hung in one thick braid down her back. His shirt that she wore to sleep in, crept up her thigh, revealing more of her creamy flesh. Sam couldn't take his eyes off her exposed legs. Didn't she ever get cold wearing nothing but that? Sam hadn't realized he spoke the question out loud.

"No. Not really." She turned and met his gaze. There was no mistaking the desire she saw there. "And it's comfortable."

"Wouldn't that be considered improper in Charlotte?" Sam couldn't take his eyes from hers.

"Yes." She nodded. "But I'm not in Charlotte."

"No, you're not." There was a husky note to his voice.

Their eyes held for a long moment before she had to look away from the searing heat in them. She moved to Marie's bed and tucked the covers tightly around the little girl. Then she patted Cody on the head. He sighed, and his tail wagged for a moment.

True smiled, such an unusual couple, big ugly dog and small adorable girl. For some reason the image of Steven and herself came to mind. A beautiful whore's daughter and a scrawny businessman. She shook her head at the thought and turned.

She was unaware that Sam had moved up behind her until she ran right into him. She stumbled, placing her hands on his chest for balance as he caught her by the shoulders.

"Whoa, be careful," he said holding her upright.

"Sorry, I didn't know you were there." She steadied herself.

She was all too aware of his nearness and his hands seemed to burn into her shoulders. She looked up into his dark eyes, the heat was still there. She knew she should move away from him and give him an apology for bumping into him. Yet all she could think of was how big his hands were on her arms and how hard his chest was as she touched him. Regretfully, she started to move away from him, but his hands held her arms and she could see an inner struggle in his dark eyes.

"You have no idea what you do to me," he whispered. Then he jerked her to him, bent his head and kissed her. His hands slid down her arms to grasp her around the waist, holding her tightly against him.

True knew she should protest and pull away, but she couldn't seem to force herself to do so. The way he was kissing her made her body hot and she seemed to go weak. She murmured something. It might have been either protest or permission, she wasn't entirely sure, as his arms went around her. He held her tightly against him and kissed her deeply.

She slid her fingers into his hair and pulled his mouth harder against hers. His arms held her captive as his mouth devoured hers. True clung to him, leaning into him to press her breasts against his muscular chest. Need raced through her and she brushed her tongue across his lips. He held her close with one arm and let his hand slide down over her hip, caressing her. He ravaged her mouth, plunging his tongue deep between her lips.

Her heart pounded in a way she hadn't thought possible, and she could feel his heart racing against her chest. She had never experienced anything like this before, nor expected that she ever would again. When Steven had kissed her, it had been proper and quick, this was exactly the opposite. Sam sent her body into a fever and she wanted more.

Unable to stop the soft sound that escaped her, she wrapped her arms around his shoulders and clung to him. She pressed herself fully against him and felt his body shudder as he let out a groan. He stepped her back until she bumped against her bed. She let out a startled cry when he lifted her slightly to set her on the bed. He pushed her legs open with his thighs to stand between them.

Sam moved his hands up her bare thighs beneath the shirt to touch her, she was so damn soft. He let his hands drift over her hips, across her waist, and along her ribs. She made a breathy sound against his mouth and he felt heat surge through him. He pushed her back until she lay on the bed, his body covering hers. His mouth moved to her neck as his hands worked at the buttons of the shirt she wore. He muttered a curse when he found his hands shaking.

True tilted her head to let his mouth explore the skin of her neck and he took advantage. He tasted and nipped her, letting his tongue swirl over her tender skin. He opened her shirt and let his hands drift up her ribs to cover her breasts. A startled gasp escaped her, and he bit back a groan. Her breasts were fuller than he had imagined, they fit his hands perfectly. He dragged his thumbs over her nipples and she let out a small cry.

True bit her lip and tried to sort out the feelings and emotions he was creating in her. His hands and mouth on her skin sent fire through her body. An unexpected heat settled in her stomach and a throbbing began between her legs. She wound her hands in his hair as his mouth drifted over the swell of her breast. When his mouth closed over her nipple and tugged, she cried out.

"Sam." She could hardly find enough air to speak as his mouth tugged and suckled. She couldn't stop the moan that escaped her as his mouth drifted to her other breast to give it the same exquisite torture.

Sam found her mouth again and pressed his body down onto hers. The feel of her breasts against his bare chest caused him to groan. His hand slid down to cradle her hip, lifting her as he pushed his hard arousal against her. She whimpered and shifted her hips under him.

A soft sound behind him stopped him still. He tore his lips from hers to look over his shoulder at Marie. She stirred in bed, rolling over to place an arm around Cody. Sam breathed a sigh of relief; she was still asleep. He was suddenly pulled back to reality as he looked at True again. His body wanted hers, but he knew he couldn't have her.

"Jesus, True…" He practically groaned the words as he moved off her and pulled her shirt closed to cover her tempting body. "I must be crazy. If Jo ever found out what I was thinking she'd kill me." His breath was ragged with desire.

"No, don't stop."

She sat up, holding the shirt closed. Her breathless plea was almost his undoing.

"True, if I don't stop now, I might not be able to." He stepped away from her. "You don't understand what could happen."

"I-I think I would like to find out," she said softly

Sam looked into her eyes, they were filled with innocence, curiosity, and passion. It was plain she was willing, but he couldn't do that to her. She was a lady, not some convenient whore. But God, how he wanted her.

Her brow puckered as she studied him. "Sam?"

He let out a long breath and reached out to button her shirt. "You should find out what it's like when you're back in Charlotte and married to a good man. Not here in the middle of nowhere with me," he said, as he finished buttoning her shirt.

She almost laughed. "Somehow I doubt that. My fiancé never made me feel like this." She had known Steven for years and never once had her body melted at his touch. She had only known Sam for a short time and her body turned liquid fire with just a look from him.

At the mention of her fiancé and the thought of another man touching her, Sam felt as if he had a knife twisting in his gut. It only reminded him that she did in fact belong to someone else, and that knowledge was painful. Very painful.

He cleared his throat. "You should try to get some sleep," he told her as he turned from her. "It's late."

He heard her move from the bed and pull back the covers to climb into it. He couldn't look at her right now and he had to force himself to remember she wasn't his. True belonged to a wealthy man in Charlotte and Sam knew he didn't have a chance in hell with someone like her. It was going to be difficult, but he couldn't let his feelings for her get the better of him.

He must avoid touching her in any way. Next time, he might not be able to stop.

Chapter Nine

True paced the cabin restlessly. Sam had left hours ago to hunt and she was going crazy being cooped up inside. He had taken Cody with him and Marie missed her playmate but didn't complain. True needed fresh air and sunshine before she forgot what they were like.

She studied Marie, who was engrossed with her doll and asked, "Marie, would you like to go outside today?"

She looked up and her dark eyes sparkled with delight. "Yes!"

True smiled at her. "Let's get bundled up."

In no time, they were dressed in their coats and gloves and stepping outside. True closed her eyes and took in a deep breath of crisp air then slowly let it out. It was warmer outside than she expected and she was glad to see bare patches of ground where the snow had melted. With any luck, it wouldn't be long before the pass was clear enough for them to get to Rimrock. She had no doubt her sisters were worried sick by now.

Marie laughed as she eagerly ran out into the snow and threw herself down to make a snow angel. True couldn't help but smile, and then acted on her sudden urge to do the same. She couldn't remember when she had last enjoyed the simple act of making a snow angel.

The two laughed and played in the snow, making snowmen and having a snowball fight.

Images of True playing with her sisters when they were children flashed through her mind. They had to be outside and out of the way as men came and went from their cabin for their mother to entertain. Their father would sit outside, take the money and drink whiskey. Joanna always tried to keep her sisters far from the cabin when the men were there, but True knew what was happening.

"Help me build another snowman," Marie called out as she began to roll the snow.

True helped her and soon they had a large snowman standing before the cabin. Sticks became arms and pinecones his eyes and nose. True stood back and admired their handiwork. This snowman was a bit lopsided, but he matched the other two small snowmen near the cabin.

"Come on, let's go in and get warmed up," True said, noticing that the sun had begun to dip down over the hill. She hadn't realized how long they had been out.

Marie followed True into the house. The fire was low, so True placed a couple more logs into it. She stripped out of her coat and gloves and began pulling the clumps of snow from her hair. Marie did the same.

"Come, let's get you out of those wet things," Marie said, pulling at True's hand.

She had to smile at the little mother hen. "You're all wet too," True pointed out.

Marie looked down at herself. "I know." She

lifted her arms and waited for True to pull her dress over her head. True laughed, took Marie's dress off and draped it over the back of the chair to dry. Marie took off her under things and hung them on the back of the other chair, then went to her bed, grabbed her nightdress from beneath her pillow and put it on.

"Now, could you get us some blankets to wrap up in?" True asked as she took off her own dress and pulled on Sam's shirt. Marie grabbed blankets off the bed and drug them over to True, who laughed. "No, you have to wrap up in one."

Marie wrapped herself up, as best she could, in the huge blanket. True swung a blanket around her shoulders and hung her wet clothes wherever she could to let them dry. Then they snuggled down on Sam's sleeping mat in front of the fireplace. True felt content and happy, sitting with Marie, listening to the little girl's happy chatter.

***

Sam stepped inside the cabin and hung his coat and hat on the pegs by the door. Cody vigorously shook the snow from his fur and trotted to his food pan. Sam's eyes searched the room for Marie and True. He didn't see them, only their wet clothing hanging around the cabin. He took another step into the room and spotted them sleeping next to the fireplace. True slept on her side her arm laying protectively around Marie, who was curled up spoon-style against True's stomach.

Sam stood and looked at them for a long time. The deep longing in his heart was painful and he felt he could watch them sleep all night. He only wished that he was the one lying in True's arms.

Bending down, he picked up Marie and carried her to her small bed. She murmured something to him.

"Shhh," he whispered in her ear as he lay her down and covered her up.

He bent and kissed her on the cheek. Marie was so precious to him; he didn't know what he would do without her. Cody jumped onto bed and lay down and Marie automatically reached for him.

Sam put two more logs on the fire, then sat on his haunches watching True sleep. The firelight glistened off her gold hair as it hung loose around her face and shoulders. His eyes traveled the length of her, the blanket draped loosely over her curves. Her calf was exposed, he studied it. The skin was very red. Sam touched her leg. It was cold. He moved the blanket up and touched her thigh, it was also very cold. Her leg suddenly jerked up and Sam drew his hand back. Then her foot came forward and caught him in the chest, knocking him backwards.

True leaped to her feet, trying to wake up enough to realize what was happening. She clutched the blanket tightly with one fist, with her other hand she brushed her hair out of her face so she could see.

Sam lay on the floor, then propped himself up on one elbow and held his other hand to his chest where she had kicked him.

True stood with her feet wide apart, ready to fight, then her eyes slowly focused on him. She blinked the fog of sleep away. Sam saw her breathe a sigh of relief when she recognized him.

Sam slowly stood, rubbing a hand over his chest, his eyes fixed on her. Her hair was tangled and hung loose around her shoulders and down her back. His gaze traveled down to her bare legs.

"What were you doing?" she asked sharply.

"Forgive me for being concerned." He walked over to the chair, sat down and started taking off his boots. "I thought there might be something wrong, your skin was awfully red."

"Sorry, you just startled me." She pulled out the chair across from him and sat down. "Marie and I went out for some air and played in the snow. We made a few snowmen and got soaked." True looked fondly at the child. "But I made her get out of her wet clothes, so she wouldn't catch cold."

Sam looked at his daughter lying in her bed. "Good thinking, I don't want her to get sick."

"Don't worry." True smiled slightly at him. "I may be from the city, but I know a thing or two."

He nodded and favored her with a slight smile. "As I'm beginning to find out."

His eyes drifted to her bare legs and he felt his need for her rush through him once again. He fought the urge to rip the blanket off her, throw her across the table and savagely take her body. But no, he couldn't do that. True was a lady and deserved better. Besides, if Jo ever found out she would kill him for touching her sister.

"Marie!" Sam stared at True with wide eyes.

She only looked at him in confusion. "What?"

"Did Marie see you?"

"Did she see me what?" True asked not

understanding what he was getting at.

"Did she see you get undressed?" he asked almost distressed. Usually he would sit with his daughter with their backs to True while she changed. This time he felt sure Marie had seen True naked.

"Well, yes. It's not like you have a dressing room here or anything." True was baffled at his reaction. "It's not the first time I've had to change in front of her."

He stared at her, open mouthed. "Did she ask questions?"

True fought the urge to laugh. "Well, of course she did, silly."

He stood and practically loomed over her. "What did you tell her?" he demanded.

True stood and looked him in the eyes. "I told her the truth." Loving the horrified look on his face True couldn't help but enjoy the moment, so she decided to embellish a bit. "She asked all kinds of questions." Her voice was low and silky as she advanced on him. Sam backed up a few steps.

"True, stop it." Sam backed away a little more.

True only smiled and took a few steps forward. "Then she wanted to know when she would—"

"I said, stop it!" Sam reached out and grabbed her shoulders.

"Sorry, I was just having a little fun with you."

But Sam didn't look at all amused as he looked down at her.

"Besides she had to find out sometime. Don't worry, I didn't explain the facts of life to her, if that's what you're worried about." True became aware of the heat of his hands on her shoulders through the blanket. "She asked a few simple questions and I answered them as best I could."

"But she's just a child."

"Would you have rather explained it to her?" True couldn't stop the grin that tugged at the corners of her lips.

"No." Sam let go of her shoulders, walked to the fire and stared into the flames.

True was disappointed when he let go of her. "Sam, I'm sorry." She moved to stand next to him, but he didn't look at her. "I didn't mean to be so…" She paused trying to think of a word. "I don't know, crude, unfeeling. I didn't mean to upset you."

"It's not your fault. It's just that I don't want her to grow up." Sam moved to the table and sat down, leaning one elbow on the table and staring into the fire again.

True hopped up to sit on the table close to him. "Do you want to talk about it?"

There was a long silence. True decided not to push the subject if he didn't want to talk about it. When he did finally speak, it startled her.

"Someday she is going to grow up and meet a man and she won't be my little girl anymore." He was silent for a long time. "Then what if she gets pregnant and…" He didn't finish. He didn't have to. True understood him. He was afraid that his daughter would die in childbirth like her mother had. "I just don't think I could live without her." Sam looked over at his sleeping daughter. "She's my whole life."

True reached out and placed a hand on his

shoulder. "I don't think you have to worry about any of that for many years to come."

Sam looked up at her, his eyes filled with sadness. She smiled at him slightly and touched his cheek. At that, he stood and went to the fire, poking at it with a chunk of wood before tossing it in.

True, still sitting on the table, swung her legs back and forth a little. "Besides she's spunky and tough. If there is a man that can tame her, he'd be worth having."

True looked at her small feet as they hung several inches from the floor. She felt uncomfortable. This man had just told her his greatest fear and she wasn't quite sure what to say to give him comfort. She had to admit, he was quite the man. A lot different than the snooty unfeeling men she knew in Charlotte.

True's discomfort gave way to feeling guilty as she thought of Steven. Yes, he was snooty and unfeeling, she only hoped that their marriage would be a good one. If it were anything like her parents' marriage, she wanted no part of it. But then, Steven's parents didn't seem to enjoy being married to each other either. They were cold and distant when they were together and True had never seen them show any affection toward each other.

She looked at Sam, his back toward her. He was such a powerful man with so much feeling, she could love such a man. She looked at her feet again. He had already stirred feelings in her that Steven never had, probably never could. She wondered if marrying Steven would be a great mistake. She cared for him, but the feelings she had for Steven were nothing compared to how Sam made her feel.

With a sigh, True hopped down from the table. "I suppose we should get some sleep."

"Yeah." Sam still stood staring into the fire, his back rigid.

She walked over to him. "Sam?" He didn't look at her or say anything. "Are you all right?"

"She was so young." Sam almost whispered and True stepped close beside him to better hear him. "She was young and so small." He stared at the flames of the fire. "But I wanted to marry her, and then before we knew it, she was pregnant. If I had only known then..." He looked down at his hands and shook his head. "She was too small to have children. I should have known." He swallowed hard. "I never should have—"

"Sam, don't do this to yourself." True moved to stand in front of him.

"If I had only known what would happen to her, I never would have—"

"It's not your fault." True put a hand on his face, forcing him to look at her. "Life is full of ifs, and if you never married her you wouldn't have Marie. You love her so dearly and Marie loves you more than anything in the whole world." She brushed his hair back. "Stop blaming yourself, you can't change the past. Things happen for a reason. We may not understand it at the time and it may hurt like hell, but we have to keep living."

She gasped as he grabbed her hand and held it to his cheek, closing his eyes. Then his arms were around her and he held her tightly against him. She let go of the blanket and it pooled on the floor at their feet. She put her arms around him and held him close, wishing she could take some of his pain away. He blamed himself for his wife's death and had been carrying so much guilt all these years. With open-hearted sympathy, she stood on tip toe and kissed him on the neck. She felt him stiffen, then pull away slightly, holding onto her shoulders.

"I shouldn't have done—" That was all she could say before his lips found hers and he pulled her against him tightly.

Fire shot through her as his mouth took hers with such hunger. She opened her mouth to him and his tongue slipped inside, exploring her. A soft, involuntary moan escaped her lips and she leaned into him.

Sam gave a shuddering groan as his hands trailed down over the curve of her hips to pull her against his growing arousal. She gasped against his lips but didn't try to pull away, instead seeming to try to get closer to him. Her fingers wound in his hair, pulling his mouth harder against hers to deepen their kiss.

Sam wanted to blame his raging emotions for his actions, but couldn't. He had a fiery need for her from the beginning and it only kept burning hotter. Now that fire was out of control and he wouldn't be able to stop himself this time. Consequences be damned.

Her hands went to his shirt, frantically pulling at the buttons. When she had them all free, she pushed open his shirt and splayed her hands across his chest. Sam's body shuddered and the feel of her hands on his skin sent desire raging through him.

She pushed his shirt off his shoulders and stepped into him.

Sam muttered a curse as he dropped the shirt to the floor, then crushed her to him. She felt so good in his arms. Too damn good. His hands went to her bottom and he lifted her. She gave a startled cry but wrapped her legs around him as he carried her to the bed. He lay her down and covered her body with his own, his mouth going to her neck. She tipped her head back, allowing him full access, and he took advantage of it. Tasting her throat, his fingers worked at the buttons of her shirt until he had it fully open. His mouth trailed kisses down across her collarbone to the swell of her breast.

"Sam." Her voice was a raspy whisper.

"I'm busy here," he said against her skin. His breath and mouth hot as he tasted her.

"Sam," she said again and pushed at him slightly. "Marie."

His head shot up and over to look at his daughter. She still slept. "She's a sound sleeper," he told her and bent his head once more.

She pushed at him again. "What if she sees?"

He drew back and looked at True. Her cheeks were flushed, her lips swollen from his kisses, and the passion in her eyes was clear to see. She was beautiful. But he understood her concern. Marie was a deep sleeper but if she happened to wake, he sure as hell didn't want her to see this. He nodded and pushed from the bed.

Using the chairs and blankets, Sam fashioned a canopy over Marie's bed. If she woke, she would be unable to see anything and be lucky if she managed to get out from under the blankets hanging over her.

He turned back to True, who lay in bed under the blankets watching him with shining dark eyes. He could see she had removed her shirt and he sucked in a deep breath of anticipation as he walked back to the bed. Quickly as his shaking hands would allow him, he removed the rest of his clothes. True brazenly looked him over before she blushed and turned her face away. Sam chuckled to himself and crawled under the blankets with her, covering her body with his.

True let out a noise that was half gasp and half moan as he pressed his body down on hers. His hard body over her, his arousal against her thigh, she had never felt anything so amazing. She pulled his mouth to hers and let her hands explore his body. He was so hard and solid.

After a long deep kiss, he lifted his head to look at her. "I should pick up where I left off," he told her, a smile tugging his lips.

She smiled back at him. "Maybe you should."

Sam nuzzled his way back to the swell of her breast. She gasped when his hand cupped her breast and he ran his thumb over her aching nipple. Then he drew her nipple into his mouth. Her body shuddered and her hands went to his hair, holding him close. His hand slid down her stomach to cup her womanhood. She instinctively opened for him. Her body melted as his hand moved over her.

Feelings True had never known washed over her as he touched her so intimately. Her body jerked and a small cry left her when his fingers gently moved over her, finding the little bundle of nerves to send urgent pleasure through her. She needed more and wanted to experience everything with Sam tonight. His mouth found hers for a deep kiss as his fingers built her pleasure until her hips were moving against him and she moaned into his mouth.

Sam swore softly as he withdrew his hand. He couldn't wait any longer, he needed True now. He reached between them to guide his aching manhood to her hot entrance and pressed against her. Slowly, carefully, Sam eased into her. She made a soft noise and he grit his teeth, fighting for control. If he lost it, he wouldn't be able to bring her the pleasure she needed.

True's hands clutched at his hips. "More," she breathed with urgency.

He felt the barrier of her virginity, though the resistance was slight. Still, he would have moved slowly, but she wouldn't let him. She shifted beneath him and pulled at his hips. He groaned and pushed into her farther and faster than he meant to. He muffled her cry of pain with his mouth. He kissed her softly and held himself still inside her. She felt so damn good, so tight and welcoming.

"Sam?" Her voice shook.

"It's all right, True," he told her gently and rained kisses across her face. He groaned as she shifted beneath him and whimpered. "The pain will ease," he told her as he kissed her softly. "Let your body accept mine."

She let out a long breath and tried to relax. "I didn't know it would hurt."

He looked into her dark eyes. "Just the first time." He brushed his lips across hers. "I'll try to be gentle with you."

She pulled his head down to capture his mouth fully. He kissed her deeply, building the burning fire in her. The pain began to fade as he slowly moved within her. Pleasure flowed over her in lingering waves as he moved his body over hers.

Nothing had ever felt as powerful as the moment when she took all of him. Nothing in his life had prepared him for the sheer rightness of joining with her. In filling her, some empty part of himself was filled. He felt suddenly alive in a way he had never been before.

She shifted her hips. "Sam, more."

Her whispered plea was his undoing, he began to move within her with more urgency. The rhythm of their loving was slow and strong, and True was with him. Her eyes held his, and holding her gaze seemed the most intimate experience of his life, more intimate than the joining of their bodies.

The fire inside him, between them, flamed higher and burned hotter as the rhythm increased. Faster, harder, he thrust deep into her. The sharp bite of her nails on his back urged him on. The soft sounds of pleasure she made was like music to his ears. Soon her hips moved against his as she matched his rhythm. Her hips rolled and the act flamed the fire into an inferno.

"God, True," he growled and kissed her deeply.

She was driving him wild, taking him to the edge far faster than he had wanted. His body spiraled toward release and he thrust harder and deeper. He swallowed her cries of pleasure with a deep kiss as he pushed her toward the edge with him. He levered over her on his elbows and pushed against her sensitive bud with each thrust. Her fingers bit into his back and her body began to shake.

"Sam," she breathed against his mouth. "Sam, I... Please."

"Let it happen," he urged, his breath coming hard.

Then he felt it, deep inside her, the clenching of her inner muscles around him like a velvet fist. He felt her shake and she filled her lungs. Sam clamped a hand over her mouth as she cried out. Her release hit her and took him over the edge of pleasure. He put an arm under her hips and pulled her to him as he groaned out his own release.

The first thing True became aware of was Sam's weight pressing her into the bed. She reveled in it. She relished the feel of him still buried inside her, and the way his ragged breath was hot against her ear. She never wanted this moment, this closeness she felt with him, to end. She wanted to wrap her arms around him and hold him there forever.

Without warning, tears stung her eyes. Feeling and emotions slammed into her and she could hardly breathe. A sound that was half sob, half laughter escaped her. The sound muffled by his hand still over her mouth.

Shaken by the sound, Sam raised his head and took his hand from her mouth. "True?"

"Sam." Was all she could say.

He drifted kisses over her face, tasting her tears as he kissed her softly. He thought he understood her tears. He knew he hadn't hurt her, and that she had found her pleasure in their loving. But it had been so intense, so unlike anything he had ever experienced before. He wished he could join her and find an escape through tears for the emotions that made his chest tight. Her body shook as laughter and sobs mingled. She held him tighter as her feelings and emotions untangled themselves.

Sam also didn't know whether to laugh or cry. What had just happened between them had been intense. Too far outside the realm of what he had always believed possible between a man and a woman. He couldn't help but smile as he raised himself to look at her.

"True, that was…" he whispered, unable to describe what he had just felt with her. Instead, he kissed her lightly on the lips.

Sam rested his forehead against hers and lay over her until his breath returned and his heart slowed down. He had to be crushing her. Reluctantly, but knowing he had to, he withdrew from her and rolled to his side, and pulled her into his arms. He held her close, his fingers sifting through her hair, and she was asleep in a matter of moments. Sam stayed awake long into the night, enjoying the feel of her body next to his and wishing he could have this with her every night.

Chapter Ten

"Daddy!" Marie's voice echoed in the cabin.

Sam jerked awake. "Shit," he growled as he leaped from bed.

"Daddy, language," she scolded, even as she pushed at the blankets covering her.

Sam quickly pulled on his trousers and made his way to Marie's bed. "Just a minute," he told her as he turned to be sure True was covered. She had her shirt on and was trying to get control of her hair as she walked to the fireplace.

"Daddy, why..." Marie shoved at the blanket. "What..."

Sam grabbed the blanket and pulled it from his daughter, she gave him an indignant look and he couldn't help but laugh. "Sorry, honey."

"Why was I in a tent?" she demanded with a huff. Cody nearly knocked her over as he jumped from the bed and headed for the door.

"You better let Cody out while I get breakfast ready," Sam told her as he helped her from the bed.

With her attention diverted, she trotted to the door and opened it for the dog. He cast a look at True to see her smiling, she met his eyes and blushed before she turned and concentrated on putting wood on the dying fire. He took the liberty of watching her for a moment. What would happen between them now?

"Can I help, Daddy?" Marie asked as she tugged at his hand.

He tore his eyes from True and looked at Marie. "You bet."

When True dressed, Sam had to fight to keep from watching her. He was sure Marie would reprimand him for peeking. True's body was perfect and he knew he could spend hours just watching her.

The three of them went about their daily routine just as they had since True's arrival. He stole glances at True throughout the day, trying to gage her reaction to what had happened between them last night. She was shy around him, but he didn't get the feeling of regret from her. That was something to be grateful for.

Outside Cody barked and Sam walked to the door to open it and look out. He smiled when he saw the two riders approaching the cabin.

"Who's here, Daddy?" Marie asked as she practically pushed him aside to look.

"It's Raven and Snow," he told her.

She gasped with excitement and pushed him aside to get a better look. "Is Hawk with them?"

"I believe so," he said with humor.

"Raven," True said from beside him as she too looked out the door. "He's the one that pulled me from the creek."

"Yes, and he's brought his wife. You'll like Snow," he assured her.

True stood beside Sam as she watched the riders draw closer, he slid his arm around her waist, and she wondered if he realized what he had done. The man and woman were dressed in warm furs, a boy about Marie's age rode behind the woman and he leaned over to wave. Marie hopped up and down excitedly and waved back, bringing a chuckle from Sam.

Raven appeared to have a dead deer draped behind him on the horse's back. They reached the cabin and slid from their horses.

"It's good to see you," Sam called out as they approached.

Raven smiled at him. "We wanted to see you before we left for our winter camp tomorrow." His eyes moved to True. "You are looking much better than the last time I saw you."

She smiled at him and was amazed at how well he spoke English. "I'm doing much better. Thank you for helping me."

"Please, come in," Sam gestured for the group to enter the cabin. Once they were inside, Sam made formal introductions. "True, I'd like you to meet Raven, Snow, and their son Hawk." He gestured to the boy playing before the fire with Marie. "They are good friends."

She nodded and smiled at them. "It's good to meet you."

Snow looked at Sam. "She is Wanderer's sister?" Her English as clear as her husband's.

Sam nodded and turned to True. "Jo lived with the Cheyenne for a time and she was called Wanderer. That was where she met Jack, or Bear, as the Cheyenne call him. Snow is Jack's half-sister."

"I see," she said with a nod. "Jo told me about

her time with the Cheyenne in a letter, though she didn't go into great detail." She looked at Snow. "I'd like to hear more about it."

Snow gave her a friendly smile. "I will tell you all you want to know. Your sister is very special to my people."

"I brought a deer for you," Raven told Sam. "I will take it to your shed."

Sam pulled on his coat. "I'll help you."

"I want to play outside with Hawk." Marie grabbed her coat.

"Don't go far from the cabin," Sam told her as he buttoned up her coat and put on her gloves.

"Okay," she said, before scampering outside with her friend.

"We'll be back soon," Sam told True.

True watched them lead the horses to the shed. Cody trotted after the men, no doubt hoping to get a chance to eat a little fresh meat.

Closing the door, she turned to Snow, eager to talk to her. She had a lot of questions in mind, thinking of the stories she had heard about the wild savages in the West. She chose a safer subject though, not wanting to offend.

"You know my sister," she said as she walked to the table and gestured for Snow to sit with her.

Snow nodded and smiled. "Yes, Wanderer saved my life and is my friend."

True frowned thoughtfully. "Wanderer, why do you call her that?"

"She has a wandering spirit," Snow told her simply.

True nodded. *Joanna had always been the*

restless one. She loved to explore and never liked to be in one place for too long. As soon as Shyfawn and True were settled with Molly, she had taken off for the West. She had traveled to Oregon and back, making friends and no doubt enemies along the way.

True smiled as Snow told her about the time Joanna had spent with the Cheyenne. She had met her husband at the Cheyenne village, though they wouldn't be married until a few years later. Joanna had left the village and Jack behind to continue traveling. When she crossed paths with Jack again in Rimrock, he won her heart and she stayed with him until she had to leave to search for Shyfawn.

Listening with great interest, True realized she knew almost nothing about her sister. She was anxious to see her again and really get to know her. The three sisters had been separated for far too long and it was past time to be together again.

True fell into an easy stream of conversation with Snow and felt very comfortable with her. They talked and laughed as they sat at the table. Snow humored True with her many questions about the Cheyenne way of life. To True, it sounded like a hard life, but Snow appeared happy.

True leaned an elbow on the table, putting her chin in her hand and smiled as she listened to Snow.

Suddenly lights flashed behind her eyes and she took a startled breath. An image of Marie and Hawk came to her. They were playing in a small field, throwing snowballs at each other, laughing and shouting with delight.

True smiled, they were playing that was all,

they were safe. Then there was a different kind of sound, it was more of a roar. The children stopped playing, then ran. A bear was chasing them. They were running as fast as they could, but the bear was easily gaining on them. He swiped a big paw and knocked Marie down, his claws and teeth digging into her soft flesh. True cried out and forced the image from her mind.

"True?" Snow's voice held worry.

"The children." Was all she said, her voice full of panic as she leaped out of the chair.

"True, what is the matter?"

True jerked on her coat. "I have to find them fast."

"What is happening?" Snow asked, pulling on her furs.

Flinging open the door True rushed out. "A bear, we have to hurry."

"A bear?" Snow closed the door behind her and hurried after True. "What are you talking about?"

"Trust me. Get Sam and Raven," she ordered as she ran through the snow.

She couldn't explain now, she had to find the children before the bear did. If he hadn't already. True followed the tracks the children had left in the snow. Soon she heard their laughter, True started running faster. Breaking through the trees she watched the kids play, her eyes scanning the area for the animal. There he was. He was at the edge of the trees, lumbering slowly toward the children. She had to get to Marie before he attacked.

"Hurry, Sam," True breathed and dashed across the space that separated her from Marie.

The bear came from the trees, moving toward the children at a fast pace. Marie screamed when she saw him coming and the two children began to run. True had to go faster or she wouldn't make it in time. The children were almost to her now, Hawk was a faster runner and farther ahead of Marie.

True lunged at Marie the same time the bear swiped his paw to make the kill. True heard the shot from a rifle, she felt the claws of the bear rip into the back of her coat, and Marie screamed as they tumbled onto the snowy ground. True covered Marie with her body, waiting for the bear to attack again.

She could hear the angry roars and she could smell his breath. Looking up she saw the wounded animal crawling toward them, he reached up and swatted at True's leg. She scooted back as quickly as she could. Unable to maneuver in her layers of petticoats, she helped Marie to her feet.

"Run! Run to Snow," True ordered but Marie hesitated, staring at the bear crawling for them. "Marie, run!" True snapped and the little girl did so.

The bear had its full attention on True now. He came toward her striking out with his giant claws, his roars filled her ears and fear nearly choked her. She pulled herself back as he struck out for her, his claws caught her leg, ripping material and skin. She cried out in pain and did her best to move out of his range, but the layers of her dress hindered her progress.

Another shot rang out and the bullet kicked up snow near the bear's stomach, showering him with powder. It only seemed to enrage him further and he came at her with a vengeance. As she scooted back, she saw blood on the white snow. It was her blood, and there was so much of it. Realizing that if she didn't get up and get the hell out of there the bear would kill her, she did her best to get to her feet, but her leg screamed with pain and her petticoats were becoming soaked with snow. He was getting so close to her.

Staring the bear in the eyes she fought back fear, True tried not to start crying. If she didn't bleed to death, he would surely kill her. She would never see Sam or her sisters again, tears sprang to her eyes at the thought.

With one last desperate effort, True tried to get to her feet. She managed to get one foot under her to push herself up just as the bear made another grab for her. His claws hooked into her dress and pulled her back down. She cried out, unable to fight her tears as they overflowed.

She was going to die.

Hearing a ferocious fit of barking she looked to see Cody barrel down on the bear. He landed in the middle of the animal, his teeth going deep. The bear turned his attention to the dog and the two fought in the snow that was growing rapidly red. There was a shout from Sam and the dog backed off as a rifle boomed. The bear jerked, and then lay still.

True sagged with relief, knowing the bear was dead and they were safe. She leaned back in the cold snow and closed her eyes. The children were safe now, she no longer felt panic and she could rest as she tried not to think about the pain in her leg.

Her rest however would have to be put off. She

heard people running for her, the harsh breathing of men, and the crying of a little girl. She opened her eyes to see Sam and Raven kneeling over her.

"Sam." Her voice was weak and her eyes fluttered shut.

"Jesus, True." For some reason his voice sounded strange.

"Daddy!" Marie cried and threw herself at him.

"Marie, are you all right." He checked her over for any damage, but saw none.

"Yeah, I'm fine." She looked down at True, tears streaming down her face. "Help her, daddy."

"I will, honey." He kissed her forehead. "You go with Snow and I'll take care of True."

She nodded and took Snow's hand, Hawk taking the other. Marie called for Cody who was growling at the bear, waiting for it to get up so he could attack again. Then, reluctantly, he left the bear and went to Marie.

Kneeling beside her, Sam looked her over, there was so much blood. He couldn't tell if most of the blood was True's or the bears. But judging from her red stained petticoats he guessed that she was hurt badly. He lifted her dress to assess the damage.

"Hey, there will be none of that," she said, trying to keep humor in her voice.

Sam spared her a small chuckle and examined her leg. Her calf had several gashes in it from the bear's claws. She would need stitches and a lot of rest. And he prayed that she wouldn't get an infection. As for right now, he had to get her to the cabin and stop the bleeding. He leaned over, gathered her in his arms and carried her back to the cabin.

The trip back to the cabin took far longer than Sam would have liked. True lost consciousness somewhere along the way and he pushed himself faster. Finally, he was at the cabin and Raven opened the door for him to enter. Snow had warm water and bandages ready for him, then she helped him get True out of her bloody clothes. When he removed her coat, he saw the back of it was shredded. He said a silent prayer that the coat had been the only thing torn up.

Sam washed her calf and prayed that there would be no infection. When her leg was clean, very slowly he began to stitch her up. For what seemed like hours he leaned over her, while he listened to Snow and Marie tell the story of how True had saved the children. That was twice he owed her for saving Marie's life.

"She was sitting at the table, then she jumped up, saying that we had to get to the children before the bear did," Snow explained. "I didn't know what she was talking about. Then she ran out the door. She told me to get you and that's what I did."

"Oh, Daddy, he was so big and I was so scared." Marie bounced to her father. Now that the moment of terror was over and she was safe, she excitedly told the story. "I saw him comin' for me." She held up her hands like claws and stalked around the room. "And then True grabbed me just in time. I'm glad she was there."

"Me, too." He looked from his daughter to the woman lying on his bed. "I wonder how she knew," he muttered to himself, and then turned to Snow.

"You say she was just sitting here and knew the children were in trouble."

Snow nodded. "Yes, she was so scared for them. She knew Sam. Somehow, she knew."

He nodded and thought back. "Just like she knew that I had gone to the pass and it was still impassable."

Snow studied him. "She is Wanderer's sister," she said as she thought.

"That's right." He didn't see why that was important.

"If Wanderer can see at night. Then who's to say that True can't see things as well?"

"That's ridiculous," Sam said, yet somehow felt it was true.

"Is it? Then how do you explain it?" She looked at Marie. "Explain why your daughter is still alive, when she should have died twice already."

Snow's words cut through Sam like a knife. She was right, if it wasn't for True, Marie would be dead. Sam knew True's sisters well and knew they each possessed a special ability. Snow was right about Jo, her eyes allowed her to see at night. He had witnessed this firsthand after seeing her follow a trail in the middle of the night. He had watched Shyfawn heal wounds with just the touch of her hands. She had healed a cut on Marie's head, and also the wounds of Travis Colton, who had been mauled by a mountain lion. He had stood by her side as she healed the deep gashes. It was very possible True had her own gift.

He wished Shyfawn was here now to heal True.

***

Raven and Snow stayed for most of the day, helping Sam look after True. Snow prepared salve and tea to help her in her recovery. Late in the afternoon they bid Sam farewell.

The next several hours were hard for Sam. True never regained consciousness and he began to worry. She had developed a slight fever, but he had managed to keep it low, thanks to the willow bark tea Snow had prepared. So far, there was no infection.

Sam was glad that Marie had Cody to play with, since he had been too busy with True to pay much attention to her. Unable to stop himself he lay on the bed next to True and put an arm around her, pulling her against his side. He tried to be gentle, not wanting to jar her leg. She nestled against him and he held her close. He closed his eyes and lay there for a long time, holding True and listening to Marie play with her doll and talk to Cody.

"Daddy?"

Sam opened his eyes to see Marie standing beside the bed. "Come here." He opened his arm and she crawled up onto the bed beside him. She scrunched her little body against his on the narrow space of the bed. He hooked an arm around her to keep her from falling off.

"Is True going to be okay?" she asked, her voice trembling slightly.

"Yes, honey," he assured her. "She's going to be fine. She just needs rest."

"We should rest with her," Marie suggested.

Sam couldn't help but smile. "That sounds like a good idea," he told her and closed his eyes.

Chapter Eleven

It was long past sunset when True started to wake up. Blinking her eyes open she looked around. The memories came back to her, Marie and Hawk, a bear, and she had been attacked. Her leg screamed with pain when she tried to move it. She bit back a cry as she shifted her body to get more comfortable.

She was in Sam's bed and she wasn't alone. Sam had his shoulder under her head and his arm around her as he slept, his breathing slow and even. She bit her lip against the pain that shot through her leg as she turned to her side. She settled more comfortably against him and looked across him to see Marie nestled at his other side sleeping. Tears pricked her eyes and she reached across him to touch Marie's face.

Sam felt True move and came awake with a jerk. "True?" He turned to look down at her and she lifted her face to his, he saw the shine of tears in her dark eyes.

"Is she all right?" she whispered.

Sam had to swallow hard. "Yes, she's fine. She's worried about you." His arm tightened around her. "So am I."

"My leg hurts like the blazes," she said softly. "And I'm so hot."

"You have a slight fever. The bear got you pretty good," he told her in a low voice. "I had to put a lot of stitches in you."

She blinked at him. "*You* stitched me up." She guessed people in the wilds of the west had to be able to do everything on their own. It wasn't like he could run down the road for a doctor.

He gave a soft chuckle. "You don't have to sound so shocked."

She reached up and stroked his jaw. "Thank you for taking such good care of me."

Sam couldn't speak. He wanted to take care of her for the rest of her life. Her hand cupped his jaw and she lifted her head to place a soft kiss on his mouth. Sam drew her closer and pressed his lips firmly to hers. He gently kissed her for a long time. She drew back and rested her cheek on his chest.

True reached across him to stroke back Marie's hair. "I'm so glad she wasn't hurt."

"It's the second time you've saved her life. I don't think I can ever thank you enough," he said quietly. "You always manage to show up at just the right time. How do you do it?"

True felt her heart lurch and she heard an undercurrent in his voice that she couldn't place. She couldn't tell him, couldn't explain it to him. She was saved from having to answer when Marie opened her eyes to see True looking at her. She squealed with delight and scrambled across Sam's chest to hug her. Sam grunted as little knees pushed into his stomach in her haste. True laughed and hugged the girl close.

"I'll get us something to eat while we are all

awake," he said and crawled out from under his daughter.

Sam had his heart in his throat as he watched the two hug for a long time. True smiled as she pulled back and inspected Marie for any damage. Sam had to swallow hard as he turned and went about lighting the lamp and getting them something ready to eat.

"I'm glad you're safe," True told Marie and kissed her cheek.

"I'm fine, True." Marie sat up on the bed. "That big ol' bear didn't get me." She took True's hand and patted it. "How are you, dear?"

Despite herself True laughed. "I'm just fine. Your dad fixed me up really good."

She nodded vigorously. "He's the best doctor in the world."

"Doctor?" True managed to sit up and bit back a groan as pain stabbed up her leg. She looked at Sam, he turned from the fire and shrugged. "You're a doctor?"

He gave her a small grin. "Guess I forgot to mention that."

She smiled back at him. "And here I thought I knew you so well."

"That's why Marie and I are here," he told her simply. "I come to check on Raven's people before they travel to their winter grounds. Many of them need medical attention. They also supply me with herbs for medicine."

"I see. A mountain man doctor," she said with humor.

"Shyfawn could have fixed you better." Marie

pulled her hair away from her forehead. "I fell on my head when I was little, and she fixed it for me. Bet when we get home, she'll fix you, too."

True blinked at the child. Shyfawn had healed her, but Jo warned her never to use her gift on anyone. Same with True's visions, people wouldn't understand and condemn them both for having their gifts.

"Marie, that's silly," she said nervously.

"No, she really did it." Marie glanced at Sam. "Didn't she, Daddy?" He nodded. "We promised we wouldn't tell, but since you're her sister I thought it would be okay to tell you. She even fixed up Travis, too. He was hurt worse than me, but she fixed him just the same."

It couldn't be possible; these people knew about Shyfawn and didn't hate her. Shyfawn trusted them enough to let them know what she could do. No doubt her husband knew and obviously still loved her. But that couldn't be, people didn't accept what the sisters could do, that was why Joanna insisted on keeping their gifts a secret.

True laughed uneasily. "Marie, that's quite a tale."

"But it's the truth." Marie pouted. "Isn't it, Daddy?"

"Yes, sweetie. True's just tired." He fixed her mussed hair. "Go play with Cody, and then you can help me get some dinner ready." She nodded and hopped off the bed and skipped away.

"Kids have such imaginations." True shifted on the bed, causing a jolt of pain to her leg. Damn, she had to stop moving. "What they don't think of."

Sam studied her. Why was she denying it? "True, you don't have to pretend. We know about Jo and Shyfawn." He walked to the bed and sat facing her.

"I don't know what you're talking about." She averted her eyes and watched Marie put her doll on Cody's back like he was a horse.

"True, I know that Jo's unusual eyes let her see at night and Shyfawn can heal with her touch." He paused for a long moment. "What can you do?"

Slowly, True looked at him. "What?"

"How is it that you know what's going to happen before it does?" Sam could see the fear in her eyes. It was true. "You saved Marie twice now and you seem to know a lot about the pass for someone that is cooped up inside all the time."

"I think you're the one with the fever." True swallowed hard. "That's the craziest thing I've ever heard."

"That's what I thought, too. But after hearing Snow and Marie tell of what happened today, it has to be true. You have visions of things that will happen. Don't you?"

True felt as if she were suffocating. He knew, all the evidence was right in front of him, yet he wanted her to say it. He accepted Shyfawn and Jo, could he possibly accept her? She squeezed her eyes shut. If he wanted the truth, then he would get it.

"Yes," she snapped and met his eyes. "I can see things before they happen. I saw Marie fall into the creek and get attacked by the bear, I saw you at the pass and that it was still impassable. There, are you happy now?" She felt tears burn her eyes.

Sam studied her for a moment, his expression softening. "Do you see everything that happens in the future?"

"No." She turned her head away. "Just some things." She sighed. "But there are things that I wish I *could* see."

"What do you wish you could see?" Sam asked, tucking a piece of hair behind her ear.

"My own future." She looked at him, then quickly looked away. "I can see what happens to other people, but never myself." Like if she had a future with Sam. "But I don't think people are supposed to see their own life before it happens."

"I don't suppose so. Do the visions come to you only when someone needs help?" he asked as he took her hand.

She shook her head and met his eyes. "Sometimes I see good things that are happening to people. I saw Jo marrying her husband. At first, I was confused at the location, but now I understand they were at the Cheyenne village." She gave him a small smile. "I was also amazed that Jo was getting married. She had never wanted to be with a man after what our father did to her."

Sam nodded in understanding. "I was there when Jack found her again, after she left the village. He had to fight tooth and nail to convince her he loved her and wouldn't hurt her."

"I'm glad he did, she deserves to have a good life." A sad smile played on her lips before she looked down at their joined hands. "I'm glad Jo and Shyfawn are happy."

"Are you happy?" he ventured gently.

She said nothing for a long time. "I'll be happy when I see my sisters again." She shifted her legs and groaned in pain. "I thought bears were supposed to hibernate," she grumbled.

Sam went along with her change of subject. "They do but it's still a little early for that. He might have been looking for a snack before he hid for the winter."

She shot him a look of irritation. "I don't find you funny."

"Daddy, I'm hungry," Marie announced as she skipped to the bed.

Sam laughed as he released True's hand and stood. "Then we better fix that. Go sit at the table and I'll dish you up something."

Marie happily did so and Sam filled a bowl with warm stew for her. He would be glad to get back home and have some good meals at the café. What would happen after he returned to Rimrock with True? Would he see her again? Things between them had changed drastically and he wasn't sure what to do. Would she go back to her fiancé after what they had shared last night? He didn't want to think about that, he would be glad for their time together and worry about the rest later.

"You better eat," he told True before he stood and went to dish her up a bowl of stew.

"Can I sit with True?" Marie asked hopefully.

Sam nodded and she scampered from the chair to climb up onto the bed to sit beside True. Sam picked up her bowl from the table and handed it to Marie before giving True hers. He sat at the table and watched the two of them as they ate and talked.

Marie was becoming very attached to True and he worried about what would happen when they had to leave True with her sisters. How devastated would Marie be when True left to go back home? How devastated was *he* going to be?

Sam paced the cabin long after True and Marie fell asleep, his mind working and only making him more confused. His eyes fell on Marie as she slept in her bed with Cody, he hoped Marie would understand that True wouldn't be with them after they left the cabin. She would never be with them again. That thought sent a stab of pain through his heart.

Letting out a muttered curse, his eyes quickly going to Marie to be sure she hadn't heard him, he stripped down to his long underwear and walked to his sleeping mat before the fire. He stilled as his eyes went to True sleeping peacefully in the bed. He watched her for a long time and the longing he felt when he looked at her made his chest ache as he stepped up to the bed.

Knowing he shouldn't but not really giving a damn, Sam pulled back the blankets and crawled into bed with her. She murmured his name and turned into him. He put his arms around her and held her close. If this was all he was going to have with her, he intended to take advantage of it while it lasted.

***

Four days had passed since the bear attack and True's wounds were red and swollen but there was no infection, for which Sam was grateful. He knew her leg hurt her, but she didn't complain, and humored Marie as she played nursemaid.

Sam stiffened when Cody got to his feet and growled at the door. He grabbed the rifle, then he paused when he heard a loud, drawn out greeting that could only come from one man. He smiled and set the rifle down. Cody barked and wagged his tail as he jumped up to paw at the door.

True saw the change in Sam. "Who is it?"

"Travis!" Marie said with excitement.

Sam chuckled at the second even more drawn out 'yoo-hoo' from the man. "Yeah, Travis."

Sam opened the door for Cody to go greet him. "Travis Colton. He works for Matt and Shyfawn." Sam reached out and grabbed Marie before she could dart outside. He closed the door and she gave him an indignant look. "We'll wait for him in here."

"Ah, Daddy," Marie said with disappointment.

True sat up straighter and winced when her leg moved. "If he came from Shyfawn's that means the pass is clear, right?"

Sam looked at her for a moment. "More than likely." He tried to keep his tone casual. The clear pass meant he would have to take her down and he wasn't ready for that. Hell, he may never be ready.

True felt an unfamiliar surge of emotion go through her. She would be leaving the cabin. Leaving Sam and Marie. She had gotten used to their daily routines and enjoyed their company so much. She would no longer sleep in Sam's arms or wake up to Marie's laughter. Guessing from the look in Sam's eyes he was having the same feelings. He finally looked away when he heard stomping outside.

"Travis!" Marie squealed as she hopped up and down. "Come in!"

The door swung open to reveal a young man dressed in warm furs. "Well, by gosh, I will." Came his deep gravelly voice as he entered the cabin.

True almost laughed at the way Marie hopped around as she held her arms up to him. The man easily lifted her up and hugged her close as he kicked the door closed, just as Cody darted in. True saw that Travis was a good-sized man. He was a head shorter than Sam but just as broad. He was young, maybe around twenty, and had dark features.

"I've missed you, Chipmunk," he told Marie.

Sam stepped up and offered the man his hand. "Good to see you."

Travis smiled and held Marie in the crook of his arm as he took Sam's hand. "Glad to see you remembered how to survive out here on your own. I was worried town life had made you soft."

"No chance of that." Sam laughed. "What are you doing running around the mountain?"

Travis jerked his head toward True. "Looking for her."

True felt her stomach lurch. It was the first time he looked at her, yet he knew she was there. What puzzled her more was that he knew who she was. She met his dark eyes and saw only friendliness, putting her at ease.

"Shyfawn sent me out to look for you," he told her. "She's worried about you." He gave her a grin. "And might I say: *hello*."

Sam slapped him on the back of his head. His fur hat tumbled off and Marie caught it. "Put your eyes back in your head," Sam snapped.

Travis laughed and Marie let out a happy screech as she put his hat on her head. It was too big and slid down to her nose, causing her to giggle. He moved to the table, toed a chair out to sit on, and gave a grateful groan when he sat and settled Marie across his lap.

Travis gave Sam a sly grin. "Now just what am I gonna tell Shyfawn? That I found her sister there?" He gestured toward the bed. "And you know what Jo will do to you," he said with a chuckle.

"You'll tell them you found her in the cabin with Marie and I," Sam told him, trying to keep his tone light in front of his daughter.

Travis smiled. "Right."

Sam scowled at him. "She is in my bed because she has a wounded leg."

Travis frowned. "What'd you do to her?"

Sam wanted to choke him. "I didn't—"

"She saved me from a huge bear," Marie said as she tipped her head back to look at him from under the hat.

Travis met Sam's eyes. "Bear?"

Sam nodded. "You know how much claws hurt."

Travis's hand absently went to his shoulder. "Yes, I do."

"You had a bear attack you?" True asked him.

"Mountain lion and he tore me to pieces. I'd be dead if it hadn't been for Shyfawn."

True stared at him and felt her face go pale. This was the Travis that Shyfawn had healed. Sam,

Marie, Matt, and Travis knew about her sister's gift and they didn't care. How many other people knew?

Sam saw the panic in her eyes. "It's all right, True. Travis knows what Shyfawn and Jo can do. Not everyone knows about them but Shy's healed Travis more than once and he's been on a trail at night with Jo as well."

She looked at Travis. "Jo let you find out about her?" That didn't sound like her sister.

Travis shrugged his broad shoulders. "I kinda figured it out. I'm a good tracker but when it came dark, she could still follow the trail. I knew something was different about her eyes. The unusual coloring must adjust to night." He looked at her for a long moment. "What can you do?"

She felt her heart hammer in her chest and fear gripped her. Her eyes darted to Sam for help. He made a gesture with his hand that told her it was her choice to tell Travis. The man wasn't stupid. He knew she would have an ability as well.

She swallowed hard. If her sisters trusted him, so would she. "I-I have visions," she said quietly. "Sometimes I can see things before they happen."

"She saw the bear chase me," Marie said as she scrambled off his lap to practically crawl over Travis to sit on the table behind him. She adjusted the big hat on her head and began to gather up his shoulder length hair.

"Handy thing," Travis said with a nod. "You have any more sisters that I need to worry about? I'd hate for one to show up and zap me with a lightning bolt."

True smiled at him and relaxed slightly. "No.

Our two younger sisters died when they were very young." She paused as she watched Marie begin to put small braids in his hair.

Travis frowned. "I'm sorry to hear that. I myself have no family, but I'm blessed with many great friends." He turned to Sam. "I thought you'd be home by now."

Sam nodded. "I had planned on it but True had a little misadventure when she got here, and the snow hit hard. The pass was socked in."

True watched in amazement as Marie braided Travis's hair. The big rugged-looking young man made no protest and carried on a conversation with Sam as if it were an everyday occurrence. She thought it might be, for Sam appeared not to notice as braids appeared and stuck out around Travis's head. She smiled to herself. She could like Travis and felt she could, in fact, trust him.

"Travis, did someone find Toby?" True ventured, not sure she wanted to hear the fate of the man.

Travis nodded as he looked at her. "Yes. Luckily Trapper Josh happened along and found Toby in time to save his life."

Relief washed over True. "Thank God."

"Toby was aware enough to see you take the horses and run," Travis told her. "At least I knew where to start looking. Problem was, that trail was too dangerous to try to take with all the snow that had fallen. I had to back track and come up through the pass. It's still pretty snowed in but manageable."

Sam stretched his legs out in front of him. "Surprised you didn't bring Heck with you."

Travis chuckled then winced slightly when Marie pulled a little too hard on his hair. "We started out together, but I sent the one-eyed wonder after the men that shot Toby and took the mules."

"Their saddles and bedrolls are in the barn," Sam told him. "I went through them but didn't come across anything that looked important or anything that might help figure out who they are."

Travis nodded. "I'll have a look at them later. But right now, I'm hungry."

"And you're pretty!" Marie exclaimed as she threw her arms in the air.

True couldn't help but laugh outright at the sight of Travis with braids sticking out all over his head. Sam laughed as well. Travis reached up with a hand to feel his head and smile.

"I guess I am." He laughed and turned to Marie. "Thank you."

Chapter Twelve

Travis spent the night with them. Marie and True took the big bed, Sam slept before the fire and Travis took Marie's bed. He was far too large for it but that didn't deter him. He had been sleeping on the snowy ground for weeks and was all too glad for a bed. Even if most of him hung off it.

A groan left him as he stood from the bed and stretched his back. "Slept like a baby."

Sam laughed as he prepared breakfast. "And you snored like a grizzly."

Travis grinned and shrugged. "I've had to keep one eye open the past week when I slept so I wouldn't get *eaten* by a grizzly. Last night I didn't have to worry about it and was just making up for lost sleep." He sat at the table and reached for a cup of coffee.

"I'm sure there's logic in there somewhere," Sam told him. "Marie, come eat."

Marie muttered a protest as she snuggled closer to True. "Can you bring it to me?"

Sam looked over at her and smiled. "No, come sit at the table."

Marie sat up and rubbed her eye. "But True gets to stay in bed."

"Because her leg is hurt."

Marie sighed and slid from the bed to walk

sleepily to the table. She went to Travis and climbed up on his lap, waiting patiently for her father to place a plate of food in front of her. Travis held her with one arm and placed a kiss on the top of her head.

True smiled as she sat up, wincing slightly as her leg protested the movement. She liked Travis and was glad that he was someone she knew she could trust. She had a feeling Rimrock was full of good and trustworthy people, so unlike Charlotte.

"How's your leg?" Sam asked as he walked up to her with a plate and handed it to her.

"It hurts," she confessed. "But I'm fine."

He reached out to press his hand to her forehead to feel for fever. "Your fever is gone," he told her absently before he turned and sat at the table. "Travis, will you take Marie back down with you today?" Sam asked as they ate breakfast.

Travis shrugged. "Sure."

"Aren't we all going?" True asked from the bed.

"You can't ride yet and need a few more days to heal," he told her. Hell, the truth was he needed a few more days with her.

True nodded. "I see."

"You want me to go without you?" Marie asked as she looked across the table at her father.

"Yes," he told her. "I think you've been stuck up here long enough. Come here," he whispered and gestured for her to stand beside him.

"Whatcha need?" She asked, scrambling off Travis's lap and skipping around the table to him.

He pulled her close and lowered his voice as if

it were a secret. "I need you to make sure Travis gets home." He leaned closer to her. "Sometimes he has a hard time finding his way around. I'm worried he might get lost."

True stifled a laugh as Travis shot him a glare. Sitting right across the table from them, it was impossible for him not to hear. Sam only gave him a grin and Travis shook his head with a smile. True was fairly sure Travis could find his way to anyplace in the world.

Sam leaned back and looked down at Marie. "You have to tell Shyfawn we found True and keep an eye on her until I get back."

Her eyes widened. "That's a lot of stuff to do."

Sam smiled at her. "Yes, it is, but I'm sure you can do it."

She nodded vigorously. "You bet I can."

Travis laughed. "Lord, help us if Marie's our ramrod."

Marie gave Travis an indignant look and he laughed, then reached out and ruffled her hair.

True smiled and shook her head – she liked Travis more every minute.

***

Sam led one of the bandits saddled horses to where Travis stood saddling his gray. "Take this one back with you and let the sheriff decide what to do with it. I have no doubt he's been stolen."

Travis snorted. "He's probably too damn drunk to do anything." His eyes quickly darted to the open cabin door, waiting to see if Marie had heard him to reprimand him.

"Probably," Sam agreed. "I guess tell Sims

about the horses, he might have heard of stolen horses in the area." If anyone knew where the animals came from it would be the livery owner.

"Marie, are you ready?" Travis called.

"Yes!" she yelled and scampered from the cabin, Cody following her.

Sam lifted her and hugged her tightly for a long time. He would miss his daughter, but he knew the best thing was to send her with Travis, as it was past time for her to be home where it was safe and warm. And, he wanted to be alone with True for a few days. Sam knew he was being selfish but he didn't give a damn.

"You be careful while I'm gone," Marie told him.

He chuckled and pulled back to kiss her cheek. "I will."

"And take good care of True."

"I will."

Travis gave him a knowing wink. "Have fun."

Sam wanted to make a rude gesture but knew Marie would catch him. "You just make sure you get her home safe."

Travis chuckled and easily swung up onto his horse. "I will."

Sam lifted Marie to Travis and he set her in the saddle in front of him. "I'll see you in a few days."

"I'll make sure he don't get lost," Marie told him proudly.

Sam smiled. "I know you will."

Travis moved his horse out at a walk, leading the other horse behind him while Cody ran ahead to lead the way home. Marie waved at Sam, he waved back and watched them until they were out of sight. He was going to miss Marie, but it was only for a few days.

Letting out a long breath, Sam went back into the cabin and closed the door behind him. His eyes went to True who sat in the bed and watched him. She was beautiful.

Sam did his best to make casual conversation with True for the rest of the morning, though his insides were in knots. Maybe this wasn't such a good idea, being alone with her like this. He felt nervous and was having extremely inappropriate thoughts, all of which involved her being very naked.

"I better change your bandage," Sam said as he began heating water.

True watched as he moved around the cabin. They were going to be alone in the cabin for several days and the thought caused her heart to flutter. She had slept in his arms for the last few nights, but her body wanted his again, she ached for him.

Sam took a deep breath as he picked up the clean bandage and pan of warm water. He tried to calm his racing heart. He let the breath out slowly as he turned and walked to her. He could do this. He had changed her bandage a dozen times. It would help if she wasn't in his bed, however, and if they weren't alone.

True said nothing, she knew the routine. She sat in the middle of the bed and moved the blankets from her wounded leg. She bent her knee and waited for him. He sat down on the bed and handed her the pan of water. He carefully began to remove the bandage before tossing it on the floor and began cleaning the wound.

"It's looking better," he said after a while. "We'll have to leave the stitches in for a couple weeks," he told her, trying to be professional when he really wanted to crawl on top of her and bury himself deep inside her.

"He really got me," she said in way of conversation, hoping she didn't sound breathless. "How bad was Travis hurt when the mountain lion got him?"

"Really bad," he told her, thankful for the distraction. "The cat tore him up and we probably would have lost him if it hadn't been for Shyfawn."

"She healed him," True said, though not surprised. Shyfawn could never tolerate seeing people hurt. Her first reaction was to heal.

Sam nodded as he began to bandage her leg. "Yes, she was determined to heal every wound, but I stopped her."

She gave him a puzzled look. "You did?"

He met her eyes. "Yes, the rest of the ranch hands saw how badly hurt he was and if he showed up in the bunkhouse without a scratch, they would have been curious as hell. He has scars across his shoulder and chest as a reminder not to play with mountain lions again." He gave her a slight smile before turning his attention to the bandage again.

True felt her eyes burn. Sam had protected Shyfawn from being discovered by the other men. He never ceased to amaze her. She had never met someone so thoughtful or so giving.

"There you go," he said as he tied off the

bandage. "You're good until tomorrow."

Sam ran his hands over the bandage and couldn't keep one from running across her soft skin to her knee. On its own, his hand drifted to caress her inner thigh. He bit back a groan and withdrew his hand to reach for the pan of water. His eyes met hers and he swore softly. Hunger reflected in their dark depths.

"Sam." She could barely find her voice as she leaned forward until she could brush her lips to his. "Please."

The groan of need ripped from his chest as he claimed her mouth. He tossed the pan to the floor, sending water flying, and jerked the blanket off her as he pushed her down on the bed. She moaned against his mouth as he rested his body in the welcoming cradle of her thighs.

True desperately clung to him as she opened her mouth to him. He kissed her deeply and her body went to liquid fire. She moved her hips against him and felt him shudder. Jesus, she wanted him. He had taught her passion and now she craved it. Craved him. His hand slid down her thigh to cup her bottom and he lifted her as he pressed his arousal against her.

"Sam." She could hardly get his name out as she tugged at his shirt.

Sam drew back enough to pull his shirt over his head and toss it away. He groaned as her soft hands moved over the width of his chest. She leaned up and her mouth followed the path of her hands. She tasted and nipped his skin and the air left him in a hiss as she flicked her tongue over his nipple.

"Damn it, True," he practically growled the words as he sat back on his heels. He gripped her arms and hauled her up with him.

She let out a startled cry as he grabbed the front of her shirt and gave a mighty jerk, sending buttons flying. He pulled the shirt from her body with an urgency that made his hands shake. He pushed her back down on the bed as his mouth found her breast and closed over her nipple. She moaned and wrapped her arms around his head to hold him to her.

Today, there would be no holding back, there was no need to be quiet. He intended to bring her to the heights of pleasure again and again. She was so passionate and his need for her was driving him to the brink of sanity. Sleeping beside her night after night and not being able to take her body had been killing him. But he would have her now and to hell with any consequences.

His mouth went to her other breast to tease her nipple. His hand slid down her stomach to the soft curls at the junction of her thighs. She eagerly opened her legs for him. She moaned as his hand cupped her, his fingers lazily moving over her. She let out a broken cry when he softly stroked her sensitive bud.

True breathed a protest when his mouth left her breast. His mouth drifted over her chest and down across her stomach. His tongue flicked across her belly button before moving lower.

"Sam?" Her voice was a husky whisper.

"Relax." His breath was hot on her skin.

She watched his head move lower, his hands

went under her hips and he drew her to his mouth. She cried out and arched her back as his mouth closed over her. Fire shot through her as he brought her pleasure even higher. Flames of desire licked over her with each stroke of his tongue. He took her to the edge of that blinding release and held her there. She moaned and moved against his mouth.

Sam pulled back. "Not yet."

He drew away long enough to shed the rest of his clothes before he covered her body with his again as she dragged air into her lungs. She opened her eyes to look into his dark gaze. He gave her a slight smile and kissed her gently. He settled his body over hers and she felt him hard and throbbing against her hot entrance. She moaned and shifted her hips. He hooked an arm under her knee to open her as he gently pushed inside her.

"Jesus, True," he groaned as he looked down at her. He buried himself to the hilt and stilled. "You feel so damn good."

True couldn't speak as she looked up at him. He filled her completely, stretching her, and causing pleasure to flood her body. She reached up and ran her hand through his hair as she pulled his mouth back to hers. She rolled her hips and felt the shudder that ripped through him.

Sam groaned and began to move; his strokes were slow and strong. His hand moved down her leg to hold her hip, pulling her to him as he pushed into her. Her cries and whimpers became more urgent and he increased the pace and force of his thrusts.

"Sam, please," she begged as he once again

held her on the brink of that rush of pleasure.

He groaned and his hand gripped her hip tightly. He began to thrust hard and deep as she cried out again and again. Her nails bit into his back as her body began to shake. He drove into her over and over until she was nearly sobbing his name.

Her release hit her hard. Her body arched and she screamed as waves of pleasure crashed over her. Her muscles clamped down on him so tight it took him over the edge. He plunged deep and his body went rigid. His harsh cry mingled with her scream as he shuddered out his release, filling her with his seed. He groaned and collapsed on top of her, his breath ragged.

True wrapped her weak arms around him and held tight. She buried her face in his neck as her body continued to ripple with pleasure. He released her hip and his hand stroked her hair before he cupped the back of her head and held her close. She felt tears prick her eyes at the tender gesture.

When they could both breathe again, he wound his fingers in her hair and pulled her head back to kiss her. He kissed her softly for a long moment before lifting his head to look at her. He saw the shine of tears in her eyes, but she gave him a smile. He returned her smile and kissed her again.

***

Sam woke with the gut wrenching feeling of dread. True's leg was healing well and she would have no trouble riding. It was past time they headed down the mountain and he was putting it off. The last three days with True had been amazing. They had talked, laughed, and made love at every opportunity. He didn't want to take her to Rimrock. He didn't want to give her up. He didn't know if he *could* give her up.

He pulled True close and held her tight. She murmured his name and snuggled into him. Would she still murmur his name when her husband held her? Sam couldn't think about it. The thought of another man holding her, touching her, making love to her, made him sick.

He cursed himself. Hell, if he was half a man he never would have touched her in the first place. She was promised to another and he knew it. He knew from the beginning that she would never be his and yet he had taken her body. He had made love to her over and over the last several days and she had given him everything she had. He had never known such passion existed until True.

With a reluctant groan, he eased his body away from hers. Careful not to wake her, he slid from the bed and began to dress. He needed air, needed time to think, to get his emotions under control. He had to force himself to accept that tomorrow he would take her to her sisters.

"Sam?" Her sleepy voice slid over him like a caress.

He paused in the act of pulling on his gloves to look at her. He shouldn't have, she was beautiful. She lay on her side, propped up on an elbow as she looked at him. Her blond hair fell wildly around her, her dark eyes drowsy.

"Where are you going?" she asked softly.

He focused on his gloves to keep from looking at her. "I..." He cleared his throat. "I'm going to take a ride and have a look at the pass." It was partly true; he knew the pass was clear but he needed some time alone and think.

True felt her stomach drop at the thought he would soon take her to Rimrock. "I see," she managed to say and looked down before he could see her tears.

Sam took a deep breath. "I'll be back later," he told her as he went out the door.

True flopped back on the bed and covered her face with her hands. She let the tears flow and tried desperately to sort out her feelings. She didn't want to leave the cabin, but knew she had to. She didn't want to be away from Sam. She would go to Shyfawn's and he would go home. When would she see him again? When would she see Marie again? True choked on a sob and curled up into a ball.

Chapter Thirteen

"Sam?" True pulled her coat closed against the cold as she entered the shed. She paused to let her eyes adjust to the dim light inside. "Are you in here?"

"Yeah." His voice sounded hollow.

She found him in the back, he didn't look at her as he slung his saddle over the stall rail.

"What're you doing?"

"Just checking the gear for the ride down tomorrow," he said quietly, still not looking at her.

She frowned at him as he went over the saddle a little too closely. "Sam, what—"

"It'll be an early day tomorrow, you should try to sleep," he said as he moved to the workbench at the back wall.

She followed him. "Sam, what's wrong?"

"True, go to the cabin and get some sleep," he said, unable to keep the edge from his voice.

She grabbed his arm and made him face her. When his eyes met hers, she about went to her knees. So many emotions raged behind those dark eyes. "Tell me," she whispered and reached out to touch his face. She let out a startled gasp when his hand shot out and grabbed her wrist.

"Go back inside," he growled the words out.

She fought against the tears and the tightness in

her throat as he glared down at her. "Sam, why are you angry with me?"

His grip on her wrist tightened and he stepped closer to her. "I'm not angry with you, I'm mad as hell about the whole situation. Tomorrow night you'll be back with your sisters and all this will just be a lovely story to tell the girls back in Charlotte."

Pain stabbed through her heart. "I'm not—"

"I'm sure you'll leave a few details out so your fiancé won't get upset with you," he snarled. As soon as the words were out, he wished he could take them back. Tears and pain filled her eyes. "True, I'm—"

He didn't get to finish his sentence because she slapped him hard. Not getting the desired effect, she balled her fist and he grabbed her wrist to stop her from hitting him again. She wanted to rage at him, scream at him, but she couldn't find the words. She wanted to beat him senseless, but she was too small. She pulled at her wrists, but he held them tight.

"Sam, you're hurting me," she snapped.

"I'm hurting you?" His voice was hard. The thought of her leaving him was killing him.

She pulled at her wrists again. "Yes. Let me go."

Let her go? He was going to have to let her go tomorrow night. His heart ached with the thought. The thought of her leaving him to marry another man was too much for him to take. His grip on her tightened as his anger boiled. He had known her for only a short time, yet she had found her way to his heart and now she was going to break it apart.

"I'll let you go," he ground out. "I'll let you go

tomorrow night and you can get on with your life. But not tonight." He roughly jerked her to him. "Tonight, you're still mine."

His mouth crashed down on hers and he held her in a bone crushing grip. True found it hard to breathe as he kissed her with a fierce need. She felt the same need as her emotions overwhelmed her. She needed him so much. She needed to feel him, to make love to him.

True frantically worked with the buttons of his coat, then his shirt until she had her hands on his bare chest. She tore her mouth from his and he groaned and shuddered as her mouth placed hot wet kisses across his strong chest. She found his nipple and gently bit down. A surge of heat went through her at the sound he made. Her hands explored him as her lips found their way back across his chest to his neck. He grabbed a handful of her hair and forced her to tip her head back so he could capture her mouth again.

His mouth never left hers as he picked her up and set her on the workbench. His hands pushed at her dress until he felt the bare skin of her thighs, he pushed them apart to stand between her legs. His arms went around her and pulled her to him as he deepened the kiss, her tongue sparring with his.

She moaned low in her throat as his hand moved between her thighs to touch her. His fingers bringing her delightful torture as they moved over her and within her. Her hands went to the front of his pants to brush against his hardness before she pushed at his pants. A ragged groan left him when she took him in her hand and stroked the hard length of him.

With a muttered curse, he grabbed her hips and pulled her to the edge of the workbench. He hooked an arm under her leg to open her to him as he roughly pushed inside her. She cried out against his lips and clung to him. Sam held himself still for a moment, savoring the feel of being inside her. Wanting to remember it forever, before he lost her forever.

His mouth went to her neck as he moved against her. There was no tenderness, just hard thrusts as he tried to ease the raging emotions inside him. Knowing he would never be with her again tore at his heart. He was trying desperately to ease that ache inside as he held her tight and pushed deep into her. He kissed his way back to her mouth and went still when he tasted the tears on her cheek.

"True?" He pulled back to look at her. Tears streamed down her cheeks; her dark eyes cloudy with so many emotions. "God, True, I'm sorry." All anger left his body in a rush.

"Don't stop," she choked out as she shifted her hips against him. "Sam, please."

He took her face in his hands and wiped at her tears with his thumbs. "Not like this." He kissed her tenderly and she whimpered. "Not like this," he said against her lips before he stepped away from her.

"Sam, you can't stop now," she protested through her tears.

"I'm not," he assured her as he took her by the hand and led her to the hay piled in the back corner of the shed.

He let go of her hand to lay back on the hay

and she eagerly followed him down. Picking up her skirts she straddled his hips and knelt in the hay. Her mouth found his as she slid down over him, drawing a moan from them both. His hands went to her waist, holding her against him. Slowly she began to move, his hands on her waist helped her find her rhythm. She leaned back, bracing her hands on his chest as she moved over him.

Sam's hands went to her bodice, he quickly worked at the buttons and slid it open. To his relief she wasn't wearing anything underneath. She shivered as the cold air washed over her heated skin. His hands moved over her ribs to cup her breasts. Her hands clutched his forearms as he caressed her. Soon her pace increased, her breathing became ragged, and her body trembled.

She cried out and collapsed on him as her climax shook her to her core. Sam grabbed her hips and urged her to keep moving as he thrust hard up into her until his own wave of release washed over him. He held her tight as he emptied himself inside her. She cried out again and clung to him, her body trembling uncontrollably.

When he had the strength, he lifted his hands and grabbed her face, making her look at him. Her eyes flowed with tears, but there was only pleasure in their dark depths. He kissed her softly before pulling back to wipe at her tears. He wrapped her in his arms and held her tightly to him.

She lay over him for a long time, listening to his strong heartbeat. Savoring the feel of him against her. His hands stroked her hair as her heart ached. She didn't want to leave him. She didn't want to go back to reality. If only she could stay locked away with him in the cabin for a while longer. Her body shivered and she wasn't sure if it was from the cold or the thought of leaving him.

"We better go in before we freeze to death," he said, his voice rumbling in his chest.

Reluctantly she stood and buttoned her bodice. She took a deep breath and turned to Sam. He didn't bother buttoning his coat or shirt as he held out a hand to her. She took it and he led her back to the cabin.

***

True fought tears as Sam helped her mount her horse. The sun was barely peeking over the horizon and she was grateful for the darkness. She didn't want him to witness her misery. They had spent all night making love and he had left the cabin before sunup to saddle the horses.

Sam remained silent as she settled on her horse and he mounted his own. He hadn't spoken more than a few words to her and wouldn't meet her eyes. He moved his horse out and her horse automatically followed as they headed away from the cabin.

True turned for one last look at the small cabin where she had found love, and then loss.

Tears burned her eyes as she turned away to focus on the trail Sam followed. He had told her it would be a full day's ride to Shyfawn's. A full day of Sam not speaking to her. She looked at his back and easily saw the tension in his shoulders, despite his big coat.

She felt her heart breaking as she watched him ride ahead of her. She thought he loved her but had been wrong. She had only known Sam for a few weeks but was sure she loved him. The feelings she had for Sam she had never had for Steven. New tears came to her eyes as she thought of her fiancé for the first time in days. She had betrayed Steven.

"We'll rest the horses for a spell," Sam said, his voice startling her out of her thoughts.

She said nothing, suddenly realizing how much time had passed. True had been so lost in her self-misery she hadn't noticed just how far they had ridden. She pulled her horse to a halt beside his and quickly dismounted, not wanting him to help her. True knew she would fall apart in a fit of tears if he touched her.

Sam didn't meet her eyes when he handed her the canteen and something to eat. She didn't have much of an appetite, but she knew she would be starving by the time they reached Shyfawn's if she didn't eat now.

She watched through tears as Sam walked away. He took out his own rations and stared down the trail as he ate. True had the sudden urge to go over to him and push him down in the snow. Anger was replacing her heartache and she would try to hold onto that.

She may have loved Sam, but he had his fun with her and was throwing her back to Steven. Could she go back to Steven? The question stopped her heart still. She could never tell him about her time at the cabin with Sam and Marie. Tears filled her eyes when she thought of Marie. She dearly loved the little girl and would be lonely without her. How would Marie feel about not seeing True anymore?

She scowled at Sam's back. Damn him for complicating everything.

Chapter Fourteen

It was well into the night when they neared her sister's ranch. True was exhausted. The moon lit up the ranch but she saw no lights on in the house or outer buildings. She was eager to see her sister, but didn't want to rouse her out of bed at this hour. A dog began to bark and True knew the entire ranch would be awake soon.

The dog met them as they rode into the ranch yard and Sam spoke to him. He quieted and whimpered happily as he recognized Sam's voice. It was obvious that Sam often visited her sister's ranch.

"Sam…" Travis's tired voice drifted to them as he walked toward them from the bunkhouse. "I was starting to worry you'd never make it."

Sam didn't answer as he dismounted and helped True from her horse. Pain shot up her leg and a small gasp left her as she held onto Sam for a moment. When she felt her muscles would support her, she drew away without looking at him. It was taking everything she had not to cry as she thought of them parting ways.

They followed Travis up the steps onto the porch and he opened the door to walk right in. True and Sam followed, hoping to be quiet enough to keep from waking her sister. She could just sleep in the parlor and see Shyfawn in the morning.

Apparently, Travis had other ideas.

"Matt, Shyfawn, they're here," he called as he walked to the dining table and lit a lamp.

True heard movement from the upper floor, and then light from a lamp accompanied footsteps coming down the stairs. She turned and saw her sister wearing her nightdress, her pregnant tummy clearly evident. Her long auburn hair was in a single braid over her shoulder. A man she assumed was Matthew followed her, wearing only his trousers, his dark hair mussed from sleep.

"True," Shyfawn whispered and tears filled her green eyes.

"Shy," True choked out and went into her sisters waiting arms.

True clung tightly to her sister as she cried. Sobs racked her body, though she wasn't sure if it were from the happiness of seeing her sister or the agony of knowing she would never be with Sam again.

"Everything's all right, honey," Shyfawn soothed as she held True tight.

"Thanks for bringing her back safely," Matthew told Sam.

"I filled them in on what happened to her," Travis said simply.

True sniffed and drew back to wipe at her cheeks. "I'm fine. Sorry to be so emotional."

"I'd say you have a right to be," Shyfawn said as she gently brushed True's hair back. "You've been through a lot."

"I better be going," Sam said, his voice void of

emotion.

True turned to look at him and her heart broke as he turned and headed for the door. She didn't want him to leave, she wasn't ready to be apart from him.

"Stay the night, Sam," Matthew said. "It's late."

He shook his head without turning to look at Matthew. "It's past time for me to be home."

He didn't say another word as he walked past Travis. True saw them exchange a look she couldn't read before Travis followed Sam from the house. Unable to stop herself, True began to cry again and let Shyfawn comfort her. Her life had been turned upside down and now it was in a tornado of confusion. She had never felt more lost in her life.

***

True came awake slowly as she felt something brush against her cheek. Lifting a hand to wipe it away, she connected with something warm and furry. A startled cry left her as she bolted upright in bed, her eyes darting to the gray ball of fur beside her and she let out a breath of relief.

"A cat," she muttered.

He meowed and studied her as he sat looking at her with big green eyes. His fur was deep gray with white on his face and paws. She smiled at him and, as he watched her closely, she ran her hand down the soft fur of his back. Deciding she was a friend, he began to purr and crawled up on her lap to rub against her.

She laughed and hugged him to her. "I like you, too."

After a moment she set the cat aside and tried to get dressed, a task made a little difficult because he insisted on being underfoot. Her leg ached when she put weight on it, but it was better than a few days ago. When she finished dressing, she picked the cat up and carried him downstairs.

True headed toward the kitchen and the smell of coffee. Entering the kitchen, she found Shyfawn busy at the stove as she prepared breakfast. True felt her heart warm, she was so grateful to finally be with her sisters again. She was anxious to see Jo and have all three of them together for the first time in so many years.

Shyfawn looked over her shoulder at True and smiled. "I see you've met Gray Cat."

"Gray Cat?"

"Marie named him," Shyfawn said simply. "Better put him out, he likes to help all the time and it's hard to get work done."

True laughed and went to the door off the kitchen that led to the back porch. Gray Cat protested, but True managed to pluck his claws from her bodice and place him on the porch, closing the door quickly before he could dart back inside.

True went to the coffee pot on the stove and poured a cup. "I'm glad my belongings made it to Rimrock," she said, looking down at her clean blue dress. "My other dress was completely ruined."

"I'm pretty sure the bandits weren't after women's clothing," Shyfawn teased.

"Travis said Toby was alive and recovering," True said before she took a drink of the hot coffee.

"He was very lucky he was found, or he would

have died out there," Shyfawn said seriously. "I was scared to death when we got the news the freight wagon had been attacked." She smiled knowingly. "But you're a Tucker and I had no doubt you'd find a way to survive."

True nodded and tried not to think of just how close she had been to death before she reached Sam. She pushed thoughts of him away and took a deep breath to calm her nerves. "I'd like to see Toby sometime."

Shyfawn nodded. "We'll be going to town in a few days, you can see him then."

"I'd like that." She put down her cup and limped over to stand beside Shyfawn. "What can I do to help?"

Shyfawn frowned and looked at True's wounded leg. "Let me heal your leg. There's no reason for you to be in pain like that."

True liked the idea but shook her head. "No, you better not. I know how healing can drain your energy. You need that energy." She gestured to Shyfawn's tummy.

Shyfawn smiled and placed a hand over her child. "You're right." She let out a long breath. "I don't like it, but I'll leave your leg alone. Now, you can help me with breakfast."

The two sisters spent the day talking, laughing, crying, and just being thankful to be together. True was introduced to the ranch hands and they all seemed very nice. She was glad to see Travis's familiar face, too, it made her feel like she at least had one friend in this untamed land.

Matthew's ranch foreman, Charlie, was a

stocky man with graying hair and a mustache. His voice was deep and booming, as was his laugh, and True had an instant liking to the man. John, their handyman, was a good-sized man with a black beard and black hair that stuck out carelessly around his head. He was quiet and reserved, not talking much as they all sat at the table eating breakfast. Wally was a skinny man of average height, his blond hair shaggy and his smile revealing several missing teeth, apparently having been knocked out in a fight. Heck was a tall lean young man about the same age as Travis and it was clear they were inseparable friends. He had a patch over one eye, with a scar running from beneath it down his cheek. His hair was sandy brown, and his grin was wide and friendly.

True enjoyed the conversation and banter between the men. They weren't just hired help; they were a close-knit family and it was clear they deeply cared for one another. Shyfawn fussed over them as if they were her own children, and they loved and accepted her. True felt longing stab her heart, as she had always longed for love and acceptance.

The men bid them good day as they headed outside into the cold to begin their days work. Matthew pulled Shyfawn close and kissed her lovingly before he left the house.

True helped her sister clean up and couldn't help but envy the love that surrounded Shyfawn. When they were finished, they went into the parlor.

"You have a good life here," True said as she sat on the sofa with her sister.

Shyfawn smiled and nodded in agreement. "I do. After I was taken, I never thought I'd be free or be able to settle down in a normal life. But Jo found me, and I met Matthew, and though we've had our disagreements, I couldn't be happier. I'm loved and surrounded by good people."

"I envy that," True confessed. "I've only been here a day and I can easily see how happy you are."

"Hullo?" a woman called as the front door opened.

Excitement rushed through True and she bolted to her feet and ran from the parlor to see Jo pulling off her coat and gloves, then dropping them on the floor by the dining table before reaching out to hug True tight. They clung to each other for a long time and True couldn't keep from crying. She wasn't surprised that Jo wasn't crying though, she had never seen her sister cry a day in her life. She had always been so strong and solid as they grew up.

"Let me look at you," Jo said as she stepped back to take in True's appearance. "You're more beautiful than the last time I saw you."

True smiled and was shocked to see moisture in her sister's unusual eyes. Dark brown eyes with flecks of blue near the pupils, she had missed seeing those eyes. Those special eyes that allowed her to see at night. Jo was still the same as True remembered. Long black hair hung in a thick braid over her shoulder and she was wearing men's clothing. She was beautiful in her own way and though she was rough on the edges, she had a big heart.

True hugged her again. "I've missed you so

much."

Jo held her tight. "I've missed you, baby sister."

The two stepped apart when the door opened again, and a big man stepped into the house. His hair was black and his skin darker, his gray eyes were piercing but friendly. She recognized him from her vision of Joanna getting married.

"True, this is my husband, Jack," Jo told her proudly.

"It's good to meet you."

"You, too," he said, his voice deep and friendly. "Jo's told me so much about you."

True thought of the letters she had received from Jo and knew her sister was deeply in love with Jack. Seeing them together only confirmed that. The way they looked at each other made True's heart ache. Though she might be miserable, she was glad for her sisters and wasn't going to dwell on her own sadness. Her family was whole again and she intended to savor every moment she had with them.

***

Sam entered the clinic and was eager to get to work to keep his mind busy, hoping it would keep it away from thoughts about True. After Sam had left Matthew's house, he had ridden home with tears in his eyes and a deep pain in his chest at the reality of not being with True anymore. In the weeks they had been together, he had developed deep feelings for her and was pretty sure he loved her. He had taken her body knowing she was promised to another and would leave Rimrock in the spring. She would leave him and what they had shared behind.

"Glad to see you're back," Doc Black greeted him as he came from the examination room.

Sam smiled at his friend and offered his hand in greeting. "It's good to be back." It wasn't a total lie. "What have I missed?"

"Luckily not a lot," Doc Black told him as he went back into the examination room, Sam followed. "A few coughs and sniffles. The Turner kids all have chicken pox."

Sam listen to Doc Black as the man went through the cabinets to take inventory on what they would have to order. Sam moved to the counter to pick up the washed bandages and began to roll the strips up before placing them on a shelf. He was glad that things had gone easy for the man, though Doc could easily handle anything that might turn up.

Doc Black had been the doctor in Rimrock since the day it was settled, and the town was lucky to have him. Being the only doctor within hundreds of miles, people came from all over to get tended to. After Sam came back from schooling, Doc Black often made house calls to the settlers in the area. He spent a lot of time in Claytonville, a small settlement a day's ride from Rimrock and named after the Clayton family who had homesteaded the area. Sam always figured Doc's visits might have a lot to do with the Widow Johnson though, as it was a known fact that Doc was sweet on her.

The bell over the front door rang, followed by, "Daddy!"

Sam smiled and set the bandages aside, then headed for the waiting room to see Marie and his mother, Milly. Marie let out a happy shriek and ran to him. He easily picked her up and held her close. She grabbed two handfuls of his short beard and leaned in to kiss him on the cheek.

"I missed you," he told her and hugged her tight.

"I missed you, too." She wrapped her arms around his neck and nearly choked him as she squeezed tight. "I miss True, too."

Sam couldn't say anything to that. He missed her as well, and he had only been away from her one night. He feared that Marie might have a hard time adjusting to not having True with them. He knew he was going to be miserable without her.

"I'm glad you're home," his mother told him as she stepped up to him.

Sam shifted Marie to one hip and used his free arm to draw his mother close. She wrapped her arms around his waist and hugged him tightly. She was short and plump, with dark, grey-streaked hair, and brown eyes that sparkled with happiness as she drew back to look up at him.

"We were starting to worry about you. I was so glad to see Travis arrive at my house with Marie. He told me you had to stay a few more days. How is Miss Tucker?"

"She's healing nicely and will be just fine," he told her, trying to sound professional, but he knew his mother caught the tension in his voice.

Milly studied him a moment. "Marie is very fond of her."

Sam nodded and let out a long breath, he knew where this conversation was going. "Marie, Doc needs help rolling bandages, would you like to help him?"

"Yes!" she said happily before she drew back to place a big wet kiss on his cheek. She wiggled and he put her down, then she skipped into the examination room.

"Yes, Marie is very fond of True," Sam told his mother.

She gave him a soft smile. "And so are you."

He let out a long breath. "Yeah, I am, but don't get your hopes up. True is engaged and when she leaves in the spring, she's going home to marry a rich man."

She nodded in understanding. "Have you told her how you feel?"

"No, and I'm not going to. She's promised to someone that can provide for her and give her the life she's accustomed to. I can't give her what he can," he told her flatly.

Milly gave him a knowing look. "Maybe you can give her something more. Maybe you can give her something he can't."

***

His mother's words echoed in Sam's head for the rest of the day and he was still thinking it over that evening, when he carried Marie up the stairs to put her to bed. He settled her in her bed, tucking the covers in around her. Picking her doll up from the nightstand, he placed it in bed beside her.

"Daddy," she said sleepily.

"Yes, honey…" He tucked her hair behind her ear.

"I miss True."

He felt his heart squeeze. "Me, too."

"I wish she was here."

Sam swallowed hard. "So do I."

"Will we get to see her again?" she asked softly.

He sat on her little bed and ran his hand over her hair. "I'm sure we will." He hoped his words were the truth, but he also knew seeing her again would be painful. "She'll be with Shyfawn all winter."

Marie sighed. "Good."

Sam sat on Marie's bed long after she had fallen asleep, lost in thought. True would be so close for months but he would never get to hold her again and that thought made pain radiate through his chest.

Was she missing him as much as he missed her?

***

True let her eyes move over the town as they drove the buckboard down the road. "This is Rimrock?" she asked skeptically.

The town was just a few buildings scattered down each side of the dusty street. Several small houses dotted the prairie beyond the town. She had seen many small settlements on her way to Rimrock, but she had expected the town to be a bit larger.

"Rimrock was one of the first settlements in the area," Matthew told her. "It's slowly growing though. It started as a trading post for travelers and trappers. But now we have a general store, saloon, restaurant, livery, church, school, and a few other small businesses. We're lucky Clu Bodine came to town," he said and pointed to a house on the hill with a large tree out front. "He sort of runs things. He helped get this town started with his freighting business. If you need anything, he can get it for you."

"Toby works for him," she said as things began to fall into place. "He talked about Mr. Bodine on our way to Rimrock."

Matthew nodded. "Yes, Clu is a good man and he'll be sure this town prospers and grows."

"Where's Sam's?" True asked without thought.

Matthew couldn't quite hide his knowing smile in time before he answered. "That building over there," he said and pointed to a two-story house on the main street. "The house next to it belongs to Doc Black, he uses it for a clinic. They treat patients there. Sam takes care of things in and around Rimrock, Doc Black goes to Claytonville a lot to doctor the folks there."

Shyfawn laughed softly. "I think it has to do more with Widow Johnson."

Matthew smiled. "I won't argue with you on that."

True took in the town and the few people milling about on the street and wondered how Shyfawn could have chosen to live in a place like this after knowing the luxuries of Charlotte. She had given up comfort and good living to carve out a life here in the middle of nowhere with Matthew. Shyfawn must love him more than anything else to give up so much to be with him.

Matthew drove the wagon down the Main

Street, then stopped before the general store. He climbed down and helped True and Shyfawn from the wagon before ushering them into the building. True looked around the room to find it filled with all manner of items.

"Good morning," an aging man behind the counter greeted them.

Matthew smiled at the man. "Good morning, Mr. Pearson."

True watched the friendly interaction between Matthew and the storekeeper as Matthew told the man what he needed. Today, they would load up the buckboard with enough supplies to last for several months. When winter fully came, they wouldn't be able to come to town and had to get what they needed now. The thought of being snowed in at the ranch for months made True a little nervous.

The bell over the door rang and True turned to see who had entered. She wasn't sure why she looked; it wasn't as if she knew anyone in town. It was a young woman wearing trousers and a big coat. Her smile was wide and friendly, her green eyes sparkled, and her black hair was stuffed under a hat, though several wild curls had escaped.

"Shyfawn," she said cheerfully as she approached them.

"Good morning, Aleena. I'd like you to meet my sister, True," she said with a smile. "True, this is Aleena Richardson."

"Oh, it's so good to finally meet you!" She took True's hand in greeting and shook it enthusiastically. "Shyfawn has told me all about you."

True smiled at her as Aleena released her hand. "It's good to meet you."

"Aleena," Matthew said as he joined the group. "Good morning."

Her eyes went to Matthew and she continued to smile. "We saw your buckboard out front. Mr. Bodine said to tell you your new stove should come tomorrow."

"Good, we can stay in town until the wagon gets here," Matthew told her.

"I'll let him know." She looked back to True. "Stop by today and see Toby, he's been asking about you," she said as she headed for the door. "It was nice to meet you," she called out to True as she hurried back to the door and left.

True watched the young woman leave. "I like her."

Shyfawn nodded. "She's sweet. She works for Clu Bodine and he looks after her. The man who raised Aleena died a few years ago. Clu gave her a job in the harness shop and she cooks and cleans for him. Gussy May took her in and Aleena has a permanent room with her."

True felt a feeling she couldn't describe wash over her. She had never known such kind people before. The entire town looked out for one another, helping each other whenever someone was in need. In Charlotte, she felt that nobody did anything without a chance for personal gain. There were a few people that were truly kind, but they were rare.

True knew she would love Rimrock and the people in it by the time spring came. That would make it all the harder when she had to leave.

Chapter Fifteen

They entered the building that served as both harness shop and freight office. True couldn't help but wrinkle her nose at the smell of leather, oil, dust, and assorted odors from sacks and crates stacked around the room.

"Hello?" Matthew called into the room as he closed the door behind the group.

"Hold yer horses," a man called. "I'll be there in a minute."

True's heart leaped and she smiled brightly. "Toby!"

There was silence for a moment. "Miss Tucker?"

Boots sounded on the wooden floor and Toby appeared from behind the stack of crates. He smiled at her and she was never so happy to see his tobacco-stained teeth. His left arm was in a sling and she had the desperate urge to hug him but controlled herself, not wanting to cause him any pain.

"I was so glad to hear you wasn't dead," he told her as he stood before her.

She laughed and reached out to take his hand, holding it tightly in both of hers. "So was I. I'm so glad someone found you in time."

He nodded in agreement and gently squeezed her hand. "I was lucky. After you took the horses, them fellas left the wagon and took the mules. They didn't even check on me, they just left me for dead. Luckily for me, Trapper Josh found me and kept me from dyin'."

"Did anyone find those men?" she asked as she released his hand.

He nodded. "They tried to trade the mules for a couple horses, but the homesteader recognized the mules. They knocked him out and stole the horses when he asked why they had Clu's mules."

"So, the bandits are still out there?"

"I'm afraid so," he said regretfully. "But I'm sure they headed out of this part of the country."

"I hope so," True said and prayed it was the truth. She didn't want those men around to hurt more people.

"Glad you're in town," a man said as he walked from the back of the room toward them. "Saves me a trip out to your place."

Matthew smiled. "Anything to make your job easier, Clu."

Matthew introduced True to Clu Bodine and they exchanged pleasantries before the men began to talk business. True looked Clu Bodine over and decided that he didn't look like any businessman she had ever met. His clothes were old and worn, stained and patched in places, his black hat was a bit battered, with a sweat stain around the band. She had no doubt it was from doing the hard work himself and not standing back to order others to do it. He had a friendly smile, but his dark eyes were bloodshot, a good indication that he drank too much and his eyes held an inner pain he couldn't let go.

"We'll let them talk shipping prices and grab something to eat," Shyfawn told her, placing a hand on her stomach.

True didn't argue and followed her sister down the street to the Gallop on Inn, a small building that housed the little café. They entered the café and Shyfawn was greeted by several people as the sisters made their way to a table. The room was small, but the big windows let in a great deal of light and gave the place a cozy feel. It also smelled of good food and True suddenly realized just how hungry she was.

"Shyfawn, it's good to see you in town," a plump little woman said as she approached their table. "And you must be True. Marie has talked nonstop about you since she came home."

True smiled. "You must be her grandmother, Milly."

"I am indeed. She told me all about how you saved her life." Tears filled her dark eyes even as she smiled. "You are a blessing to our family. Marie is at the clinic with Sam, you'll have to go see them before you head back home."

"We'll head back home tomorrow," Shyfawn told her. "Tonight, we'll stay with Gussy May."

True gave her a perplexed look. "Who's Gussy May?"

"She's one of the original settlers in Rimrock. We don't have a hotel here, so she takes folks in overnight to help make ends meet. She comes across gruff but she's nice."

"Yes, she's one of a kind," Milly told her. "I'll get you each a plate of the special."

"One for Matthew, too, he'll be along soon," Shyfawn said and Milly nodded before leaving. "We'll go to Sam's after we're done here. It's probably time your stitches came out."

True could only nod as her chest grew tight with emotion. She desperately wanted to see Sam and Marie again. She had a feeling she would be overflowing with happiness and at the same time, feel the stabbing pain in her heart knowing she was no longer in their lives.

***

Marie's excited shriek echoed through the building and Sam was out the door and into the waiting room in the blink of an eye. His heart lodged in his throat when he saw True standing there with Marie in her arms, the two hugging each other tight. Shyfawn stood by them and smiled at him as he came into the room.

"I was scared I'd never see you again," Marie said as she drew back to look at True.

"Now why would you think that?" True asked as she held Marie on her hip. "I'll be here all winter and we'll see each other."

Her eyes moved to Sam and he couldn't breathe for a moment. Jesus, he missed her. Seeing her there with Marie brought up too many memories of their time in the cabin and the longing he felt threatened to choke him. Her smile faltered and he had a feeling she was having the same memories.

"Sam," Shyfawn said, breaking the tension of the moment. "We were in town and I thought maybe you should look at True's leg."

He nodded. "Yeah, the stitches could probably come out today." He was glad he sounded professional. "I'll finish up with Sims and we'll get to it."

Sam walked back into the room where Sims waited patiently. He could hear Marie chatter happily as he closed the door and the sound of True's voice slid over him, bringing up too many feelings. Pushing aside all thought of True, Sam rubbed liniment onto Sims shoulder and covered it with a cloth.

"That should do it," Sam told the man as he wiped his hands on a rag.

"Thanks, Doc," the man said as he slid his shirt back on. "This damn cold weather makes that shoulder ache terrible."

Sam nodded in understanding. Sims had had an accident several years ago, dislocated shoulder and torn muscles caused by a fall from the livery loft.

"I'd recommend staying inside where it's warm, but I know you better than that," he said with a smile.

Sims smiled back as he pulled on his coat. "The livery don't run itself. Aleena's a big help but she can't do all the work." Sims paid Sam and headed for the door. "Later."

Sam followed him out and Sims bid good afternoon to the women before he left the building.

Sam's eyes found True seated in a chair with Marie on her lap. The two talked happily and Sam didn't want to interrupt them. He would have stood there all day watching them but Shyfawn cleared her throat and brought him back to reality.

"Right," he muttered. "Miss Tucker, whenever you're ready."

She looked up at him before helping Marie from her lap and getting to her feet. Shyfawn held onto Marie's hand to keep the girl from following True into the room.

"It won't take long," he told Shyfawn. He closed the door and took a calming breath before he turned to face True. "Hop up on the table," he told her and moved to get his scissors.

True swallowed hard and did as he instructed. She watched him move around the small room. Her eyes traveled over him, she missed looking at him. She missed having his strong body near. She just missed *him*. She lowered her eyes when he turned to her.

"Turn and stretch your legs out on the table," he said quietly.

She did so and he moved to her injured leg. He pushed her dress and petticoats to her knee before removing her boot. She watched his large hands work and had to bite her lip when he touched her skin. His touch was gentle as he looked her stitches over. She missed his hands on her skin and had to blink back sudden tears.

"It looks good," he told her. "You've healed very nicely."

She swallowed back the emotion. "I had a good doctor," she managed to say.

He finally met her eyes. "You were a good patient." His hands absently caressed her leg. He saw the shine of tears in her eyes and had to look away. "This shouldn't hurt," he said as he bent over her leg. "It might pull a bit and we have a lot of them to take out."

She could only nod as she watched him work. He gently cut the stitches and pulled them from her skin. It felt like forever as he pulled the stitches free. The sting of the stitches being pulled away was irritating her, but she refused to complain about it. She was thankful to be alive and it gave her a good reason to be near Sam. She studied his face as he worked, he was so handsome. Before she could stop herself, she reached out and brushed his hair from his forehead, which fell right back in place.

Sam stilled and lifted his head to look at her. She pushed his hair back again and let her fingers trail over his short beard. He swallowed hard. "True, don't." His voice was barely a whisper.

True felt her heart break and tears filled her eyes. She quickly looked down and lowered her hand. Of course he would want to keep things professional. What they had in the cabin was gone and she was nothing more than another patient to him. She had given him her body and she was sure he had her heart, because it hurt like hell. She wanted things to be as they were, but he was throwing her back to Steven and all too eager to send her back to Charlotte.

Sam muttered a curse at his now shaking hands. One touch from her could send his body into whirling sensation. He wanted nothing more than to lay her back on the table and take her body. He knew he could never do that. He had let her go once and he would never be able to do it again. She belonged to someone else and had a life far away from here. He had no right in trying to keep her. He couldn't give her the life she was used to. He was a poor small-town doctor, not some wealthy businessman.

When Sam finally pulled the last stitch free, he almost sighed with relief. He was amazed he hadn't cut a hole in her leg with the scissors he was shaking so badly. He moved to a shelf and took down a small tin of salve and a rolled-up bandage. He returned to her and rubbed the salve over the scratches. They were going to scar.

He wondered if Steven would think her imperfect now. He clenched his teeth against the thought of that man touching her. He couldn't keep his hand from caressing the marks as he rubbed the salve over them. He carefully began to wrap her leg with the bandage. To him the marks were a sign of strength and selflessness. Her willingness to sacrifice herself for his daughter.

When he was finished, he braced his hands on the table and let out a long breath. He fought back the emotions that flooded him.

"I'll never be able to thank you enough for saving Marie's life," he managed to say, though his throat was tight.

"I'd do it again in a heartbeat," she whispered.

Sam couldn't speak, so he busied himself with pulling her boot back on. With that done, he pulled down her dress and helped her from the table. That was a mistake. His hands were on her waist and her hands gripped his arms. He looked down into her dark eyes and swore at the emotion he saw there.

He pulled her into his arms and held her, needing to comfort her. He needed to comfort himself with the act of holding her to him. She clung to him and pressed her cheek to his chest.

"Damn it, True," he growled and held her tight.

"Sam, I—"

"Daddy!" Marie pounded on the door. "Daddy, are ya done yet?"

Sam reluctantly pulled away from True. "I swear that child has no patience," he said as he moved to the door, silently grateful for the interruption. "Yes, I'm done." He opened the door and Marie hurried in.

Marie skipped over to True. "Are ya all better?"

She gave the girl a smile. "Yes, I'm all better."

"Told you Daddy was the best doctor in the world," she said with pride.

"That he is."

"Shyfawn said you were gonna go to Gussy May's," Marie jabbered happily. "Can I come, too?"

"Marie," Sam scolded. "It's rude to invite yourself—"

"I think that would be fine," True said quickly before meeting Sam's eyes. "If you don't mind?"

He looked at her for a moment and let out a long breath. "Sure, she can go."

Marie gave a happy hoot and took True by the hand. "Come on."

"Okay..." True laughed and followed Marie as she fairly dragged her from the room.

Shyfawn laughed and followed them.

"Someone's excited."

Sam swore under his breath and followed them to the door. He watched as they walked toward Gussy May's quaint two-story house down the street. Being near True was killing him and Marie appeared determined to bring them all together. He swore again, Marie was going to be heartbroken when True left – and so would he.

***

True tiptoed from her bedroom in her sister's house and crept down the stairs as quietly as she could, not wanting to disturb Shyfawn and Matthew as they slept. She was restless and unable to fall asleep, maybe fresh air would help settle her nerves and slow the whirling thoughts in her mind.

When she reached the bottom of the stairs she went through the kitchen to the back door. Slipping into her boots and coat she quietly opened the door and stepped out. The cold crisp air bit at her cheeks as she closed the door and walked to the bench on the porch. Heaving a deep sigh, she sat down and leaned back as she tugged her coat closed and crossed her arms.

Looking out over the moonlit ranch yard, True felt some of the tension leave her.

It had been a month since she had left the cabin and she still wished she was back there with Sam and Marie. She was happy to be with her sister, but she missed being near Sam.

Her breath steamed in the air when she exhaled and watched the snow slowly come down. Winter had set in and it would be many months before she saw the spring flowers come. She would be leaving in May and heading back to her life in Charlotte to be with Steven. Her chest squeezed at the thought of her fiancé. How could she marry him now? She had betrayed him, and she knew she didn't love him. She couldn't be with someone she had to keep secrets from, and she didn't want to live under a cloud of lies.

The door opening warned her she was no longer alone. "True?" Matthew's voice was low as he stepped out onto the porch. "Is everything all right?"

She looked over at him. "Yes, I just needed some air."

He chuckled and sat down beside her. "You lie about as good as your sister."

"I'm not lying," she informed him. "I did need some air."

"But something is wrong, isn't it?" he asked quietly.

True let out a long breath. "I don't know, Matt. I came west to see my family and try to get my head clear," she said to him. "I feel more confused than ever."

Matthew put his arm across her shoulders and pulled her to him. She barely knew Matthew but felt so relaxed with him and his small gesture of comfort tore at her emotions. She turned her head to his shoulder and let her tears flow. She secretly wished it was Sam's arm around her. If it had been Sam, there would be no tears of sadness.

Matthew was silent for a long time, then as if guessing her thoughts, he said, "He's a good man."

Her heart surged. "What? Who?"

Matthew chuckled. "Don't pretend you don't know. Sam."

She let out a groan and leaned into him. "I know he's a good man."

"You're engaged to Steven," Matthew said softly. "Sam is the kind of man that respects that."

She nodded and felt new tears. "I know."

"He won't try to persuade you to change your mind," he told her, his voice gentle. "No matter how much he wants to and, believe me, he wants to."

"Matt, you can't be sure of that," she managed to say.

"I'm not blind, True. He cares about you, that's plain to see."

She choked back a sob. How could he care about her? He had taken her body and sent her on her way. No, she couldn't blame him. She had been more than willing to give herself to him. Sam had known she was engaged to Steven and he was stepping out of the situation to make it easier for her to go back to Charlotte.

Matthew tightened his arm around her shoulders. "It's up to you, True. In the spring you can go home to Steven or you can stay here with Sam."

"I'm just so confused, Matt," she sobbed. "I want to stay but I don't fit in here. My family is here but my life is in Charlotte."

"You have a lot to think about and all winter to do it. Who knows," he said with a shrug. "By the time spring gets here maybe you'll fit in and have a life here."

She could only nod. He was right, but she had a

feeling when the time came to choose it wasn't going to be easy.

***

True and Travis dismounted their horses in front of the freight office and climbed the steps to go inside. It had been two weeks since they were last in town but True knew Clu would be sending the freight wagon east and she had letters she needed to send. One to Aunt Molly and one to Steven. It was the last wagon to leave for the winter and wouldn't return until spring. Toby would stay at Clu's warehouse in Kansas and store the incoming freight from the east before loading up in the spring to be delivered. She admired Clu for working hard with his men and having such an organized system to deliver goods to the isolated people.

Travis held the door open for her and followed her inside. She removed her gloves and reached into her coat pocket to pull out the letters. Each letter explained her ordeal with the bandits and being trapped in the cabin with Sam and Marie. As well as she couldn't marry Steven and may stay longer with her sisters. After what she had done with Sam, she couldn't marry Steven.

"Miss Tucker," Toby greeted her as he came from behind a stack of crates. His arm was no longer in a sling and he appeared to be able to move it with no pain. "What brings you by today?"

True smiled brightly at him. "I'm going to send a couple letters with you." She held up the envelopes.

"Sure thing." He reached out and took the envelopes to place them in a canvas bag that hung from a peg on the wall. "Lots of folks sending out letters this trip."

True watched the letters drop into the bag and felt both relief and apprehension. Her engagement to Steven was over, now what would happen? She decided not to worry about it until spring – or rather try not to worry about it at all.

"Clu not in today?" Travis asked as he looked around.

Toby shook his head. "Mr. Bodine hit the bottle a little hard last night. He won't be in for a few more hours."

Travis shook his head with disapproval. "That stuff is going to kill him."

"Is Aleena here?" True asked hopefully. She liked the girl and wanted to see her again.

"No, she hasn't been feeling well. Doc Sam gave her something for her cough, but Mr. Bodine ordered her to stay home until she felt better." He smiled as he thought. "She wasn't very happy about it."

"I don't imagine," Travis said before he offered his hand to Toby to shake. "Safe travels ahead."

"Thanks." Toby released Travis's hand.

"You be careful tomorrow, Toby," she told him, worry thick in her voice.

He smiled his tobacco smile. "Don't worry about me, Miss Tucker."

"You still be careful," she ordered and couldn't keep from hugging him. Not caring that he smelled of tobacco and that rank whiskey he liked to drink.

Toby held himself still for a moment before he hugged her back. "I'll be back before you know it."

True drew back and smiled at him before she left the building with Travis. Once outside he slid his arm across her shoulders to offer comfort as she wiped the moisture from her eyes. Toby was her friend and she knew she would worry about him until he came back.

"Let's go grab something to eat before we head home," he suggested.

"I'd like that," she told him as she slipped her gloves back on.

"True!" Marie's voice rang out.

True turned to see Marie running down the boardwalk toward her. She smiled as Marie threw herself into her outstretched arms and she lifted the little girl to hug her close. Marie's arms and legs went around her as she clung tightly to True.

"Marie, it's so good to see you," True said past the tightness in her throat. "I've missed you."

"I miss you," she said as she still clung to True. "Daddy misses you, too."

True felt her heart grow tight and her eyes burned. "I miss him, too," she whispered and squeezed her eyes shut against the tears.

True held Marie close and savored the feel of the little girl in her arms. In such a short time Marie had become a big part of her life. The thought of never seeing Marie again when she left to return home broke her heart. She pulled back to look at the girl. Her dark eyes shown bright with happiness. Her black hair was in two long braids, hanging over her shoulders. She was so beautiful.

Feeling something against her leg, True looked down to see Cody, his tail wagging happily.

"Hi, Cody." He wiggled and whined softly.

"True."

She looked past Marie to see Sam standing there. Her heart squeezed and her breath caught. He was so handsome. She let her eyes drift over his tall broad frame. Images of his hard body over hers flashed in her mind and she felt color rise to her cheeks. His dark eyes looked at her with hunger and she knew he was having similar thoughts.

"Mr. Barkley," she managed to say, though her voice sounded breathless. "It's good to see you. I hope you've been well."

Sam frowned at her formal greeting. "Been well enough, Miss Tucker." He looked past her. "Travis," he said in a more friendly voice, but with a disapproving look.

Travis gave him a wolfish grin. "Afternoon, Sam."

"I'm on my way to Jack's to check on Sunny, his cast should be ready to come off," Sam told them. "I was taking Marie to her grandmother's until I get back."

"Can I go with True?" Marie asked hopefully.

Sam looked at True for a moment. "I'm sure she's busy, honey."

True gave him a hard look at the tone in his voice. "I am not," she snapped.

Sam gave her a small grin. "Then I guess she can go with you."

Marie squealed with delight and hugged True's neck tightly.

"I was taking True to the café to eat before we head back, I'll tell your ma we're taking Marie with us," Travis told him.

"I'll come by and pick her up later," he said to Travis. "I need to check on Shyfawn as well."

Sam stepped up to True and leaned forward. She watched as he lowered his head towards her, and then turned to kiss Marie on the cheek. True felt her heart jump at the nearness of him and breathed in his scent. Her body heated and she found it hard to breathe.

"Be good," he told Marie and pulled back.

"I will," she said and hugged True's neck.

Sam reached up to tweak her nose and she swatted at him. He smiled at her, and then met True's eyes. He let his hand drop to hers for a moment and even through the gloves she felt the heat of his touch.

Travis cleared his throat a little too loudly. "You better be going, Sam."

Sam scowled at him and said nothing, but True didn't miss the look of irritation he gave Travis, who grinned and put a hand on True's lower back to guide her down the boardwalk. She also saw Sam's angry glare at Travis and heard Travis chuckle with amusement.

Chapter Sixteen

Sam stepped up onto the porch of Matthew's ranch house and smiled when he saw Cody laying by the door. He lay on a rug and Gray Cat lay curled up on top of him to keep warm. He chuckled softly and bent to pet each animal before he opened the door and went into the house.

"Hello?" he hollered as he closed the door behind him.

Shyfawn was setting the table and looked up to smile at him. "Hello, Sam."

"Daddy!" Marie ran from the kitchen and threw herself at him.

Sam laughed and scooped her up in his arms. "Did you miss me?"

"Did you have to cut Sunny's leg off?" she asked, her face serious.

He smiled at her and kissed her cheek. "No, I didn't. He still has two legs and is doing just fine."

True stepped into the room and drank in the sight of Sam. He easily held Marie with one arm and smiled lovingly at her. She felt her heart break a little and had to swallow hard, longing nearly choking her as she looked at the two of them.

"Can we stay for dinner?" Marie asked Sam.

"I don't know, it's going to get dark in a few hours, we should head home."

Marie looked disappointed and tucked her head against his shoulder. "True and I were making something special."

Sam's eyes moved to True and he had to take a calming breath. She was beautiful. Her big dark eyes stared at him intently and her expression held both hope and dread. He frowned as he studied her. Her skin appeared pale and she had circles under her eyes. She wasn't sleeping. He understood that because Sam hadn't had a decent night's sleep since he had returned home. He would wake in the night reaching for her only to find his bed empty. He wanted her near now, even if it was only for a little while.

"I think we can stay for dinner," he said quietly, not sure if he was speaking to Marie or True.

Marie squealed with delight and pushed at him to put her down. "Come on, True." She ran to True and grabbed her hand. "We have to finish cooking."

True laughed as Marie nearly jerked her arm out of its socket as she pulled her toward the kitchen. "I'm coming."

Shyfawn laughed and stepped up to Sam. "She is sweet."

"That she is," Sam said still looking at the empty doorway.

She linked her arm through his. "Your daughter or my sister?" Sam looked down at her and she gave him a knowing smile. "I'm not blind, Sam. You care about True."

He gave her a sad smile. "It doesn't matter. She's going back to Charlotte to be married."

She patted his arm. "She'll be here all winter." She gave him a wink. "You'll have plenty of time to convince her to stay."

Sam chuckled. "You're impossible."

"I know." She laughed. "Matt's down at the barn if you feel like escaping." Shyfawn cast him one last smile and went to the kitchen.

Sam swore under his breath and went outside to find sanctuary in the barn. A good male conversation about horses, cattle, and guns was just what he needed. Cody looked up at him as he left the house and got to his feet, spilling Gray Cat onto the rug. Sam laughed, walked to his horse and led him to the barn where his nose was assailed with the scent of hay and horses.

"Matt?" he hollered as he walked in.

"Be down in a minute," Matthew called from the loft as he pitched hay into a stall below.

Sam smiled up at his friend. "Don't you have hired help for the manual labor?"

Matthew laughed. "They're out doing it. They're out there in the cold wind checking cows and I'm in here where it's warm."

Sam chuckled as he unsaddled his horse. "I should have known you had a good reason for working."

"Sunny's leg all healed up?" he asked, as he pitched more hay into the stall.

"Yep, he might have a small limp, but he's all right." Sam put his horse into one of the stalls and he happily chewed on the hay.

"Good." Matthew put the pitchfork aside and descended the ladder to stand before Sam. "I imagine I'll be seeing a lot more of you now."

Sam's brows drew together in confusion. "I suppose so. Shyfawn will have her baby in a month or so."

Matthew grinned at him. "I'm talking about True. I just want to know if you plan on coming courting."

Sam felt pain stab his heart. "She's not mine to court."

Matthew frowned at him. "She's not yours to do a lot of things with but you want to anyway."

Sam jabbed a hand through his hair and swore. "What the hell am I supposed to do? She's promised to someone else."

"You should have thought of that before you bedded her," Matthew growled.

"Who says that I...that we... Damn it, how'd you know?" Sam snapped.

Suddenly, Matthew burst into laughter. "I'll be damned."

Sam stared at him. "What?"

"I seem to recall we've had this talk before. Only it was you lecturing me about carrying on with Shyfawn."

Sam thought back. Matthew was right. Sam had given him a similar speech and Matthew's response had been exactly the same. Sam couldn't help but smile. He had loved seeing Matthew squirm. Now that the shoe was on the other foot, he didn't like it so much.

Sam let out a long breath. "You're right," he admitted. "I'm in a hell of a fix."

"That you are," Matthew agreed. "In the

meantime, let's go in and warm up."

Sam wasn't going to argue and felt he was composed enough to see True again. He mulled over Matthew's comment as they walked back to the house. Could he come court True? Would she want him to? He wasn't sure he was brave enough to find out.

***

"We better be heading to town soon," Sam said as they sat in the parlor after dinner.

"Ah, do we have to, Daddy?" Marie slumped in her chair.

"Yes, we do." He chuckled as he got to his feet and lifted her into his arms, causing her to shriek with delight.

"I'll get your horse saddled," Travis said and headed for the door. He leaned close to Sam and whispered. "If you don't put a claim on her, I will."

Sam elbowed Travis in the ribs and Travis laughed. An unexpected possessiveness washed over Sam at the thought of Travis courting True. He felt as if True was his, even though he knew it wasn't the reality of things. She belonged to Steven.

The dogs barked and Travis paused at the door. "Someone's riding in fast."

Matthew went to the door. "Who is it?"

"Looks like Clu," Travis told them. "He's hell bent. I'll bet he's here for you, Sam. I'll get my horse for you, he's a runner," he said before he leaped from the porch and ran for the barn.

The entire household stepped out onto the porch. Clu slid his horse to a stop in front of the house and vaulted from the saddle. He ran to the porch steps and stood there breathing hard from his ride.

"Sam, I'm glad I found you, your ma said you came here," he managed to say between breaths.

"What happened?" Sam asked even as he moved to True and handed Marie over to her.

"It's Aleena, she's really sick," he told Sam, worry in his voice. "Gussy May thinks it's pneumonia. Doc Black is in Claytonville tending to the Ryker family, so I came for you."

"I'll get you a fresh horse, Clu," Heck said, jogging to the barn.

Sam looked at Marie. "Stay here with True and Shyfawn."

She nodded and clung tightly to True.

Sam went back into the house, the women and Matthew followed, getting out of the cold. Sam slipped into his coat and put his hat on.

"I'll have Travis take Marie into town later," Matthew told him.

"Be sure you bundle up for the ride to town," he told Marie as he leaned in to kiss her cheek.

"I will, Daddy," she said as she clung to True's neck. "Don't forget your gloves."

Sam chuckled. "I won't." He met True's eyes and let his fingers trail down her arm before he turned and went outside. True walked to the window and watched as he mounted and rode away at a gallop with Clu. She watched until he was out of view and held Marie tight.

"Is Aleena gonna be okay?" Marie asked softly.

"I hope so, honey," she said and sent up a silent prayer for the girl.

"I should go," Shyfawn told them. "I could help her."

"No," Matthew said flatly. "If it's pneumonia, it will take too much of your energy and you can't risk anything happening to you or the baby because of it."

True turned to look at her sister. "He's right. I know you don't like it, but you can't help her."

Shyfawn nodded in understanding and slid her arm around Matthew's waist to lean into him. "I hate feeling this helpless."

Matthew kissed her temple. "Sam will help Aleena."

True blinked back unexpected tears and held Marie close. She hoped Matthew was right.

***

Sam looked up to see Travis, Heck, and Marie enter Gussy May's house. Marie ran to him and he lifted her into his arms to hug her tightly.

"How's Aleena?" Heck asked as he closed the door behind him.

Sam continued to hold Marie, she didn't appear to want to let him go just yet. "She's very sick and the next few hours will tell. I've done all I can for her for now."

Travis let out a long breath. "She's too stubborn to let this get her, she'll fight it."

Sam gave him a slight smile. "I have no doubt about that."

"Can we see her?" Heck asked hesitantly.

Sam nodded. "Just don't wake her, she needs rest. Clu is with her right now."

Heck nodded and went up the stairs, followed

by Travis, while Sam held Marie tightly. His job was a continuous reminder of how precious life is and how easily it can be taken away. A few days ago, Aleena had been a strong healthy young woman, now she lay weak and deathly sick. He hoped she pulled through. Gussy May would be lost without her. The girl had a big place in the heart of the cantankerous woman and she loved Aleena like a daughter. Even Clu would be lost without her. She had become a big part of his life since he had taken her under his wing. She might work for him, but she also kept him in line and his drinking had slowed a great deal.

Sam often wondered what Clu was trying to drown at the bottom of a whiskey bottle. He had been there himself after Piper had died and understood the pain that drove a man to numb himself with whiskey. Sam had pulled himself from the bottle because Marie needed him. Maybe Clu was cutting back on the drink because he felt Aleena needed him.

"Is she gonna die, Daddy?" Marie asked softly.

Sam hugged her tighter and savored the feel of her small body as he held her. "I don't know, honey."

***

Sam entered Aleena's room and was pleased to see her sitting up in bed talking to Clu as he sat in a chair beside the bed. She had given him a good scare and Sam was sure he was going to lose her, but she had pulled through. She smiled at him as he stood by the bed, her eyes bright and alert, though her face was still gaunt and she looked exhausted.

"How are you feeling today?" he asked her with a smile.

"I'm great," she told him.

"She's full of sass," Clu said as he stood and stepped away to allow Sam room to examine Aleena. "Thinks she can go back to work soon."

She scowled at Clu. "I can."

"Not yet," Sam told her as he set his bag on the dresser and pulled out his stethoscope. "You need more rest."

"Told you," Clu said triumphantly.

"Before you swear at him, let me listen to your lungs," Sam said with a grin. He listened to her breathe and was relieved that her lungs sounded good and strong. "You're going to be just fine," he told her as he stepped back and put his stethoscope away.

"Good to hear." She fixed her green eyes on Clu. "And I'll come back to work when I damn well feel like it."

"Aleena! Language!" Marie hollered from outside the door.

Sam laughed. "You can come in now."

Marie scampered through the door and ran to Aleena's bed. Crawling up onto it she threw her arms around the girl and hugged her tight. Aleena laughed and returned the hug.

Sam smiled as he watched the two of them. Marie had insisted on coming with him to check on Aleena and he had gladly let her. She often accompanied him when he made calls, he felt her infectious happiness was good for his patients. Marie sat on the bed facing Aleena, took her hand

and began talking rapidly about how worried she had been about her dying.

Sam caught Clu's eye and jerked his head toward the door. The man followed him downstairs and into the kitchen to find Gussy May preparing lunch. The aging woman's gray hair was pulled up in a haphazard bun and worry lines added to the wrinkles on her face as her sharp blue eyes met Sam's. The woman may always put on astern façade, but it was clear she loved Aleena like a daughter.

"Aleena's going to be just fine," he said confidently.

Gussy May let out a long breath of relief and absently wiped her hands on the apron covering the front of her dress. "Thank God."

"She still needs a lot of rest so don't let her do much work for a while," he said firmly.

"Do you know how hard it is to keep her still?" Clu asked. "She works for me." He paused and thought. "In fact, I think she's starting to take over, she does so much. She helps Gussy May and works at the livery for Sims."

Sam laughed and nodded. "I know it won't be easy but try very hard. Assign her small jobs and make sure she doesn't do more than that."

Clu chuckled and shook his head with humor. "Wish me luck."

Chapter Seventeen

Sam pulled the sleigh up in front of Matthew's house. Travis trotted up from the barn and greeted them. He held his arms out to Marie and she leaped at him. He caught her and swung her around, bringing a delighted shriek from her. Cody leaped from the sleigh and was instantly met by Matthew's dog to play in the snow.

"What brings you out here today?" Travis asked as he settled Marie on his hip.

"We came to see True," Marie told him happily.

Travis grinned and looked at Sam. "Really." He drew the word out. "Is that so?"

Sam glared at him. "Yes, that's so. I'm putting a claim on her," he informed Travis as he took two toboggans from the sleigh.

Travis grinned at him. "It's about damn time."

"Travis!" Marie scolded.

Travis cringed and looked apologetically at her. "Sorry, Chipmunk."

Sam laughed and jerked his head to the house. "Let's go in." He placed the toboggans near the bottom of the steps leading up onto the porch.

Travis followed Sam into the house, then set Marie on her feet before he turned and went back out to unharness Sam's horse and stable him. Sam helped Marie out of her winter clothes. She didn't wait for her father as she turned and ran into the house.

"True, we came to claim you!" Marie shouted as she ran into the house.

"Damn it," Sam grumbled.

"Daddy, language!" she hollered as she ran.

Sam frantically removed his coat and boots, throwing them in a pile on the floor. "Marie!" He ran after his daughter. Sam slid to a stop in the kitchen to see True lift Marie to sit on the counter.

True laughed. "You came to what?"

"We came to cl—"

"Visit," Sam interrupted as he stepped up to them. "We came to visit."

Marie frowned at him. "But you told Travis—"

"Never mind what I told Travis," he said, giving Marie a look that willed her to be quiet.

She let out an aggravated sigh. "We brought toboggans," Marie said excitedly, her thoughts momentarily diverted.

True looked at Sam. "That sounds like fun."

He smiled at her. "That's what we thought, so we decided to come out and make a day of it."

Shyfawn entered the kitchen from the washroom. "That sounds like a good idea." She placed a hand on her belly. "I'm afraid I won't be able to go with you."

"Sure you can," Marie said with a big smile. "Daddy said we would make a big fire and you can sit there and stay warm."

She looked at Sam. "I would like that."

***

In no time at all the entire ranch was outside at the base of a hill in the pasture tobogganing. The men had built a fire and had provided stumps for seating around it. Shyfawn and Matthew sat contentedly by the fire and talked as they watched the group play in the snow. Sam and True were at the top of the hill, seated on the toboggans.

Sam looked at True. "I'll race you."

True smiled at him and pushed off, getting a head start. "Let's go!" she yelled.

"No fair!" he called and rushed after her.

"Go True!" Marie yelled from the bottom of the hill.

True couldn't stop laughing as she raced down the hill. She dared a glance over her shoulder to see Sam barreling after her. She cried out as the front of her toboggan jerked and she was thrown sideways. She landed in the snow and rolled before she came to a stop sprawled on her back and covered with snow. She couldn't help but laugh at the sky.

Sam saw her pitch into the snow and rolled from his toboggan. He scrambled to where she lay buried in the snow laughing. He dropped to his knees beside her and laughed with her. She was beautiful. Her nose and cheeks red from the cold. Her smile lit up her face and her dark eyes danced with joy.

"Did I win?" she asked between laughter.

He looked at her for a moment. "I think maybe we both did."

She held her hand out to him. "I think I'm stuck."

Sam took her hand and pulled her to a sitting position. He reached out and brushed the snow from her face. She could only stare at him and smile. She had never been happier. Since she had met him, she had laughed more, cried more, and been confused as hell. Her only explanation might be that she loved him.

Sam helped her to her feet.

"Are you all right?" He couldn't quite read her expression. She was happy but looked unsure of something.

She nodded. "Yes, I think I am."

"Come on." He took her hand and they walked down the hill to the fire.

Sam placed Marie on a stump close to the fire to be sure she would warm up. The little girl was having so much fun and wasn't ready to go back to the house yet. True took a stump between Marie and Shyfawn to warm her hands and feet by the fire. Sam was content to stand nearby and watch the ranch hands act like children as they continued to toboggan. Travis and Heck raced up the hill. Pushing and shoving at each other.

Shyfawn laughed. "I don't think those two will ever grow up."

Matthew put his arm around her shoulders and watched the two young men. "Don't give up on them. They just might surprise you."

True watched, and for the first time that she could remember, she felt happy and content. The people on the ranch, as well as in town, were truly good people. Her eyes went to Sam as his attention stayed on Travis and Heck as they wrestled in the snow. She was happy and content with Sam. But how did he feel about her?

True bit her lip, she hadn't told Sam that she had sent a letter to Steven, breaking off the engagement. She couldn't marry Steven now. Not after being with Sam, not after what they had done. She had betrayed Steven. Even if she told him about Sam, she knew Steven would call off the engagement and scandal would follow her everywhere. She could never tell him and that was just one more secret between them, she didn't want that.

Sam accepted her just as she was and there were no secrets between them. He knew about her visions and didn't condemn her. He knew about her terrible childhood and the fact she was just the bastard child of a drifter and it didn't matter to him. She knew he cared about her, but did he love her? If he did, could she stay in Rimrock with him and give up the life she knew?

Sam turned and caught her staring at him and worry creased his brow. He moved to squat down between Marie and True. "What's wrong?"

She gave him a small smile and lied. "Nothing."

She could clearly tell he didn't believe her, but he didn't push for the truth and she was grateful for that.

**

True lay in bed and stared at the dark ceiling as she willed her body to relax and tried to sleep. She was having no luck at all. Her mind was filled with Sam and she could think of nothing else. Being near him made her heart leap with joy while her stomach twisted with uncertainty.

What good was this gift if she couldn't see her own future?

A small smile tugged her mouth, she couldn't see *her* future but maybe she could see Sam's. She closed her eyes and concentrated on Sam. Pain stabbed her head as she forced the vision and lights flashed behind her eyes as images rushed through her mind until they slowed and she could see them clearly.

The image of Sam seated on Marie's bed filled True's mind. He sat there and watched his daughter as she slept, reaching out to gently stroke her hair back. She felt the tears burn behind her eyes as she watched them for a long time. She refocused her mind to push farther into Sam's future. Images flashed by to settle on Sam once again. He stood holding a newborn baby with black hair.

"Black hair," True whispered.

If Sam was holding their child, the baby's hair would be light brown or blond. She held in a sob as her heart broke, she wasn't in Sam's future. Sam lifted eyes shining with tears as he smiled at someone. True wanted to see the woman and clung to the vision desperately. He walked to a bed where a young black-haired woman lay propped up with pillows. Sam lay the baby in her outstretched arms and kissed her forehead lovingly.

True's breath caught. It was Marie.

A man entered the room and rushed to kneel beside the bed to gaze at Marie and the baby. His hazel eyes filled with tears as he smiled at her and gently touched the baby. Sam stepped back and left the room to give the couple privacy. Outside the door he smiled at someone and reached out a hand to take a feminine hand in his. True watched as he pulled the woman close and the image snuffed out.

"No," she protested and desperately tried to get the vision back.

Pain slashed her head; she was pushing her mind too hard and she needed to stop but she had to see who the woman was. Who was Sam reaching for? Lights danced behind her eyes again and she saw images of Sam swirl around her. She tried to grab an image of Sam holding a woman close while he slept but she couldn't hang on and it slipped away. Tears leaked from her eyes as frustration washed over her.

"Why can't I see who she is?" she whimpered.

"Because you aren't meant to."

True let out a startled scream as Shyfawn's voice filled the room. She sat up and scrambled for a match to light the candle by the bed. She turned to the door to see Shyfawn standing there in a nightdress watching her. True hadn't heard her sister come in.

"Shyfawn, what are you doing here?" she asked when she could find her voice.

Shyfawn walked across the small room to sit on the bed facing True. "Your thoughts were keeping me up."

A small smile tugged True's mouth. "You can still sense when I have a vision?"

She nodded. "I felt your pain. You were forcing this one."

Tears streamed down her cheeks. "Why can't I see my own future? I see other people's future events and some I wish I had never seen but they come to me anyway. I want to know what happens to *me*."

Shyfawn reached out to tuck a strand of hair behind True's ear. "We aren't supposed to know our own future. We are meant to live our lives as the days come and go."

"I just want to know where I belong," True said and began to cry.

Shyfawn gently placed her palm against True's forehead and closed her eyes. True felt her sister's hand warm and her skin tingled as the pain in her head left her. Shyfawn opened her eyes and stroked True's cheek before she took her hand to hold it tightly.

"That is something you must decide for yourself. You have to listen to your heart and go where it leads you," she said softly.

"My heart is confused," she confessed. "I love Charlotte and I love the life I had there. I know now that I didn't really love Steven and I could never marry him, but my life is in Charlotte." She had to swallow hard and felt new tears fall. "Then I see what you and Jo have here and you're both so happy."

Shyfawn gave her a soft smile. "It's Sam, isn't it?"

She nodded. "And Marie. The time I spent with them in the cabin was so wonderful. I think I love Sam."

"I think you do, too," she gave her sister a

knowing look. "You and Sam... were together?"

True felt herself blush and she nodded. "We were. It was amazing. I had no idea making love would be like that."

"Only if it's with the right man," Shyfawn told her. "I think Sam's the right man for you."

New tears tracked down her cheeks. "He might be, but I don't know if I can stay in Rimrock. It's so different here and life is hard."

"I won't argue with you on that. Life out here in this untamed land is very hard but I wouldn't trade it for the world," Shyfawn told her honestly. "I'll take Rimrock over Charlotte for the rest of my life."

True gave her a smile and blinked back her tears. "I can understand why, you found people that love you and accept you. You don't have to keep any secrets from Matthew."

Shyfawn nodded. "Yes, it's a blessing to finally not be afraid anymore. I always feared being branded a witch or being burned at the stake if anyone ever found out about my gift."

"I didn't want to have secrets from the man I would marry someday. I never could have told Steven about my visions," True said regretfully. "He never would have accepted me for what I can do or what my family was really like. How did you tell Matthew about what you could do?"

"I didn't," Shyfawn said. "He caught me healing a cut on Marie's head. He was shocked, naturally, but he loves me and accepted me without hesitation."

True nodded, thinking of how Sam had reacted

to her ability. He didn't act surprised at all and he didn't act differently toward her. "Sam figured me out. I'm guessing since he knew you and Jo so well, he instantly assumed I had my own gift. He accepted me, and I know that's something that Steven would never have done."

Shyfawn squeezed her hand. "Sam is a good man, True. Give him a chance. You have until spring to decide if you belong here or in Charlotte."

True hugged her sister tightly and couldn't keep from crying. She knew Shyfawn was right. She needed time to think and when spring came, she would know her answer.

***

Sam stood on the porch of Matthew's house and took a deep breath of courage. He could do this. Last night he had come to a decision and he wasn't going to chicken out now. There was too much at stake and he had too much to lose if he backed down now. Raising a slightly unsteady hand, Sam knocked loudly and waited. He usually just walked in, but this was an official visit.

Matthew opened the door. "Sam, this is a pleasant surprise. Come in."

"Thank you," he said as he stomped snow from his boots before entering.

"What brings you here?"

"I, my friend, came courting," Sam informed him.

"I appreciate it, Sam, but I'm married."

Sam shot him a look of irritation. "You ass."

Matthew laughed and slapped him on the back. "She's in the parlor."

Sam grumbled at him as he removed his winter clothes before walking through the house. He took a deep breath and entered the parlor. True sat on the couch with Shyfawn. A quilt spread over their laps as they sewed. They stopped talking when he came in.

"Sam." True wasn't sure if she said his name out loud or not. Her eyes drank in the sight of him and she felt her heart pound in her chest.

"Morning ladies," he said hoping the butterflies in his stomach didn't slap him to the ground.

"Sam, please come in," Shyfawn said and stood. "I'll get you something to drink."

"Shyfawn, I can do that," True said as she gathered the quilt and set it aside.

"Nonsense, I need to get up and move around." She rubbed her stomach. "I'll be right back.

True managed to find her voice as she looked at Sam. "What brings you out today?"

"Well I came to…uh…" Sam started, she looked at him expectantly with those beautiful eyes. "Um…how are you feeling?" he stammered.

She blinked at him. "Fine."

"Good." He took a calming breath. Christ, he felt like a fool. "Are you sleeping better?" He noticed she still had the dark circles under her eyes, so he knew she wasn't.

She frowned. "Sam, what is this about?"

He ran his hand through his hair. "I…uh." Jesus, it wasn't like he hadn't courted a woman before. Why was he such a mess? "I'm just worried you might not be well."

What the hell was wrong with him?

Her brow furrowed. "What do you mean?"

"True I…" He what? "Damn it."

True stood to face him. "Sam, what is wrong with you?"

"I came to court you," he blurted.

True's eyes widened in shock as she looked at him. "You came to court me?"

"Yes, damn it." He jabbed a hand through his hair again. "I know you're engaged, and I know you plan on leaving in the spring, but I came anyway." He stepped up to her.

"Sam, I—"

"I can't let you leave without a fight," he told her softly. "You've stirred something inside me I thought was long dead. In the end the decision will be yours and if I only have until spring with you, I'll accept that."

True felt the tears fill her eyes as feelings and emotions slammed into her. This was what she wanted, to be near Sam and now that it was within reach she was scared. She loved Sam. But could she live in Rimrock and leave everything she knew?

Sam felt his gut twist and his heart stop at the turmoil in her dark eyes. "I didn't mean to upset you." He had to swallow hard as he cupped her cheek. "I can't watch you leave without trying my damnedest to keep you here."

True covered his hand with hers. "Sam, I…" She took a breath to calm her heart, but it did little good. "I would like for you to come courting."

Sam about went to his knees and he couldn't speak so he kissed her. He kissed her because he had to. She made no protest as she wound her arms around his neck. Sam kissed her long and deep, holding her tightly to him. Jesus, it felt good to have her in his arms again and by damn he was never going to let her go.

"Slow down there, Romeo..." Shyfawn laughed and the two broke apart. "Do I need Matt to chaperone you two?"

Sam felt himself blush and gave her a grin. "No. Sorry, I got carried away."

"I'll just leave the tray of tea and cake for you." She set the tray on the small table near the drinks cabinet.

"I'll leave you to talk." She pointed at Sam. "You behave."

"Yes, ma'am," he said quickly.

True looked at him and smiled brightly. When Shyfawn left the room, Sam pulled True to him and kissed her for a long time. His heart was filled with happiness and hope there was a future for them.

Sam pulled back and took her by the hand, then led her to the sofa to sit with her.

"Since it's winter, I couldn't bring flowers." Sam dug into his pocket. "I brought this." He closed his hand around the object. "Don't laugh."

True smiled. "I'm almost scared to know." She held out her hand and he dropped it into her palm. She stared at it. "You brought me a rock."

"You don't have to say it like that," he said with humor. "It's not just any rock." He turned it over.

True gasped to see shiny lavender crystals. She held it up and examined it. "It's beautiful. Where did you find this?"

"There's a system of caves in the hills near Matt's ranch," he told her. "We've explored them for years and have found some amazing rock formations."

"I'd like to see it sometime," she said as she looked the beautiful gem over.

"I'll be sure to take you," he told her hopefully.

She smiled at him. "Thank you for this."

They spent several hours in the parlor talking and he couldn't keep from holding her hand. He missed touching her and being near her. Sam hoped she would stay, when spring came, and he intended to convince her she belonged in Rimrock with him.

Chapter Eighteen

True sat at the large dining table and looked around at her family and new friends as they sat together for the Christmas meal. The hired hands were all there and Jo and Jack had come for the day as well. True was glad to have both of her sisters with her on this special day.

Her eyes settled on Sam as he sat across the table from her with Marie at his side. Did she love him? She was pretty sure she did. Did he love her? She thought back to the last few days in the cabin with him and how tender he had been with her as they made love. She remembered his anger at bringing her back to her sisters to get on with her life, then go back to Charlotte and to Steven.

Sam looked up and caught her watching him. She blushed, and he gave her a soft smile. His dark eyes held hers and she had no doubt he was remembering their time in the cabin as well. Travis coughed and reached for his drink; accidentally bumping Sam hard on the shoulder. Sam glared at him and Travis chuckled as he gave True a knowing wink. Her cheeks flamed and her eyes quickly lowered to her empty plate.

True fidgeted a moment as she listened to the buzz of conversation around her. When she felt she could look up without blushing, she shot Travis a look of irritation. He grinned at her and Sam quickly elbowed him in the ribs.

"Get along," Marie ordered as she shook her finger at the two men, causing everyone at the table to laugh.

Shyfawn stood and rubbed a hand over her belly. "You men go to the parlor and have a drink. We'll take care of this." She gestured to the table.

The men stood and made their way to the parlor, while True, Shyfawn, Jo, and Marie cleared the table. They finished up quickly and joined the men, who were talking and laughing. True felt a warm contentment wash over her as she sat on the sofa beside Sam. This gathering of friends was far different than the gatherings she had attended in Charlotte. Here there was no stuffy putting on airs or fake smiles, this group was relaxed and truly cared for one another.

Matthew left the room to return shortly with a basket of gifts. "Time for the good stuff," he teased.

All stood to collect the gifts they had brought from the basket. True pulled out her bundle wrapped in checked cloth before she sat beside Sam again. She watched the small gift exchange take place in the room and smiled happily.

"Marie," True called and Marie left Travis's side, as he examined a new knife, to walk to True. "I have something for you."

Marie smiled and took the bundle as True handed it to her. "For me?"

"Yes, I hope you like it."

Marie pulled off the ribbon and opened the cloth. A puzzled look crossed her face as she took out the deep burgundy material. She held it up to reveal a dress and her face lit up as she squealed with delight. She stood back and held the dress to her chin and let it drape over her.

"I think she likes it," Sam laughed and absently reached behind True to place an arm around her, his hand resting on her waist.

"It's beautiful." Marie threw herself at True and hugged her tightly. She pulled back and looked at Sam. "Can I put it on, Daddy?"

He nodded. "Yes, you can."

"Shyfawn." Marie hurried to her and grabbed her hand. "Come help me."

She laughed. "I will." She put a hand on her belly and got to her feet with Matthew's help. The two disappeared through the door.

Jo smiled at True. "So that's the dress you've been working on all this time."

True nodded. "Yes, she loved the color and the dress needed far too much mending for me to wear again, so I used the material to make a dress for her."

"She's going to love it," Sam assured her. "She talks a lot about having a pretty dress like yours someday."

She smiled at him. "I remembered how much she liked that dress before it was ruined by the bear."

They heard Marie running through the house long before they saw her. She ran into the middle of the room and twirled. The full skirt billowed around her. Her dark eyes shone brightly and her black hair was loose, swinging around her as she twirled. She stopped when she was dizzy and faced Sam. The dark burgundy dress looked beautiful on her.

"I'm pretty," she said with joy.

Sam smiled lovingly at her. "You're always pretty. Right now, you're downright beautiful."

She ran to hug him and he held her tightly. He loved her so much, she was beautiful and happy, and he wanted to remember this moment forever. He eased his hold and she moved to True to hug her.

True smoothed a hand over the girl's hair. "I'm glad you like it."

She looked at True and smiled brightly. "I do. Thank you."

Shyfawn came in and leaned on the doorframe, hand on her belly. "You look very lovely."

"That she does," Travis said and got to his feet. "Such a lovely lady I can't resist." He gave her a sweeping bow. "May I have this dance?"

She gave him a puzzled look.

"John, music," Travis barked.

John picked up his fiddle and began playing a lively tune. Heck pulled out his harmonica and joined in as Wally and Charlie clapped in time to the beat. Marie cried out in delight and threw herself at Travis. He stooped over and took her hands in his and danced her around the room. Matthew stood and took Shyfawn's hand. She tried to decline as she patted her belly, but in the end Matthew won. Jack moved to Jo and took her in his arms to dance as well.

True laughed as she watched them and knew she loved this place. Shyfawn was so lucky to have these people in her life. Jo was happy for the first time in her life and had finally found peace. True wanted all that her sisters had.

"True," Sam said softly.

His voice startled her and she looked at him. "Yes?"

"I have something for you." He reached into his shirt pocket.

She watched as he drew out a black ribbon. She held out her hand and he dropped it into her palm. Attached to the ribbon was a rounded white object. She studied it. It was polished and shone brightly.

"Is this a tooth?" she asked and looked up at him.

He chuckled. "Don't look at me like that. It's probably not considered an appropriate gift where you come from."

She gave him a smile. "I would say not."

"It's an elk ivory," he told her. "The Indians use the ivory teeth to decorate their clothes and make jewelry."

She rubbed her thumb over the smooth surface. "Thank you."

He took it from her and tied the ribbon around her neck. The ivory settled into the hollow of her throat. "I wanted you to have it." He lightly touched the ivory. "This way you'll always remember the mountains." He let his fingers trail gently across her skin before he lowered his hand.

True felt the tears flood her eyes. "I could never forget the mountains."

"Don't hog her all night." Travis was suddenly there and wearing a very wide grin.

Before she knew it, Travis was whirling her around the room. She was grateful for the distraction. Her emotions were in a jumble. She saw Sam lift Marie and dance with her. True smiled at Travis and savored the complete joy of the day.

"Sam!" Shyfawn cried.

All stilled and turned to see Shyfawn leaning heavily against Matthew as a puddle pooled around her feet. True felt her heart hammer in her chest. The baby was coming! She wasn't ready for that yet. True realized with total clarity that it wasn't up to her when her sister gave birth.

Taking a deep breath, she let it out slowly to calm herself, she could do this.

Chapter Nineteen

True held the baby in her arms, his tiny body moved and wiggled as he tried out his muscles. Jo poured clean water into a pan and he let out an angry squall when True placed him in the pan of warm water to clean him. Jo was ready with a cloth to dry him and a warm, tiny blanket to wrap him in. True held him close and smiled through her tears.

"He's perfect," she told her sister as she moved to the bed and placed the baby in Shyfawn's arms.

Shyfawn held the baby close and kissed his head. "He's beautiful."

"Yes, he is," Jo agreed as she brushed back her sister's sweat-soaked hair.

The door opened and Matthew came into the room, followed by Sam. Matthew quickly moved to the bed and sat down beside Shyfawn. His eyes were fixed on the small bundle in her arms. Shyfawn turned her face up and smiled at him. Tears shown in his eyes as he leaned down and kissed her softly.

True felt her eyes burn and she watched them as they inspected their son. She was so happy for her sister. Shyfawn was so in love and now had a family. True couldn't keep her eyes from moving to Sam, he was watching her intently. His image blurred and she left the room. She needed air.

True descended the stairs quickly and almost bumped into Jack. "Sorry," she mumbled.

He carried a sleeping Marie in his arms. "It's all right," he whispered.

A smile played on True's mouth as she looked at the sleeping girl. "She's going to be upset that she missed seeing the baby tonight."

Jack nodded in agreement and smiled. "I'm glad you will be the one that deals with her wrath in the morning."

She let out a groan. "Thanks."

"I'll put her to bed and I'm calling it a night," he told her as he stepped aside for her. "Go out for some fresh air, you look pale."

True wasn't going to argue, but before she could escape, the ranch hands filed out of the parlor. They were laughing and stopped still to look at her, their faces a little more serious. She couldn't help but smile, it was clear they had been freely drinking the whiskey. John and Wally quickly wiped what appeared to be tears of happiness from their eyes.

"Is Shyfawn all right?" Travis asked with worry.

She gave him a reassuring smile. "Yes, she's fine. It's late and you boys should head to bed."

Before they could reply, True turned and fled for the back door. She needed air and time alone. She wasn't entirely sure why her emotions were in such a jumble. Shyfawn's labor had been relatively easy and both she and the baby were doing well.

True reached for her coat that hung on the peg by the back door and swung it on as she pushed open the door and stepped out. Closing the door quietly behind her, she drew in a deep breath of cold winter air. She let it out slowly and moved to the porch railing to look out over the dark pasture. The chill of the air helped calm her nerves.

She heard the door open and turned to see Sam come outside. He tugged his coat closed and pulled the door shut behind him. She drank in the sight of him, her heart fluttered, and her eyes suddenly burned with tears.

"Are you sick?" Sam asked, worry in his voice.

"No," she said and turned to look out over the pasture again. "I just needed air."

"You did good up there," he told her as he moved to stand behind her.

True suddenly couldn't speak and had to swallow hard against the sudden emotion that choked her. She took a step back to lean her body against Sam's. He wrapped his arms around her and pulled her close as she knew he would. She needed his strength and needed him to comfort her. He didn't ask any questions and for that she was grateful, he only held her close and she savored it. It had been too long since she had felt his arms around her like this.

Sam lowered his cheek to rest against her hair as he tightened his arms around her and let out a contented sigh. She felt pretty darn content herself. She let out a heaving sigh of her own and leaned her head back against his shoulder as she closed her eyes.

"Are you all right?" he asked softly.

True had to swallow hard. "I'm not sure."

"Tell me what you're thinking." His voice was

a gentle whisper against her hair.

She didn't answer, her thoughts were a mess and she had no idea how to articulate them in a way he, or she, could understand.

"Remember the night we watched the elk?" she asked, as she touched the ivory necklace at her throat.

"It's a night I'll always remember," he assured her as his mouth lowered to her neck. "That's the night I kissed you for the first time."

A shiver went through her that had nothing to do with the cold as his mouth brushed her skin.

"I-I miss our time together." She swallowed hard as emotion filled her voice.

"So do I," he whispered and kissed her neck. "You don't have to go back to Charlotte."

She heard the hope in his voice and squeezed her eyes tightly shut against the burning tears.

"Sam, it's my home. It's the only life I know, I belong there." Even as she said the words, she heard the doubt in her voice.

His body tensed and he pulled in a deep breath as he lifted his head to rest his cheek against her hair. "Have you ever thought maybe you belong here? That you could have a life and a home here?"

"Charlotte is where Aunt Molly and my friends are," she tried to reason, more to herself than Sam. "It's where I…" She couldn't finish the sentence. *Is Charlotte where I belong?*

"It's where you plan to get married," Sam muttered as he released her and took a step back.

She turned to face him. "No, Sam, I—"

"I understand," he said softly, though there was

an edge to his voice. "I know Steven can give you things I can't."

True reached up to fidget with a button on his coat as she tried not to cry. There was so much that Sam could give her that no man ever could. Sam accepted her with all her flaws and her visions. He made her feel things that she had never felt in her life and she knew she would only feel with him. Could she give up everything she knew to stay in Rimrock with Sam?

True looked up at Sam and blinked away her tears. It was too dark to make out his features, but she could feel the tension in his body. He placed two fingers under her chin and tilted her face up as he lowered his head. A soft whimper of both need and heartache escaped her when his lips met hers.

His hand left her chin to slide to the back of her neck to hold her close as he deepened the kiss. She eagerly opened her mouth to him as his tongue swept in to taste her. Her hands pushed open his coat to wrap her arms around him and hold his body to hers. He tunneled his fingers into her hair to cradle the back of her head as he kissed her.

The kiss quickly turned passionate, hungry, and urgent as their need for one another consumed them. She moaned into his mouth as she leaned into him and savored the feel of his strong body against hers. She had missed the feel of him, his taste, and this burning need her body had for his. This was something only Sam could make her feel.

When they could no longer breathe, he pulled back to rest his forehead against hers. "We should go in," he told her. "It's cold."

"Not yet," she almost begged, not wanting to be away from him yet.

"Come here," he told her as he stepped back and took her hand to lead her to the bench.

True didn't argue and eagerly went with him. He sat down and, without hesitation, she lifted her dress and straddled him. She felt his body tense with surprise but before he could object, she took his face in her hands and kissed him deeply. Any protest he might have made left him in a ragged groan as his arms went around her.

The desperate need raging inside her pushed away any thought and all she wanted to do was feel the release Sam could give her. She took his hand and pushed it under her dress and layers of material to her womanhood. A pleased sigh left her when his fingers began to work their magic on her and soon her pleasure built.

His mouth went to her neck as her hands worked at his belt and trousers until she held the hard length of him in her hands. A shudder went through him as he gently bit down on her neck. Yes, this is what she wanted. What she needed. She pushed his hand away and shifted over him.

"True," he groaned as he pulled his mouth from her neck. "We can't do this here," his protest was half-hearted, and he didn't try to stop her.

True looked at him in the darkness and guided his shaft to her opening. A pleased sigh escaped her and a curse left him as she slid down over him. She settled over him and savored the feel of him inside her. She had missed being with Sam like this.

His hands held her hips tightly. "Jesus, True."

The words left him in a rush of breath.

He urged her to begin to move and she gladly obliged him. Her hands cupped his jaw as she kissed him, moving her hips in a way she knew he liked. In the cabin he had taught her pleasure and she had eagerly learned how to please him. Within moments they were both breathing hard, their breaths steaming on the cold air around them as their movements became urgent.

True felt her core tighten as her pleasure built to a fever pitch. When she went over the edge, she buried her face in his coat and clenched her teeth against the cry of pleasure that wanted to rip free. The last thing she wanted was for the entire ranch to hear her. She would die of embarrassment and Jo would kill Sam.

Sam groaned through clenched teeth as his arms tightened around her and his body shuddered out his own release.

They held each other tightly for a long time as their bodies stopped trembling and their breathing returned to normal. Her body was satisfied, and an overwhelming feeling of contentment washed over her as she breathed in Sam's scent. So many nights she had dreamed of being with him again, but this was far better than her dreams.

Sam eased his hold on her and lifted a hand to her cheek to bring her head up to kiss her gently for a long time before he looked at her in the darkness.

"I've missed that," he told her softly.

She felt her face heat unexpectedly. "So have I," she confessed.

He kissed her again before he urged her to

stand. "We better go in before Jo comes looking for you."

True nodded and busied herself with pushing her skirts back down with suddenly shaking hands as he fixed his trousers. She had never intended to make love to Sam tonight and this was only going to further complicate things between them. Would he think this meant she would stay in Rimrock now?

She may want Sam, but her life was in Charlotte.

He took her hand and led her back into the house and helped her out of her coat to hang it up before removing his own. She busied herself with adding more wood to the kitchen stove to help keep the winter chill from the room and stood there to warm her cold body. She had been too focused on Sam to notice that she was chilled to the bone.

"Damn, it's cold out there," Sam grumbled as he moved to stand beside her as they faced the stove, holding their hands over it to warm their fingers. "But it was worth it." He leaned over to give her cheek a lingering kiss before he focused on warming his hands again.

True could only nod as she felt the tears burn her eyes. Damn her emotions. They had been so overwhelming lately and it was beginning to irritate her. She had never been this emotional until she had met Sam and her world turned upside down.

"True, are you all right," he asked softly.

"Yes," she lied and blinked rapidly. "I'm fine."

His hand reached over to take hers and he took a step away from the stove and urged her to face him. "No, you're not. You're trembling and trying very hard not to cry."

She looked at their joined hands and her vision blurred. "It's just been a long day. I-I'm tired."

He cupped her cheek and made her look at him. "What else?"

The lamplight from across the room flickered shadows over his face but she could easily see the worry in his dark eyes. How could she tell him when she didn't understand it herself? Her emotions, her mind, and her heart were all warring with each other and it was tearing her up inside.

He swallowed hard and his voice was hesitant. "Do you regret what happened tonight?"

Did she? No. She would never regret being with Sam. It complicated things, but she didn't regret it. She had missed him and had been lonely without him since he had brought her to her sisters. When he had come to court her, her heart had sung with happiness while her mind told her they would only end up getting hurt. She didn't belong in Rimrock and they both knew it. Tears spilled from her eyes at the thought of leaving him.

Sam pulled in a sharp breath as hurt filled his eyes, he released her and stepped back. "You do regret it."

Panic filled her; he had mistaken her silence as regret. "Sam, I—"

"I get it," he snapped and took another step back from her. "You wanted it just one more time before you left in the spring. Now you realize you were once again unfaithful to Steven and regret it."

She gaped at him as her heart squeezed

painfully in her chest. "No, that's not it."

"Then what the hell is it, True?" he demanded harshly. "I get so many mixed signals from you. Sometimes you act like you want to be with me and other times it feels like you're trying to push me away."

True pressed her lips together and fought not to sob as her tears ran freely. He was right. She liked being with him but knew it would be that much harder to leave in the spring. Yet, would she be able to leave?

Sam swore savagely as he turned from her and dragged a hand through his hair. "Was I just wasting my time?" he asked as he turned to face her, his dark eyes snapping with anger. "Was coming to court you a mistake?"

She fought to find her voice as she tried not to cry. "I like seeing you. I just... I don't know if..." Her words trailed off as emotion took her voice.

"You don't know if I'm good enough for you, is that it?" he demanded harshly. "I know I'm not some dandified son of a bitch with lots of money and I don't fit into your society, but—"

"Stop it!" she cried. "Do you think all I care about is money and society?"

"I don't know!" he snapped. "What the hell *do* you care about? Because I'm pretty damn sure it's not me."

True clenched her fists in anger. "Your place is here in Rimrock, this is where your life is. Mine is in Charlotte and you knew that. You told me you'd respect my decision."

"In the spring," he bit out as he closed the small

distance between them. "If you've already made your decision, you should have told me."

"I haven't made my decision!" She was afraid that statement might be a lie.

"Then figure it out!" Anger and hurt filled his eyes as he looked down at her. "Who the hell do you want, me or Steven? I told you I wasn't going to let you leave without a fight, but if you don't want me—"

"I never said that!" she sobbed.

"Then what the hell is—"

"Sam." Jo's voice filled the room; her tone held a warning.

True turned to see her sister standing in the doorway leading from the dining room. Her eyes were snapping with anger and thankfully she wasn't wearing a gun. Jack appeared behind her and placed a hand on her hip before he hooked his fingers in her belt. True had a feeling it was to hold Jo back in case she decided to hurt Sam for yelling at her.

"True, you should go to bed now," Jo said coolly.

True blinked away her tears before she looked at Sam and her heart twisted painfully in her chest. She had never meant to make him angry. Tonight had been going so perfectly, and she had messed everything up. She pulled her eyes from his and brushed past him to go to the door. Jo kept her glare on Sam as she stepped aside for True to pass.

Somehow, she managed to get her shaking legs to walk to her bedroom. In the faint glow of a candle on the bed stand she saw Marie curled up in the bed, Gray Cat lying beside her, and a sob choked her. She loved Marie so dearly and the thought of leaving her in the spring tore out True's heart. She would leave and never see Marie or Sam again.

"True?" Jo's voice was soft as she entered the room. "Do I need to kill him?"

She turned to her sister and wasn't sure if she should laugh or cry. "No," she managed to say.

Jo's eyes softened and she stepped forward to hug True. "Everything will be all right," she said gently.

True could only cry as her sister gave her a very rare show of tenderness. She desperately wanted to believe Jo, but she had a feeling that she had just ruined everything with Sam.

Chapter Twenty

Sam paced Matthew's house restlessly as he waited for the family to wake up and start their day. The sun was barely up and he still hadn't slept, his mind had gone over everything that had happened between True and him the night before. Where had everything gone wrong? The night had been so full of happiness and celebration, before it had turned into anger and misery.

"Damn it," he growled as he dragged a hand over his tired face.

True had made love to him and it had been so wonderful. He had missed the intimacy they had shared the last few days in the cabin before they both had to face the facts of reality. He had been a fool for thinking he could court her and keep her in Rimrock.

Sam thought of the harsh words he had said to her and his stomach knotted painfully. He had been so angry and hurt they had just spilled out. He had voiced his fears, but it had come out all wrong and now he would more than likely lose her forever. Jack had stayed in the kitchen with him for a long time talking over the situation between Sam and True. His friend had urged him not to give up on True. No doubt Jo had told True to tell him to go to hell.

An excited shriek from upstairs made him smile. Marie was awake and had received the news about Shyfawn's baby. Her thundering feet echoed above as she ran for Shyfawn's bedroom and the wailing of baby Tim could soon be heard. Sam laughed softly and made his way up the stairs to Shyfawn's room. He saw Marie sitting on the bed with Shyfawn, examining the fussing baby.

"How are you feeling?" Sam asked Shyfawn as he walked up to the bed.

She smiled at him. "I've never been better."

Matthew groaned tiredly and yawned as he stood by the bed looking at Shyfawn and Tim.

Sam laughed. "Welcome to months of no sleep my friend."

Matthew smiled. "He's worth it."

Shyfawn held the little boy in her arms and looked lovingly at him. "Yes, he is."

Marie wrinkled her nose as she looked at the baby. "It's so small."

"You were that small once," Sam told her as he squatted down by the bed.

Marie drew back and frowned. She studied the baby for a moment then held her hands before her and examined her fingers. "No, I wasn't."

Sam laughed softly. "Yes, you were, and Tim will grow just like you have."

Marie gave Sam a serious look. "Will I be a sister or an aunt?"

Sam smiled at her. "Neither actually. We're not related to them, we're just good friends."

Marie looked disappointed. "Oh."

"How about we call you a cousin?" Shyfawn

suggested and cast a look at Sam. "I think that is an accurate guess."

Marie thought about it and nodded. "That'll do. Does he have all his toes?" Marie asked and tugged at the blanket the baby was wrapped in.

"Yes, he does," Shyfawn assured her as she pulled the blanket back to show her Tim's feet.

"Marie, when you're done, please get dressed," Sam said, and she waved her hand in acknowledgement as she continued to inspect Tim.

Sam laughed and left the room, passing Jack and Jo's closed bedroom door before he came to True's. It was open and his heart lurched at the idea of seeing her this morning, but when he looked into the bedroom, he found it empty. His nose caught the smell of coffee and he knew she was already getting breakfast ready.

Taking a deep breath of courage, Sam went down the stairs and entered the kitchen to see her placing more wood into the stove. He stood in the doorway and lifted an arm to lean against the doorframe as he watched her. He sent up a silent prayer that she would speak to him today and forgive him for being an ass. Whatever time he had left with her he didn't want to spend it with her being angry with him. If she even wanted to spend time with him after last night.

"True," he said softly.

She yelped and whirled to face him, her hand over her heart. "You startled me."

Her eyes were red and puffy and looked as if she hadn't slept at all last night. He had thoroughly upset her and it gave him a small hope that she might care about him. He wasn't about to let that small amount of caring get away, so he would beg for forgiveness and hope she didn't laugh at him or kick him in the kneecap.

He pushed away from the door and walked to stand before her. "True, I'm sorry for what I said and how I acted last night."

She swallowed hard and looked down at the buttons of his shirt. "You were angry with me and I understand. I-I know I frustrate you and I don't mean to."

"I know," he said gently and reached up to stroke a hand over her hair. "You have a big decision to make and me pushing you doesn't help. I'll back off and give you space and time. Spring is a few months away and I should let you decide without trying to influence you."

She nodded as she reached up to fidget with a button on his shirt.

"I don't regret it," she whispered softly.

His brows drew together. "What?"

She looked up at him and her eyes were shining with unshed tears. "I don't regret what we did last night."

Relief left him in a sharp exhale. "I'm glad to hear that." He cupped her cheek and his thumb caressed her soft skin. "I promise it won't happen again. I don't want to use that as a way to convince you to stay."

She nodded in understanding, but he saw the hurt in her eyes. "It complicates things."

"Yeah," he said and lowered his hand before he stepped back. "I won't push you for a decision.

We'll know in the spring."

She looked as if she wanted to say something but the sound of feet coming down the stairs made her turn and focus on getting mugs down for coffee. Sam turned to see Jo enter the kitchen and her unusual eyes instantly went hostile. He knew Jo well and he knew not to make her angry, the lump on his nose was proof of that. She had hit him and knocked him flat on his ass. When the black spots cleared from behind his eyes, he had fully intended to hit her back. He took a swing at her, but she was fast and he had been very drunk. He hadn't fared well in that fight.

Jo continued to glare at him as she helped True prepare breakfast. Sam left the room and went into the parlor as his mind drifted back to the day Jo had hit him. He had just lost Piper and had lost himself in the bottom of a whiskey bottle for a while. Jo had hit him and informed him that Marie needed her father and not a drunken ass. He had left Marie with a wet nurse, buried his wife, and had been drunk for days after that.

When he had sobered up, he focused on raising Marie. When she was old enough, he had taken her to Boston with him and attended medical school. He had helped Doc Black for years, but he knew if he was going to be any good at helping people, he needed the proper education. He had done a lot of good for the people in Rimrock and he was needed here. He knew he could never leave the small town, too many people depended on him.

Sam slouched down in the chair and glared at the ceiling as his mind once again overthought the situation with True. She had been right though. His life was here in Rimrock and hers was in Charlotte. He wasn't going to give up on her yet, though. She might think her life was in Charlotte but he knew she belonged here, with him.

***

True sighed happily as she walked the house with the baby as he fussed. It had been three months since Tim had been born and True was loving her role as Aunt and sister's helper. And Tim had grown so much in the short amount of time he had been on earth.

"You're spoiling him," Matthew teased as he came into the house.

She smiled at Matthew. "That's my job."

He stood at the door, not wanting to track mud through the house. The weather was getting warmer and she was grateful for that. The past three months had been filled with cold temperatures and endless blizzards. Now the snow was beginning to melt, but Matthew told her that the spring blizzards could be bad. He pulled off his gloves and she didn't have to ask to know he wanted to hold his son.

"Maybe you can get him to settle," she told him and transferred the baby to Matthew's big hands.

He smiled. "I'm his pa, I can do anything." Matthew tucked Tim against him, and the little guy instantly went from fussing to cooing happily.

"Show off," True teased.

She stood there and watched Matthew hold his son with such love. She had no doubt Sam had held Marie with such gentleness. It was something she wished she could have seen. Sam loved Marie dearly and True knew he would always be a great, and very protective, father to her.

Unexpected tears burned her eyes as she thought of Sam and Marie, she hadn't seen much of them the last few months and she missed them. The weather had kept everyone from traveling to visit and she was hoping this break in the weather would give Sam incentive to see her. The few times he had come, things between them had changed and it wasn't a change she liked. He had told her he would give her space and wouldn't push her, but she missed spending time with him. She missed his voice and the way he touched her in small ways when he was near. But she knew with the warmer weather, she would see him again soon.

Her mind drifted over the past few months and she couldn't help the feeling of contentment that went through her. Her life had changed so much, and she was growing to love it at Matthew's ranch. She could see why Shyfawn chose to stay here and not go back to Charlotte. Now she was married with a beautiful baby.

Something in True stilled and she felt herself go numb for a moment. Months. Her hand trembled as it went to her stomach. She tried to think of her last monthly. It happened before Christmas, but she couldn't remember having one after that. Nothing after she had made love to Sam Christmas night.

"True?" Matthew's voice held worry. "You've gone white. Are you all right?"

She swallowed hard and tried to remember how to breathe. "I'm fine," she said quietly, but had a feeling Matthew knew she was lying.

***

True's day passed in a cloud of fear and confusion. What would she do now? What choice did she have? Maybe her suspicions were wrong.

At dinner she tried to stay present and visit with everyone but her mind kept drifting. Travis kept looking at her and she swore he knew exactly what she was thinking. She had the sudden urge to get up and run to her room but managed to control herself.

She was relieved when dinner was over and the ranch hands filed out to the bunkhouse. Matthew insisted on helping Shyfawn clean up and wash the dishes, so True took a drowsy Tim and went into the parlor to sit in the rocker with him. It took only a few moments of rocking for him to fall fast asleep.

Gray Cat meowed and she looked to see him sitting on the floor before her, scowling at the baby in her arms. She smiled at the cat. "Don't worry. I'll love on you later."

With his tail twitching, he sat, waiting impatiently for someone to come take the baby so he could jump in True's lap.

"You're a natural," Shyfawn said from the doorway.

True lifted her eyes to look at her sister and felt the tears flood her eyes. "That's a good thing."

"I'm so glad you're here to help me," she told True gratefully. "I don't know what I would do without you."

She gave Shyfawn a small humorless smile. "I need the practice."

"Don't worry, honey, you'll have plenty of

time to practice before you start your own family," she said with a smile. "And I can come help you when the time comes."

True blinked and tears spilled from her eyes. "It may be sooner than you think."

Shyfawn's brow furrowed. "What do you..." Her voice trailed off and her eyes widened with realization.

Chapter Twenty-One

"You're what!" Jo's angry voice echoed through the house.

"I'm pregnant, Jo." True sat on the sofa in the parlor and tried not to cry. She had never seen Jo so mad in all her life.

"God damn it, I'll kill the son of a bitch for this." Jo clenched her fists at her sides.

"No, please—"

"What did he do? Did he rape you?" Jo's body shook with anger.

"No, I gave myself to him." Tears streamed down True's cheeks. "Jo, I love him."

"You love him!" Jo threw her arms into the air. "Well that just fixes everything now, doesn't it?"

"Jo, calm down." Shyfawn sat next to True and put an arm around her shoulders. "Can't you see she needs your support?"

"Support!" Jo roared. "She's going to get all the support she needs from me, since that slimy bastard can't come to grips with what's happened."

True choked back a sob, stood up and went to the window, her back to everyone in the room. She really didn't want to talk about this in front of Matthew and Jack as well, but everyone was going to find out eventually anyway.

Jo was quiet for a moment. "He doesn't know,

does he?" Her voice was cold and hard.

True shook her head. "No." She turned to face her sister. "I haven't had a chance to tell him. Please, don't tell him, and for God's sake don't try to kill him."

Jo looked into her sister's eyes. "I promise nothing." She took a ragged breath to calm herself. "You love him?"

"Yes, more than anything," True said as she cried.

Jo stared at the floor. "Does he love you?" She slowly looked into True's eyes. Seeing the pain there she wished she hadn't asked.

"I think so." True was openly sobbing now. "He's never actually said it."

"Did you tell him you loved him?"

"No." True dropped to her knees and buried her face in her hands. "I couldn't tell him. I was so unsure where I belong, Charlotte or Rimrock."

Jo knelt next to True, facing her. "Look at me," she demanded.

True slowly looked up. "Jo, I'm sorry. I know I've disappointed you, but I couldn't help myself. I love him so much."

"No, True, you haven't disappointed me. I know what it's like to fall in love." She looked up at Jack, then back to True. "And have too much damn pride to admit it. If you love him, don't leave him. You'll regret it the rest of your life if you do."

"I'm scared, Jo."

"There's nothing to be afraid of," she said softly. "You belong here, in Rimrock with us. With Sam."

"How can you be sure?" she asked with a sniff.

"Because I'm usually right about everything," she said casually. "But you're going to have to tell Sam about the baby soon. You won't be able to hide it much longer."

True swallowed hard and nodded. "I know."

"Now pull yourself together," Jo told her. "All this emotion can't be good for the baby."

Fresh tears streamed down True's cheeks. "Jo, I love you so much." She threw her arms around Jo and hugged her.

"I love you, too." Jo held True tightly and let her cry.

Shyfawn walked over to them and knelt with them to hug both of her sisters to her. Jack and Matthew left the room, leaving the three sisters alone.

***

Sam sat at his kitchen table thumbing through a medical book and read the same page for the fifth time. He couldn't focus on the book because his mind was filled with thoughts of True and their time at the cabin. Those had been the happiest times in his life. The three of them being together in the cabin felt like the family he had been denied. He had no doubt that Marie would want True as her mother and Sam knew he wanted her for his wife.

A loud knock on his door brought him back to reality. He swore softly and got to his feet, preferring his daydreams about True to reality. He went to the door and opened it to see Jo standing outside. Her eyes were hard as they looked at him and she looked more serious than usual. He thought she looked worried and angry as well.

"Jo, what are you doing here?" Sam stepped outside to face her. "Is Shyfawn all right?"

Without a word Jo's fist came out and struck him in the face. Sam's head snapped back and his jaw hurt where her fist had connected. Blinking away the black spots that began to gather behind his eyes, he stared at her as he rubbed his jaw, tasting blood from his cut lip.

"What the hell was that for?" he demanded, not believing that his friend had punched him.

"I ain't supposed to tell you," she said angrily before she turned on her heel and walked back to her horse. She swung up and rode off without a backward glance.

What on earth had he done to deserve that? Sam stood there for a long time as she rode through town toward the direction of her ranch. Surely, she hadn't rode all the way into town just to punch him in the face. Yet, she rode out alone and with no supplies. He wasn't sure why she was angry with him, but he was damn sure he wouldn't make her angry again.

Sam closed the door and stepped away from it as he touched his lip and drew his fingers away to see blood. Jo sure knew how to throw a punch. But then, he knew that already.

"Daddy, I need help!" Marie stated as she hurried into the room, and then stopped in her tracks, staring at him. "What happened to your face?"

"I bit my lip."

She shrugged and held up her ragdoll for him to

see. "Dolly broke her leg."

Sam saw the ragdoll's leg had been ripped and the stuffing was sticking out.

"Yes, she did," he said with a small smile. "As soon as I stop bleeding, we'll get her fixed up."

***

True sat in the parlor with her sisters and was enjoying the afternoon. Her sickness had eased and she was grateful, some days it was worse than others. Sam had come to see her a few days ago and she felt too sick to see him. Truth be told, she couldn't face him yet. She knew telling him about the baby had to be done, he was going to notice soon. She was able to hide her small tummy with her winter coat and a shawl when she was in the house.

A knock at the front door startled her from her thoughts. Was it Sam? She glanced at Jo, who shrugged, and Shyfawn smiled.

"Could be," Jo muttered.

"Be nice to him," Shyfawn warned.

"Just because you told me to," Jo grumbled.

"Go let him in," Shyfawn told True.

Jumping from the chair she ran to the door and flung it open. Her smile faded when she saw the man on the other side of the door. Her spirits sank and her heart hammered.

"Steven, what are you doing here?"

"Well, that's a fine how do you do for your fiancé," he said.

"Fiancé? Didn't you get my letter?" she asked, still in shock that he stood before her.

He took a deep breath and let it out slowly. "I

did. I feel that the ordeal you suffered with the bandits upset you a great deal and I'm sure you weren't thinking clearly when you wrote the letter. It's almost time for you to return to Charlotte and I thought I would travel back home with you."

She blinked at him in disbelief. "Steven, my thinking is just fine."

He stood there for a moment as she stared at him. "Aren't you going to invite me in?"

She didn't want to, but it was better than talking in the cold doorway. "Yes," she muttered and stepped aside for him to enter before she closed the door behind him.

Steven pulled her into his arms and hugged her quickly. "I was so worried about you," he said and stepped back, putting proper distance between them.

True didn't have time to react to the hug. It was quick and her only thought was he wasn't Sam. Sam was big, solid, and strong. Steven was smaller and so very different. Sam's touches were tender and lingering. Steven's were quick and impersonal, if he touched her at all. It amazed True how one touch could mean so much.

"Please, come into the parlor," she finally said and led him into the house.

Shyfawn stood as they entered, she gave True a perplexed look. "Good afternoon," she greeted.

"Shyfawn, this is Steven Edwards Jr," True managed to say.

"True's fiancé," he quickly added. "Mrs. Reeves," Steven said and crossed the room to her. "It's good to finally meet you," he said as he picked up her hand and lightly kissed her knuckles.

"Mr. Edwards." Shyfawn had gathered her composure at the shock of seeing him. "You've come along way, please, sit down."

"Thank you." He seated himself in a plush chair. Steven saw Jo by the liquor cabinet and looked down his nose at her. "Would you be so kind as to bring us some refreshments?" he ordered.

"I ain't so kind," she said coldly.

"True, the hired help around here is very rude," he snorted.

"Steven, she's not my hired help. That's my sister, Joanna McCord."

"Your *sister*?" Steven's brows knitted together as he took in the men's clothes Jo wore. "That is your sister?"

True sighed. "Steven, we need to talk."

"I should say so," he said. "You've never mentioned your sister dressed like that."

"There is a lot I've never mentioned."

His eyes drifted over Jo again. "Indeed."

"This may take a while." True perched on the edge of the chair across from him. "Steven, I do appreciate you coming all the way from Charlotte to see me, but there was no need. I'm doing very well here with my family." She shifted nervously. "I sent you that letter to explain everything. I told you that the engagement is off, I just can't marry you. I've been in Rimrock long enough to know I belong here, and I've decided I won't be returning to Charlotte. I'm planning on staying here in Rimrock with my family."

"And I understand how the trauma of thinking of being attacked by bandits again could make you feel you need to stay," he told her. "There is no need to worry about that now. Your sister has had her baby and I'll travel back to Charlotte with you and protect you."

Jo let out a snort that clearly stated she didn't believe Steven could protect True from anything.

"Steven, I'm not going back," she told him flatly. "I called off the engagement."

"Only because you were afraid to travel back home," he told her in a tone that one might use for a child. "You don't need to be afraid now and we can go on with our plans."

"Steven," she said firmly. "I called off the engagement."

Steven's blue eyes went hard. "Nobody has ever called off an engagement to an Edwards."

True sighed. What had she ever seen in this man? "Consider this a first then. I just don't love you."

"What does love have to do with anything?" he snapped. "You were the perfect candidate for bringing me sons with good bloodlines."

"She's a woman, not a horse, you son of a bitch!" Jo's angry voice filled the room.

"Jo," Shyfawn cautioned.

"Well, I never," Steven huffed as he looked at Jo.

"Maybe that's the problem. You probably need a good ass kicking."

"Please Jo, let me handle this." True watched her sister pace to the other side of the room and look out the window.

Taking a breath to calm her nerves and

irritation, True focused on Steven again. "Steven, about those bloodlines, my mother wasn't a duchess and I don't know who my father was."

Steven blinked at her. "What are you talking about, Molly said—"

"It was all a lie," True interrupted. "She made the story up. My mother was a whore and my father was just some man passing through." Before he could say anything, she continued. "After I escaped the bandits, I was stranded in the mountains with Sam and I fell in love with him. I knew that he was the one I wanted to be with. Not you."

Steven stared at her. "You are just the bastard child of some whore." He looked astounded and stood abruptly. "You lied to me! I had big plans for you. Well, I'm glad I found out now before it was too late."

"So am I." True stood to face him. "I can't believe that I was actually considering marrying an arrogant ass like you."

"How does your mountain man feel about you being a bastard?" Steven asked coldly, his eyes snapping with anger. "Did you lie beneath him like a whore?"

She glared at him. "And he was more pleasurable than you could ever be!"

"Why you uppity, no good, conniving little bitch," Steven raised his hand to hit her.

Before he could bring his hand down, Jo lunged at him. Steven lost his balance and fell to the ground. Jo went down with him, punching him hard in the face. She straddled his chest and delivered two more blows before True grabbed her and pulled her to her feet. Jo managed to kick him in the ribs before True pulled her away.

"I think he's learned his lesson, Jo," True said frantically as she tried to keep a hold of her sister.

"Excuse me," Shyfawn said as she stepped around True and walked from the parlor.

"Nobody treats my family like that and gets away with it!" Jo bellowed.

Steven scrambled to his feet and raced for the door. Jo broke True's grip and went after him. It was then True saw Shyfawn open the front door and step to the side to hold it open. As Steven reached the door Jo tackled him, they went through the open door and landed on the porch with a thud. Jo's fists flew at the man as he tried to protect himself, hollering all the while.

"Jo, please stop, I think he's had enough!" True tried to pull her off Steven but she refused to budge.

True heard a shout from the barn and looked up to see Jack running toward them. Matthew hot on his heels. Jack leapt up the steps, grabbed Jo by the waist and yanked her off Steven. Matthew moved to Shyfawn and pulled her into his arms as he quickly checked her for any damage.

"Let me go!" Jo roared. "I ain't done yet!"

"Damn you!" Steven almost sobbed as he held a hand to his bloody nose.

Jack held his struggling wife in his arms. "Can't I leave you for two seconds without you trying to kill someone?"

"He deserved it and he still does!" she said trying to kick at the man on the floor of the porch.

"You better get out of here before I turn her

loose," Jack warned.

With one last glare at True, Steven scrambled to his feet and ran for his horse. Leaping up into the saddle he rode away at a dead gallop toward town.

"Get back here, you coward!" Jo yelled, trying to break free of Jack's iron grip.

"Jo, I think he has had enough, you beat him to a pulp," Jack informed her trying not to laugh as he set the fuming woman on her feet, his arms around her waist.

"Damn it," Jo muttered.

"I think he learned his lesson," True said to her. "Jack, does she attack people often?"

Jack nodded. "But that's one of the reasons I love her." He kissed Jo on the side of the neck. She smiled and leaned back into his chest. Her anger forgotten.

Shyfawn laughed. "You'll get used to it."

True looked at her, thinking of how Shyfawn had calmly stepped around the brawl on the floor to open the door. She knew Jo would either throw the man out or chase him down. True smiled at her. "Apparently, *you've* gotten used to it."

Shyfawn nodded. "She's a handful."

Jo looked at True. "Are you okay?"

"Yes, I'm just fine." She placed a hand over her stomach. "For a second there I didn't think you would make it to him before he hit me."

"He was going to hit you?" Jack growled. Then nodded. "No wonder she tried to kill him."

Chapter Twenty-Two

Sam stood in the examining room rolling bandages when the door burst open and a thin man entered holding a bloody handkerchief to his nose. There was a long deep cut on his cheek and blood flowed from it, his face was swollen and badly bruised. He ignored Sam and sat down on the edge of the table.

"What can I do for you?" Sam asked as he placed the bandages on a shelf.

"You can fix me up, is what you can do," the man snapped.

Sam walked to the washstand and poured clean water into a pan. "What happened to you?"

"Do you know Jo McCord?"

Sam smiled slightly. "Yeah, I've had the pleasure of patching her up once or twice."

"Well, next time don't do such a good job. I thought that uppity bitch was going to kill me." Steven removed the bloody handkerchief from his nose.

"What did you do to make her mad?" Sam asked as he carried the pan to where the man sat and placed it on the table beside him.

"Nothing. I had merely gone there to visit Miss Tucker."

"True?" Sam tried to sound casual, but his heart

leapt. He began washing the man's face clean of blood.

"Yes, she is—was my fiancé."

Sam felt his stomach flip. This man was Steven! "Was?"

"She sent me a letter telling me that the wedding is off. I came to change her mind and convince her to go back with me. The little bitch refused. Ouch!" Steven whined.

"Sorry," Sam muttered as he roughly checked the man's cuts and broken nose. "Why won't she go back?"

"Seems she fell in love with some barbarian mountain man."

Sam's heart almost stopped. She fell in love, with him? True had refused to see him the last time he had gone to Shyfawn's to visit and he was sure her feelings for him had changed.

"And that's not the half of it," Steven continued. "I found out that she's not really the daughter of a duchess and that she is really some bastard's leavings with her whore of a mother."

Sam guessed that this was probably when Jo got mad. He fought back the urge to throw the man out.

"Maybe she just wants to follow in her mother's footsteps and be a whore to this mountain barbarian she claims to love."

Sam lost control then. He stepped back and punched Steven square in the face with such force that the man toppled over backwards off the table. Sam grabbed him by the shirt front and hauled him to his feet.

"I am that barbarian!" He ground the words out between clenched teeth.

Sam hit the man again. He fell back against the wall and slumped to the floor. Reaching down Sam grabbed the unconscious man by the back of his coat and dragged him to the front door, then opened the door and grabbing Steven by the belt too, pitched him out into the snowy street.

Sam gave one last look at the snooty man crumpled on the ground and went back into the building, closing the door with a bang. How could True have ever considered marrying such a man? Steven had said that True loved the mountain man – him. Could that be possible? He would just have to find out. Tomorrow he would have his mother watch Marie and he would ride to Matthew's ranch and find out how True felt.

Then, he intended to ask her to marry him.

"Daddy?" Marie's voice drifted down the stairs.

Sam swore under his breath, very softly, and headed for the stairs. No doubt Marie had clearly heard the commotion with Steven. "Yeah, honey?"

She walked down the stairs toward him. "What was all the noise?"

"Uh, the wind blew the door shut," he told her.

She looked perplexed but didn't ask any more about it. She nodded and turned to go back up the stairs and he stood there for a long time.

The decision to ask True to marry him wasn't his alone to make.

Ascending the stairs, Sam went to where Marie was playing. He sat on the bed and watched her for a long time as she happily played with the carved wooden animals Travis had made for her. He loved her so much and wanted her to be happy.

"Marie, come here please," Sam said. When she looked up he motioned her over.

She stood and skipped over to Sam, then climbed up onto his knee. "Whatcha need, Daddy?"

He circled his arms around her. "I need to ask you an important question."

She tipped her head and gave him a puzzled look. "What?"

"You like True very much, don't you?"

She nodded vigorously. "You bet I do."

"So do I." He brushed her hair from her face. "You know she was planning on leaving in the spring."

"Yes," she said, and sadness filled her eyes. "I don't want her to go."

"Neither do I, honey," he said feeling a pain in his heart. "I want her to stay. I'm going to ask her to stay."

Marie looked at him and smiled. "You are? I bet she'll stay if you ask her to."

"That's what I'm hoping. I want her to stay here with us," he told her. "Would that be all right with you?"

Her dark eyes sparkled. "Just like in the cabin? I would like that a lot, Daddy."

He nodded. "But she has to say yes."

"I hope she does," Marie said, her happy face fading. "I want her to stay here with us. I miss her."

Sam let out a long breath. "Me too, honey."

**

True took a deep breath of the fresh morning air as she and her sisters made the trip to town. Matthew and Jack had left for town a few hours before to take care of business. Shyfawn and True rode in the wagon and Jo rode alongside on her big black Appaloosa, his rump blanketed white with black spots. True held Tim in her arms as Shyfawn drove the buckboard. He occasionally fussed but appeared to be enjoying the bumpy ride over the rutted road. The trip would take several hours, but Shyfawn managed to keep up a steady stream of conversation. Jo only grunted or chuckled but didn't say much.

True had to shake her head as she watched her sister. Jo was always alert, waiting for any sign of trouble. No doubt the many years of traveling, and then searching for Shyfawn, had taught her to always be cautious. True often wondered about what Jo had gone through in her search for their sister. Jo had to leave the man she loved to do so. Thankfully Jack had loved her deeply enough to forgive her for leaving.

She sighed to herself. Both her sisters were so happy and loved their husbands intensely. She wanted that happiness for herself. She needed to tell Sam about the baby. She knew he wouldn't turn her away, he cared for her, that much she was sure of.

"Stop thinking about him." Jo's voice startled her.

"I can't." She shook her head, her throat tightening. "I have to talk to him. I have to let him know about the baby."

"You'd better tell him soon because you won't

be able to keep it a secret much longer." Jo moved her horse closer to the wagon.

"I know. I'm just scared." She looked up at Jo. "What would you do?"

She shrugged casually. "I'd string him up by the balls and—"

"Jo!" Shyfawn interrupted.

True fought back a chuckle. "What would you do if you were me?"

"Oh." Jo bit her lip and thought hard. "I'd still string him up by the balls."

"No, you wouldn't," True pointed out.

"You're right." Jo stared up at the sky. "But I'm not you. This is something you have to decide on your own. I had to leave someone I loved very much to find Shy," Jo admitted. "I was worried he wouldn't want me when I got back. I left him without saying goodbye because I knew he'd try to stop me. When I came back, Jack still loved me and we're together and I've never been so happy." She looked at True. "My advice to you is, if you love Sam don't let your fear push him away. You have a chance at happiness, grab onto it with both hands and hold tight." With that she kicked her horse into a trot ahead of the wagon.

"Does she do that often?" True asked Shyfawn as Jo rode away.

"Do what?"

"Open up like that and let her feelings show."

Shyfawn nodded. "Every now and then."

"I never thought I'd see the day that she'd get married. Did she know Jack a long time before they married?"

"Yes. You know Jo, she's restless and always on the move. She was traveling through the area and helped an Indian girl out of some trouble. She was shot doing it. Snow's father took her back to the village and they looked after her."

"I met Snow when I was in the mountains with Sam. She talked about Jo but called her Wanderer."

"Yes, that was Jo." Shyfawn nodded. "Snow is also Jack's half-sister. Jack was called Bear by the Cheyenne and lived with them from time to time. I don't know what all happened to her, but Jo ended up staying with the Cheyenne for quite some time. Jack had fallen in love with her when he first saw her. Jo pushed him away, not wanting anything to do with men after what our father did to her. I think she left the Cheyenne village because she was afraid of her feelings for Jack." She smiled at True. "They found each other again and love won."

"How long were they apart?"

"I don't know for sure. Jo helped Jack's sister, Raychel, out with some trouble she was having on her ranch and there she met Jack again. She was with him until she received your letter saying I was missing. Jo left him to come look for me. She thought that she had lost him forever, she was afraid he'd never forgive her for leaving without a word."

"She's been through a lot, hasn't she?" True asked, and then realized that she knew next to nothing about Jo.

"Yes, she has."

They rode in silence the rest of the way to town. True's thoughts drifted to Jo and all that she had sacrificed to keep True and Shyfawn safe. Her thoughts went to Sam, she had to tell him about the baby today. She couldn't hide the fact any longer and Sam would soon know the truth.

True glanced at Shyfawn. She envied her sister, she had a wonderful husband, a son, and a life that she loved. True silently wished that she could one day have those things. Her brow puckered as she thought. "Shyfawn?"

"Yes, True?"

"Jo's been married as long as you have, right?"

She nodded. "That's right."

"Why don't she and Jack have any children?" True felt uneasy at asking such a private question about her sister. "Does she ever say anything to you about her and Jack and how they, uh, get along?"

Shyfawn laughed. "Oh, I know they get along just fine."

"I just thought that they would have children by now."

Shyfawn shrugged. "It takes some folks longer to start families than others. And they're happy the way things are now." She chuckled. "Could you imagine Jo as a mother? Her kids would be total hellions."

True laughed at the image that came to mind. Knowing Jo, she would have them shooting pistols and throwing knives as soon as they were able to walk.

***

Upon reaching town they left the wagon at the livery.

"I better go see if that husband of mine has put us in debt yet," Jo told them.

"That's fine, I think we can manage," Shyfawn said as she held Tim close. "We'll find you later."

Jo fixed her unusual eyes on True. "Go talk to Sam."

True swallowed hard and nodded. "I will."

With that Jo rode off and True walked down the board walk with Shyfawn. They entered the mercantile and purchased supplies for the ranch. They took time looking through a catalog filled with so many things True took for granted. In Charlotte it was simple to order a new stove or bathtub, in Rimrock it took months to get such things.

"Why don't we find Jo and the men and eat at Milly's before we head back," Shyfawn suggested as she closed the catalog.

"I would like that very much." True patted her belly as they walked toward the door and left the mercantile. "I'm starving."

Shyfawn laughed. "I guess we'd better fix that."

True felt her smile fade. Eating at Milly's might have to wait. She was sure that the woman would notice her rounding tummy when she removed her coat and she didn't want Sam to hear the news from his mother first. She bit her lip. She would have to tell Sam and she might as well do it right now. Jo had told her to grab happiness and hang on, she would be happy with Sam. She only prayed that he truly wanted her.

"Shyfawn, I'd like to talk to Sam now," she said hesitantly, not sure why she was so nervous. Sam was an understanding man and being a doctor, the news of her being pregnant shouldn't surprise him.

Shyfawn gave her a small smile. "I'll walk over with you."

"Thank you," she said and blinked back tears. She could do this.

True looked down the street at the building Sam used and tried to stay calm. Both of their lives were about to change forever.

"There you are," Matthew said as he stepped out of the freight office with Jack and Jo.

"Where are you headed?" Matthew asked.

"I'm going to Sam's," True said hesitantly.

Matthew gave her an understanding nod, but before he could say anything shouts erupted down the street. True turned to see three men come out of the saloon in what appeared to be a vicious brawl. She could only stare, she had never seen men fight like this. Soon the men broke apart, reaching for pistols. Matthew instantly shielded Shyfawn and Tim with his body as he urged her back into the freight office. Jo reached for True as the pistols fired. She saw one man fall backwards into the dirt just before something slammed into her shoulder. She staggered back as Jo caught her to keep her from falling.

"True!" Shyfawn screamed from inside the freight office and Tim began crying.

True felt intense pain in her shoulder and warm blood ran under her bodice.

"Jo," she breathed.

"Goddamn it," Jo growled. "Get her to Sam!"

True's vision went hazy and she felt herself being lifted by strong arms. She managed to get her eyes to focus and saw Matthew. He swiftly carried her away and she didn't know where she was going as long as the pain stopped. True's head spun and blackness took her.

Chapter Twenty-Three

To Sam it seemed that the morning dragged on forever. After his mother came to take Marie for the day, everything had gone to hell. First, little Tommy Reed had fallen out of a tree and broken his arm. Then, his mother needed looking after because she had fainted and hit her head. At this rate he would never get a chance to ride out and see True. Finally, Tommy's mother came to and he sent her and her son home.

Sam heard gunshots and hollering coming from the center of town and headed for the door, flinging it open and squinting against the bright sun. People ran every which way, women and children ran into stores, men took cover and drew their guns. Two men fought in the middle of the street in front of the saloon, another man lay dead. Jack and Jo were running for the brawlers to stop them and Shyfawn was running toward Sam with Tim in her arms.

"Sam, she's been shot!" she called.

Sam looked past her to see Matthew carrying someone. Long blond hair almost dragged the ground as he carried the unconscious woman.

His heart plummeted. True.

"Get her inside quick." Sam stepped aside and let Matthew in. "What happened?" he asked as Matthew laid her on the table.

"She caught a stray bullet from one of those drunk bastards fighting in the street," Matthew explained taking Shyfawn in his arms.

"We had to bring her here." Shyfawn looked at Sam. "I can't heal her with that bullet still in her."

"Matt, get her coat off, but be careful." He handed Shyfawn a pair of scissors. "Cut her bodice away and cover her with a blanket."

Shyfawn carefully placed Tim on the floor in the corner of the room, he squalled in protest, then she did Sam's bidding as he washed his hands and got his tools ready for use. He quickly returned to where True lay and forced his heart to calm. Taking a deep breath, Sam began probing the wound for the bullet. He felt the metal click against the instrument he probed with, and gently he began pulling the bullet out. There was so much blood, he would have to hurry if Shyfawn was to heal it. Soon the bullet was free.

"She's all yours," he told Shyfawn.

Shyfawn pulled up her sleeves. "Give me some room."

Sam backed away as he watched Shyfawn use her gift of healing on her sister. Placing her hands over the wound Shyfawn closed her eyes and concentrated. After a long moment, she took her hands away and swayed slightly. Matthew put an arm around her to steady her and led her to a chair to sit down.

Examining True, Sam could see that the wound was completely healed. He washed the blood from her shoulder and pulled the blanket up under her chin.

Jo burst into the room followed by Jack. "How is she?"

"Fine," Shyfawn said weakly. "Sam got the bullet out and I fixed her up."

"Thank goodness." Jo leaned back against Jack.

Jack put his arms around her and pulled her back against his chest, holding her tightly. Then he sighed. "Matt, come with me and help me get those men to the jail. Jo and I knocked them out, but we better lock them up. When the sheriff sobers up, we'll explain what happened."

"Okay." Matthew cast a look at Shyfawn. "Are you going to be all right if I go?"

She smiled at him. "I'll be fine," she lied as she fought the urge to faint, a consequence of using her gift.

"I'll take care of her," Jo assured him.

Matthew placed a kiss on Shyfawn's lips and followed Jack from the room. Shyfawn rested in the chair and Jo cleaned the blood from her sister's hands as they waited for True to wake up.

"She'll be fine," Sam assured Jo. "But she'll need to stay here and rest for a day or two."

He didn't miss the look that passed between the two sisters. He ignored them, they probably feared for True's virtue, if they only knew. Taking out his stethoscope he pushed the blanket away enough to listen to her heart and lungs. He had to make doubly sure that everything was fine.

He listened to her heartbeat and it was strong. He put the stethoscope away and his eyes drifted over her as she lay pale beneath the blanket. He frowned when his gaze landed on her stomach and he moved to her side to slide his hands beneath the blanket. His hands moved over True's stomach and felt the unmistakable mound of a child there. His heart hammered in his chest as his eyes lifted to Jo.

"So, now you know," Jo said coldly.

Dawning realization washed over him. That was why Jo had punched him in the face that day. Why hadn't True told him? He looked at Shyfawn for answers, but she only shook her head. She managed to get to her feet with Jo's help. She swayed slightly and Jo steadied her. When Jo was sure Shyfawn would be all right, she went to pick up Tim, who was still fussing.

"This is between the three of you," Shyfawn said simply and headed for the door. "We'll wait in the other room." When Jo hesitated, still glaring at Sam, Shyfawn took her by the arm and pulled her out of the room, closing the door behind them.

Sam looked at True. "The three of us." He felt his throat tighten. "Oh, True, why didn't you tell me?"

Sam pulled a chair up next to the table and placed his hand over the baby inside her. Their baby. Never in his wildest dreams had he ever thought about it happening. Hell, he should have known it would happen, he should have expected it. She was pregnant and she hadn't told him. Why? It didn't matter, he knew now, and he was never going to let her go.

"Sam?" True's voice startled him.

He pulled his hand away and got to his feet. "I'm here."

"What happened?"

"You were shot, Shy healed you," he told her as he leaned over her and brushed her hair back.

"Shot?" True's memory slowly came back to her. Panic seized her, the baby. "Am-am I all right?"

"Yes, you're just fine."

"Thank God." She breathed a sigh of relief.

"True, why didn't you tell me?"

"Tell you what?" She held the blanket to her chest and sat up, her head spun, and she closed her eyes. "I didn't know I was going to get shot."

"Damn it, True, why did you keep it from me?" He took her hand.

Her eyes held his as he glared at her. Were those tears shining in his eyes? His big hand drifted to her tummy and covered the roundness there. She swallowed hard and lowered her eyes from him to look at his hand. He knew.

"Why didn't you tell me?" he asked softly.

True swallowed hard. "I didn't realize I was pregnant until a month ago. And I was scared," she said as tears spilled from her eyes. "I didn't know if you'd want me."

"Oh, True. I do want you." He took his hand from her stomach and brushed the tears from her cheek. "I came courting, I was wanting to do things right. I've wanted you from the beginning. The first day I met you I felt something deep inside for you." He placed his hand on her stomach again.

"I wasn't sure how you felt." She tried to get off the table and he stopped her. "You brought me back and stayed away for so long."

"True." Sam trapped her in the circle of his

arms. "You were an engaged woman that would be leaving for Charlotte in the spring."

"Sam, please." She pushed at him, but he held her tight.

"At the time I thought I was doing the right thing by staying away," he told her gently. "But the thought of you leaving to marry someone else killed me. I had to come court you, I had to try to convince you to stay. I had no idea you called off the engagement and intended to stay until yesterday."

"I couldn't very well go back and get married while I was carrying another man's child." She turned her face away.

Sam swallowed hard. "No, I don't guess you could." He felt a stab of hurt. He wanted her to stay because she wanted to be with him, not because she was ashamed to go home.

She choked back a sob. "Sam, I..." She what? Her mind was confused and her emotions were muddled. She couldn't seem to think straight. "I'm tired," she managed to say.

He took a deep breath and stroked her hair back. "You lost a lot of blood and will need rest for a few days," he told her gently. "You'll stay with me so I can keep an eye on you."

She wanted to argue but she couldn't. She only nodded as she lay back down and closed her eyes. She couldn't look at him, didn't want to see the hurt and confusion on his face.

"Your sisters will want to see you, then we'll take you to a more comfortable room," he said and moved away from her.

True nodded but didn't say anything.

**

True came awake and blinked her eyes open to look around the dark room. She shifted on the bed and her muscles protested. Shyfawn may have healed her shoulder but it still hurt like hell. She felt weak from her loss of blood and knew she needed more sleep. What had awakened her?

There was a dim light coming through the open door. True sat up with a groan and waited for her head to stop spinning. She swung her feet off the bed to the floor and nearly stepped on Marie. The little girl slept on the floor next to the bed covered up in blankets. Cody lay beside her as always. He lifted his head to look at True before he lay down again.

True felt tears spring to her eyes as she looked at the sleeping girl. Marie had been keeping watch over her. She sat there a long time just watching her sleep. She wanted to be a part of Marie's family so very badly. Sam cared for her and she knew that. He had come courting and didn't want her to leave. Why was she so scared? They were going to have a baby, and in her heart she knew they should be together. She wanted to be with him.

Very carefully she stood and stepped over Marie and the dog. She went to the hall and followed the dim lamp light down the stairs and to the dining room. She saw Sam seated at the table looking through a medical book. Her throat grew tight and his image blurred. Jesus, how she loved him. She blinked several times before she entered the room.

Sam looked up from his book. "True." He got to his feet and his eyes moved over her as she stood there in one of his shirts. "Are you all right?"

She swallowed hard. "I think so."

He let out a long breath and stepped around the table. "I've missed seeing you in my shirt."

She walked to stand in front of him. "I've missed wearing it." She also missed the way he looked at her, hunger and desire flared in his dark eyes.

Sam couldn't keep himself from reaching for her. He put an arm around her waist and drew her close as he leaned back against the table. The act made him eye level with her. He placed his free hand on their child. Jesus, he wanted this so much, but he was scared to death of losing her.

True felt tears clog her throat and placed her hands over his. Their eyes met and her tears overflowed when she saw the shine of moisture in his eyes. She brushed his hair back before trailing her fingers through it.

"I can't lose you, True," he managed to say, his voice tight.

"Sam—"

"I know you have a good life in Charlotte. You can have a good life here, too," he told her softly. "I can't let you go. Especially now." He rubbed a hand over their child. "I want a family with you."

"But—"

"Damn it, True." He stood and took her face in his hands. "When are you going to realize I love you? I want you to stay with me," he said fiercely, his thumbs caressed her cheeks as her tears escaped.

"Stay in Rimrock and be my wife."

"Oh, Sam." She dropped her head and cried into his shoulder.

Sam put his arms around her and held her as she cried. His eyes burned. After a long time, her tears slowed and she looked up at him. He blinked the beginning of tears away as she pushed his hair from his forehead and touched his face.

"Sam…" Somehow, she found her voice. "I want to stay. I want to be your wife," she said with a smile.

Sam nearly went to his knees as relief and joy washed over him. He pulled her into his arms and kissed her. She wound her arms around his neck and kissed him back. His tears mingled with hers and he didn't give a damn. He pulled back and rested his forehead against hers.

"Sam…" Her voice was a whisper. "I love you. I have for so long."

He could only stand there, his forehead pressed to hers. "You scared me there for a minute. I thought you might say no."

"That word never crossed my mind," she told him quietly.

"Daddy?"

Sam looked up to see Marie standing in the doorway with tears in her eyes. "Come here." He held an arm out for her.

Marie clung to the doorframe with one hand. "Is she staying with us?" she asked as tears spilled down her cheeks and her lip trembled.

True's tears renewed as a flood. "Yes, honey. I'm staying with you."

Marie let out a cry and ran to them. Sam lifted her and she clung to them both. Sam held them tightly. Nothing had ever felt so right. This was his family, the family he had always dreamed of. Sam held them both for a long time, feeling whole for the first time in years.

After a long time, Sam drew back and looked at his daughter. "Marie, it's late and you should be sleeping," he told her gently. "I'll put you to bed."

"True, will you tuck me in?" she asked almost desperately.

True smiled at her. "Yes, honey, I will."

Sam carried Marie to her room and lay her in bed. He pulled the blankets up over her and kissed her cheek before he stepped back. True stepped up to the bed and gently brushed a hand over Marie's hair before she bent to kiss her as well.

"I'll see you in the morning," she promised. "We have to make plans for a wedding."

Marie smiled brightly. "Are you going to be my mama?"

True felt her eyes fill with unexpected tears as emotion washed over her. She looked at Sam, not sure what to say. She didn't want him to feel like she was trying to push away the memory of Marie's real mother.

Sam gave her a small smile. "Yes, Marie," he said and looked at his daughter. "True will be your mother."

"I'm glad," she said happily as she snuggled down into her bed.

True kissed her again, whispering, "Good night."

Cody moved swiftly next to the bed, nearly tripping True, and lay down. She laughed softly and bent to pet the dog on the head and he happily flapped his tail on the floor. She then walked to Sam, who stood by the door. His dark eyes were intense as he looked at her.

"You should be in bed, too," he told her softly.

"So should you," she said, her voice unsteady.

Sam pulled the door half closed behind him before he followed her to her room. He caught her hand and turned her to face him. Without a word he pulled her close to kiss her deeply for a long time. She wound her arms around him and kissed him back just as eagerly.

He drew back to look at her. "Sleep with me tonight," he said softly.

True heard the need in his voice and nodded. She desperately wanted to sleep in his arms again. He took her hand and led her to his bedroom. He closed the door behind them and slid his arm around her waist to walk her to the bed. He pulled back the blankets for her and she slid in to lay down. She wished the lamp was lit, she wanted to watch him undress.

When Sam slid into bed beside her, she instantly went into his arms and he pulled her close. She sighed and nestled into his strong embrace, listening to his heart beat – this was where she belonged. She wanted him to make love to her, but she was still weak from the loss of blood.

She was quickly falling asleep and he seemed perfectly content to just lay there and hold her. Thoughts of sleeping with him like this for the rest of her life filled her mind as she drifted off into a peaceful sleep.

Chapter Twenty-Four

Two days passed and True was feeling remarkably better, the soreness in her shoulder was gone and her strength was back. She had never been happier in all her life while spending time in Sam's house with him and Marie. They would spend the days together and at night True would sleep in Sam's arms.

True was in Sam's small kitchen making breakfast when he came in. "Good morning," she told him as she cracked eggs into a pan.

"Yes, it is." Walking up behind her, he put his arms around her, and then kissed her neck.

She smiled and butterflies swirled in her stomach. "Is Marie up?"

"Yes, she'll be down soon." He moved to pour himself a cup of coffee. "I think last night better be the last time you stay here."

She whirled to face him as something close to panic filled her. "What?"

"For now," he said quickly, setting his cup down before gently stroking her cheek. "As much as I want you to keep staying here, you probably should go to Gussy May's. Townsfolk will consider you well enough that you shouldn't be here, and gossip will start about us."

She smiled at him. "Sam, they're going to

gossip when I have a baby in a few months."

He nodded in agreement. "Then we better get married soon."

Her heart fluttered with happiness. "How soon?"

"Is tomorrow too soon?"

She wrapped her arms around him and leaned into him as she smiled. "Not soon enough."

Sam lowered his head and kissed her gently before he drew back to look at her. "We better wait until tomorrow. I'll send someone out to let your sisters know to be here in the morning. Besides, we need to get married fast before Jo decides to kill me."

She laughed and hugged him tightly as she rested her cheek against his chest. "She won't kill you. I told her not to."

He chuckled and held her close. "That's good to hear."

***

True settled down for the night in her bed in the room at Gussy May's. She wanted to be with Sam, wrapped in his strong arms, holding her to him as he slept. Though she knew after tomorrow she would be with him every night, she still wished she was in his bed with him now.

She let out a heaving sigh and closed her eyes. Sleep took her quickly as her mind thought of her happy future with Sam and Marie.

The vision danced behind her eyes as she slept. Aleena screamed and struggled with a man in the darkness of her room. Who was he? He punched her and she fell to the floor, her body alarmingly still.

True watched as the man tied and gagged her before he left the room. Another man was creeping down the hall in the darkness, they talked in hushed voices, though True couldn't make out the words she knew something bad had happened to Gussy May.

True came awake gasping for breath as she sat up in bed and willed her frantic heart to slow down. Throwing back the covers, she left the bed and rushed for the door. She had to check on Aleena and make sure the girl was all right. She opened her door and crossed the small space to Aleena's door. She carefully opened it and peered in to see her sleeping peacefully in bed. A relieved breath left her and she closed the door silently. She went to Gussy May's door and heard the woman snoring as she slept. She was all right too.

True went back into her room and closed the door to lean back against it. Everything was fine in the house. Her dream had meant nothing. Yet, if it was in fact a vision, how long did they have before the men came? Maybe she was just over-reacting.

True couldn't shake the uneasy feeling and went about getting dressed. She would go to the sheriff… And tell him what? That she had a vision of intruders? The man would never believe her.

Sam. She would go to Sam and maybe with a man in the house the intruders wouldn't come. Yes, that's what she would do. True finished dressing and put on her boots before she swung on her coat.

She quietly went to the bedroom door and slowly opened it, not wanting anyone to hear the squeaking hinges. She stepped out into the hall and looked around. It was dark but the moon cast faint light into the room. She heard boots walk softly up the stairs and ducked back into her room. They were already in the house!

A startled cry from down the hall was cut short and True heard the sounds of a struggle before something crashed to the floor. Her heart hammered hard in her chest. She had to get help. She leaned back against the door and tried to think of what to do. She could go out the window to go for help before they realized she knew of their presence. She was on the second floor and could break a leg jumping from that height. She placed a hand over her tummy, or worse.

True had no choice but to leave her room and run down the stairs to get help. She listened, hearing the footsteps down the hall. Summoning her courage, she quietly opened the door and stepped out. A hand clamped around her throat and shoved her back against the nearest wall. The force of her hitting the wall caused the picture hanging near her to clatter to the floor. True fought for air as she struggled to get free of the hand holding her throat. His body pressed against hers to pin her to the wall and help keep her still.

"Is that her?" a man asked quietly as he came from Gussy May's room.

"I can't tell, it's too dark," the man holding True answered in a low voice.

Aleena's door flew open and she came out, no doubt to investigate the sound of the crashing picture. In an instant the man in the hall grabbed hold of her and threw her to the floor. Her scream was muffled by his hand over her mouth.

True gasped for breath as the man's hand tightened on her throat. She couldn't black out, she had to get away from him and she had to help Aleena. A match flared by her face as he struck it with his thumb. The sudden brightness hurt her eyes.

"This is the one we want," he said before snuffing out the match. "Tie that one up and gag her," he ordered.

True was about to pass out and her struggles were weakening as he choked off her oxygen. When he released her, she doubled over and gasped frantically for breath. Her reprise was short lived, for he stuffed a rag in her mouth and tied her hands behind her back.

"The old woman is taken care of," the man tying Aleena said.

Aleena screamed from behind the gag and fought the man as he tried to bind her wrists. True heard the solid sound of a fist striking flesh before Aleena went silent.

"Come on," the man shoved True ahead of him, toward the stairs.

True renewed her struggles, she had no intention of going anywhere with this man. He swore at her before he turned her and punched her on the cheek. She staggered and felt herself falling before someone lifted her and threw her over his shoulder. She lost consciousness as he carried her down the stairs and out the back door.

***

The morning sun was shining brightly as a

strong knock sounded at Sam's door. He hurried to the door and opened it to see Matthew.

"Sam, it's True. She's gone," Matthew told him.

Sam felt the air slam out of his lungs. "She left?"

"No, she was taken," Matthew quickly explained. "Shyfawn found Aleena and Gussy May tied and gagged. Someone snuck in last night and took True. I sent John to tell Jo."

"Damn. Marie is getting dressed." Sam quickly dressed in his winter gear.

"I'll stay and bring her over," Matthew told him.

"Thank you," he said and went out the door.

He ran the distance to Gussy May's and went in without knocking. "Gussy May?"

"Sam," Shyfawn called from the kitchen. "We're in here."

Sam rushed into the kitchen to see the women seated at the table. Both Aleena and Gussy May had bruised cheeks and Aleena had a cut on her forehead. Sam knelt beside Aleena and looked at the cut on her head, it was accompanied by a large bump.

"Aleena, are you all right?"

She nodded. "Yes, they just knocked me out. Aside from a headache, I'm fine."

His eyes moved to Gussy May. "Did they hurt you?" he asked, thinking the question silly. He didn't think there was anything or anyone in the world that could hurt Gussy May.

"No, they didn't hurt me," she assured him.

"Just tied and gagged me. But you'll be looking for a fella with a black eye."

Sam favored her with a slight smile. He should have known the cantankerous woman would have given the men a good fight. He focused on Aleena's cut again. She wouldn't need stitches, but she would have a good-sized lump and headache for a while.

The front door opened and the sound of boots could be heard coming into the house in a rush. Sam looked up to see Clu enter the kitchen. His dark eyes instantly went to Aleena and worry filled them. She tried to put on a brave face, but tears filled her eyes as she stood.

"Aleena, are you okay?" he asked as he moved to her, nearly knocking Sam aside to examine the cut on her head. "John told me men broke in last night and attacked everyone." He looked at Sam. "They took Miss Tucker?"

Sam nodded. "Yeah, they did."

"I'll take care of things here," Clu told him. "You better get a few men together and go after her."

"Already done," Travis said as he entered the room.

Sam looked past him to see Heck. "Where's the sheriff?"

"That drunk son of a bitch is passed out in the jail cell," he growled. "So, we locked him in," he said with slight satisfaction.

"Hell of a lot of good he is," Travis grumbled.

Clu nodded in agreement. "I think we'll be looking for a new sheriff."

"About time," Travis muttered. "He's been

worthless since the day he got here."

"Travis, Heck." Sam turned to them. "I need you two on this."

They said nothing, only nodded. Without a word they went out the back door. Their eyes intently scanning the ground and taking in everything.

Matthew put a hand on Sam's shoulder. "Don't worry, if anyone can find her, it's those two."

Sam nodded. "I know."

"Daddy?"

Sam turned to see Marie enter with Matthew. He opened his arms, beckoning to her, and she ran to him and he lifted her into his arms to hold her close.

"What happened?" she asked, her eyes swimming with tears. "Matt said True's gone."

Sam brushed her hair back. "Yes, she's gone. Someone took her, but we'll get her back."

Tears spilled down her cheeks and she tucked her face against his neck. Sam held her and fought back his own emotions as fear and anger threatened to overwhelm him. He had a good idea of who had taken her, and he was going to kill the bastard. He looked out the window to see Heck and Travis talking. After a while Heck jogged off in the direction of the livery. Travis came back into the house, his expression sober.

"Not much to go on," he said grimly. He looked at Sam. "I'm sure it was the city fella. Found one good footprint and nobody around here would wear boots like that in this weather."

Sam nodded. "I thought as much."

"Three horses rode out," Travis told him. "One was carrying two people, so he'll tire fast. We should be able to catch them fairly quickly."

Sam nodded and shifted Marie in his arms. "Marie, honey, I need you to stay with Shyfawn."

She lifted her tear streaked face to him. "Are you going after True?"

"Yes, I am." He brushed at her tears and kissed her cheek.

Her lower lip trembled. "Bring her back, Daddy."

Sam swallowed hard. "I will, honey."

Sam set her down and she went to Shyfawn and took her hand. Sam gave them a reassuring look before he left and headed for the livery. Matthew followed him.

"Any idea's on where he might have taken her?" Matthew asked.

"I'm guessing he'll head back east with her," Sam told him. "He wasn't happy about her calling off the engagement and making him look bad."

Matthew nodded. "He's a tenderfoot so unless those two other horses belonged to guides, he won't easily find his way. You'll find her soon," he assured Sam.

"I intend to. Stay in town and keep your eyes and ears open for anything."

Matthew nodded. "I will."

The pounding of horse's hooves caused the men to stop and look at the two riders coming into town. Jack and Jo were riding in fast, the anger on Jo's face made it clear she had received the news about True being missing. Sam did not want to be on the receiving end of that anger. They pulled their horses to a halt and swung down to stand before the two men.

"We met John on the road, he was coming to tell us about True," Jack said quickly. "Is she really gone?"

Sam nodded. "Yes, we think it was Steven."

"That son of a bitch!" Jo bellowed with rage. "I'm going to kill him."

"Get in line," Sam said as his own anger surfaced. He looked at Jack. "I could use your help in going after her."

Jack nodded without hesitation. "You got it."

"I'm coming, too. She's my sister and I'll be damned if I sit and do nothing." Jo turned to her horse.

"Jo, wait," Jack said as he caught her by the arm. "You can't go," he demanded, looking down at her.

"The hell I'm not." She glared at him, refusing to back down.

"We can handle it," he told her firmly. "You're not going."

"Damn it, I'm going."

Jack shook his head. "You're staying here."

"She's my sister," Jo snapped.

"I don't care, you can't go!"

"Why the hell not?"

"Because you're pregnant!"

"I don't care, I'm still…" She stared at him, her anger fading into confusion. "I'm what?"

Sam and Matthew shared a look of surprise.

A long breath left Jack. "You're pregnant, Jo."

Jo shook her head. "No, I'm not."

He nodded. "Think about it. Two months."

Jo appeared to be thinking and her eyes went wide as realization hit her. She stared at him, at a complete loss for words. Sam figured that had to be a first for her. In the many years he had known Jo, never once had he seen her speechless.

Jack smiled at her. "We're going to finally have a family and I'm not going to risk anything happening to you."

Jo continued to stare in stunned silence at Jack for a long time. He laughed and after a moment she smiled as she threw her arms around Jack to hug him tightly. Sam jerked his head in the direction of the livery and Matthew followed him. The couple needed a moment for themselves.

Matthew chuckled as they walked. "I'm happy for them, but can you imagine Jo as a mother?"

Sam smiled. "She just might surprise us."

"Her kids will be shooting and throwing knives by the time they are three," Matthew teased.

Sam couldn't disagree with Matthew's thinking. If they had a son, he would be well prepared and skilled for anything life threw at him. If they had a daughter, she would be anything but ladylike. Sam was happy for his friends and pleased that their children would grow up together. He sent up a silent prayer for True and their baby and vowed to bring them home.

They entered the livery to see Travis and Heck waiting patiently for him. Sam moved to his horse, thankful that Heck had saddled him to save time. Damn it, why did this have to happen? He should have done more than just punch Steven and suddenly wished Jo had killed the bastard.

Heck swung up on his horse. "I'm guessing that city fella has a hell of a lead on us and someone is guiding him."

"He about has to," Travis said. "There's no way that tenderfoot could do this on his own. He's hired someone to take her and guide them out of the area."

Sam nodded. "Travis, you and Heck see if you can follow the trail he made as far as you can. Hopefully the snow hasn't wiped it out completely. Jack and I'll head for Miller's Crossing. They'll have to stop there to rest the horses and with any luck we'll catch them there."

Travis moved to his grey and hoisted himself into the saddle. "If we lose the trail we'll head for Miller's Crossing."

"If you come across them, be careful," Sam warned.

"You bet." Travis turned to Heck. "Come on, Winkey, we get to find dimples in the snow."

"Ten dollars says you lose the trail and I won't."

"You're on." Travis smiled, and they rode out.

Sam growled in frustration. "I wish they'd take this seriously."

Matthew chuckled. "They are. They usually bet five and have a wrestling match about it before heading out. They're dead serious about this."

Sam shook his head and mounted his horse. He had been away from the ranch too long. He had known Travis and Heck for years. The two were great friends and worked flawlessly as a team. If they found True, he knew she would be safe. They might act like children most of the time, but when they were on a mission to help someone, they were all business.

"Just relax," Matthew told him. "They know what they're doing."

"I know, but I'm still damn worried." He looked at his friend. "Take good care of Marie."

He nodded. "You know we will."

Jack rode up and grinned at them.

Sam chuckled. "Congratulations."

"Thanks, Jo's still pretty shocked about it," he told them. "But she's happy. I'll admit, I've been wanting a family for quite a while."

"You'll have it," Matthew assured him. "Ride careful and get everyone home in one piece."

Jack and Sam nodded and galloped out of town toward Miller's Crossing. Steven had a good lead and Sam hoped they would catch the bastard soon. If he hurt True in any way, Sam was going to make sure the man died slowly and painfully.

Chapter Twenty-Five

True came awake with a pounding head and an aching body. She discovered her hands were bound behind her back. She lay on her side and cold air bit at her cheeks. *What is happening?*

"Are you finally going to wake up?" a man asked. His voice was very familiar.

"Steven?" she whispered and forced her eyes open.

True blinked rapidly against the bright sunlight and looked around to see Steven walking toward her. What was he doing there? What had he done? She forced herself into a sitting position and he squatted down before her. His eyes were cold and he had a triumphant smirk on his mouth.

"Steven, what's going on?" she asked as she looked around the small camp to see two other men saddling four horses.

He sighed heavily. "I'm afraid I can't go back to Charlotte without you," he said flatly. "I've made too many plans to have them spoiled now."

She was utterly confused. "Plans? What are you talking about?"

"Our plans, my dear," he said sweetly. "We're getting married and we'll be the toast of society. With my fortune and your aunt's fortune, we'll be living great.

She stared at him in disbelief. "Don't you dare try to swindle Aunt Molly out of her money."

"I'm not going to, you are."

"I won't and I'm not marrying you," she stated in a confident voice.

He gave her a sympathetic smile. "You're just not thinking clearly. Once you're back home you'll change your mind, and everything will be just like it was."

"I don't love you," she snapped. "I love Sam."

Steven's eyes hardened. "Forget about him, you'll never see him again."

"We're ready when you are," one of the men said as he walked toward them.

True looked up at the man and her heart leaped with fear. She knew this man. She cast a look at the other man waiting with the horses. Jesus, they were the men that had shot Toby.

"Steven, what are you doing with these men?" she demanded. "They're bandits."

He smiled at her. "I know. I needed someone to guide me to Rimrock from Ft. William. Luckily for me, these two gentlemen were available. When you refused to come back with me, they agreed to force you to come along."

"For a sizable price," the man said with a wicked grin, showing several missing teeth, with the rest discolored and rotting. "Don't be forgettin' that."

Steven spared him a glare as he stood. "How can I? You continually remind me."

Steven reached down and grabbed her arms to pull her to her feet. It took her a moment to get her legs to work and the pounding in her head threatened to make her black out. She wasn't sure which man had hit her, but she had no doubt she had a bruise on her jaw. She had no choice but to go with Steven as he pulled her toward the horses.

"Steven you can't do this," she protested.

"I can and I will," he snapped and stopped beside a horse. "Get on."

"I can't with my hands tied," she told him, hoping he would untie her and she might have a chance to escape.

Steven gestured to the two men and they roughly hoisted her up into the saddle. Tears of frustration burned her eyes and she lashed out with a foot to kick one of them men in the chest.

He swore at her and backed away. "Don't make this harder than it has to be."

"Go to hell," she choked out as she tried not to cry.

"Let's go," Steven said as he mounted his horse.

True blinked back her tears as she watched the two bandits mount their horses and lead the way. Steven took the reins of her mount to lead it as they rode farther away from Rimrock.

Sam would know she was missing by now and would be out looking for her. She only hoped he got to her before Steven could take her away forever. She had a feeling Sam would follow them all the way to Charlotte to get her back.

***

"We need to rest the horses," one of the bandits said as he pulled his horse to a halt.

"We'll rest them tonight, Richard," Steven snapped.

The man glared at him as he dismounted. "We rest them for a while now or they won't be worth a damn the rest of the day."

Steven swore and dismounted. "This is taking too long."

He stepped up to True's horse and roughly pulled her from the saddle. She cried out and somehow managed to get her legs under her before she fell. Steven pulled her along and shoved her down onto a dry patch of ground beneath a tree. She supposed she should be grateful for that, a foot over and she would have landed in the snow.

She glared up at her ex-fiancé. "Why are you going through all this trouble to take me back?"

"Because no Edwards has ever been refused by a woman," he informed her. "And I will not be the first."

Tears of frustration stung her eyes. "I don't love you."

"It doesn't matter. People in Charlotte don't know the truth about you. They still believe you to be the daughter of a Duchess." His voice was harsh. "And it will stay that way. Being married to you will give me a great deal of influence in society."

"Stuff society," she spat. "Steven, your plans are all useless," she informed him. "I've been with Sam and I'm pregnant."

Steven stared at her, his expression one of angry shock. "What?" The word was low and precise.

She had to swallow hard and she wished her

hands were free to cover her tummy. "I'm pregnant," she told him, her voice unsteady. "With Sam's baby."

Without warning he lashed out and slapped her hard. She cried out and nearly toppled over at the force of it. When she looked at him, she saw pure rage on his face and fear for both herself and her child made her heart pound frantically.

"You damn whore!" he bellowed and hit her again.

This time lights danced behind her eyes and she fell over into the snow. The cold against her face helped to keep her from blacking out. She lay stunned for a moment as she listened to Steven rant and rave. This was a side of him she had never seen before. Steven had always been too cool and collected for her liking. She knew one day, after they married, the real man behind the businessman façade would come out.

"How could you do this to me?" he demanded as he grabbed her hair and pulled her to a sitting position again.

She had to blink her eyes several times to keep the black spots at bay. "Because I love Sam. Not you."

"This changes nothing," he growled, his face inches from hers as his hand tightened in her hair. "You're still coming with me and if you put up any kind of fight," a cold smile curled his lips, "I'll make sure you never have that baby."

Her eyes widened with horror at the meaning of his words. Steven would more than likely beat her until she miscarried or take her to a doctor to terminate the pregnancy. She had no choice but to go with him. If she wanted to keep Sam's child alive, she would have to do what Steven said.

He released her with a shove and stepped back. "Now, I believe it's time we had something to eat."

True stared at him as he instantly changed back into the sophisticated businessman she had always known. The transformation was eerie, and she could only draw one conclusion from it: Steven was crazy as hell. She and her baby might be trapped with this mad man for weeks to come. She closed her eyes and whispered a silent prayer that Sam would find her in time to save them both.

***

"What do you think?" Jack asked as they looked down the hill at the cabin and corrals of Miller's Crossing.

Sam let out a long breath. "We can't just walk in there, he knows us. Somehow we have to figure out if they're in there or not."

"Looks like we wait and watch," Jack said and crouched down next to a tree.

Sam fetched his canteen from his horse, crouched next to Jack and took a long drink. Jack handed him a piece of jerky. They were in for a long wait.

"We'll get her, Sam," Jack said after a long while.

"We better," he said softly. "I'm not sure I'll survive if we don't. I can't lose her, Jack."

"You're not going to lose her," Jack said firmly. "We won't let anything happen to her." He chuckled. "You found someone who can finally put up with you, we're not about to let her get away."

Sam couldn't help but smile. "Yeah, I'm glad she can put up with me because I'm head over heels for her."

"Really? Couldn't tell," Jack teased.

Sam gave him a look. "You have no room to talk."

"I know, I fell for Jo the first time I saw her," Jack confessed with a smile. "She was threatening my life at the time, but I knew she'd catch onto my charms and I'd win her over."

"There's something about those Tucker women," Sam said with a smile.

"Yep, we all fell hard and fast," Jack agreed.

"I didn't know it was possible to love someone so deeply," Sam said after a moment. "I mean, I barely knew her, and at times I wanted to choke her, but I..." He looked at Jack. "I can't really explain it. I liked being with her, I wanted her, and I fell in love with her. It all happened so fast."

Jack nodded. "That's how it was with Jo."

Sam was quiet for a moment as he thought. "I knew Piper for years and I loved her very much, but with True it's different."

Jack met his eyes. "You and Piper were practically kids when you got married. A man changes in six years."

He nodded. "I guess I have. I loved Piper but True is my life and Marie loves her so much. We can't lose her."

Jack clamped a hand Sam's shoulder. "You won't."

Sam caught a flash from the corner of his eye.

"What was that?"

Jack's grey eyes scanned the hill behind the cabin. There was another flash. "Travis." Jack pulled out a silver whiskey flask from his coat pocket and caught the sun with it.

"Holding out on me," Sam teased. "I could use a good drink."

Jack chuckled. "We'll need it more when this is over."

Sam watched the flashes of light across the valley. "What's he saying?"

"I have no idea," Jack told him and sent a couple flashes back.

Sam groaned. "We're in trouble."

"We'll wait here," Jack said as he took a drink and handed the flask to Sam. "Travis and Heck will go in."

Sam took a long pull and gave the flask back. The whiskey felt good as it burned down his throat and warmed his stomach. Sam stood as he saw Heck ride out of the trees toward the cabin. He saw Travis on foot coming down the hill to the back of the building.

Jack stood. "When Heck goes inside, we'll ride down. He'll keep them distracted."

Sam nodded, he hoped whatever plan Travis and Heck had was going to work. He was putting his family in their hands. Heck stopped his horse before the cabin and swung down, he looped the reins over the hitch rail and stepped up to the door. He knocked. A moment later, the door opened and he disappeared inside.

"Where'd Travis go?" Sam asked as he

searched the area for his friend.

"Corral," Jack said simply.

Sam looked to the corral and saw Travis in with the horses, looking them over. Three of the horses looked like they had been ridden hard and he was sure True and Steven were in the cabin. Travis left the corral and disappeared into the barn.

Sam saw Heck at the door of the cabin. He waved them down. "Son of a bitch," he growled. "She's not there."

Sam and Jack mounted their horses and rode down the hill to the cabin. They saw Travis come out of the barn. They pulled their horses to a halt in front of Heck.

"Where is she?" Sam asked.

"Gone," Heck explained. "They were here. Miller said that they traded their horses for fresh mounts and rode out hours ago." Heck pointed down the road. "Said they headed east."

"Was she okay?" Sam asked, fear and anger hitting him hard.

"Miller said she had a bruise on her face and looked scared."

"They rode those horses hard to get here," Travis said as he joined the group. "They have fresh horses and are hours ahead of us."

"Damn," Sam grumbled as he checked the sun. "And it will be dark soon. You won't be able to track them."

Jack let out a long breath. "Maybe I should have let Jo come after all. She can track at night."

"We'll find them," Travis told them before he let out a shrill whistle. "There aren't many places they can go. They'll camp tonight and more than likely head for Ft. William, we'll catch them there for sure."

Sam looked when he heard the pounding of horse hooves. Travis's grey horse galloped down the hill toward them. He watched as the animal came to a halt beside Travis and nudged him with his nose.

Travis absently reached out to stroke the horse's neck. "We'll find them," he told Sam confidently before he took hold of the reins and swung up onto his horse.

When everyone was mounted, they headed east, away from Miller's Crossing. Heck picked up the trail and they followed at a steady pace, not wanting to tire the horses. They would be lucky if they caught up with Steven before Ft. William.

Chapter Twenty-Six

True flexed her cold fingers before she tucked them inside the sleeves of her coat. At least Steven hadn't tied her hands today. He still led her mount, but maybe one day he would let her have the reins and she could attempt an escape. No, she couldn't risk his wrath if he caught her again. Not to mention his helpers were far more competent and would capture her in no time.

True glared at the backs of the two men that rode ahead of her. She never thought she would see the two bandits again and she wished that they had indeed left the country. Not that it really mattered, Steven would have found some other low life to do his dirty work for a price.

"Steven, I can't believe you hired these men to help you," she told him softly as he rode beside her, not wanting the other two men to hear her. "They are scoundrels."

Steven smiled at her. "I know. I ran across Richard and Chuck in Ft. William. They know the country and I needed a guide to help me get to Rimrock. Now they'll help us get back to Ft. William and keep heading east," Steven informed her.

She glared at him. "You shouldn't have taken me, Steven. I don't want to be with you."

He leaned toward her. "That's too bad for you and I'm not giving you a choice. I could never show my face in society again if I was jilted by the daughter of a Duchess."

"I'm the daughter of a whore," she reminded him.

"Nobody but the two of us know that."

"I'll tell everyone the truth," she challenged. "To hell with your society."

He gave her a cruel smile. "You'll keep your mouth shut if you want that precious baby."

True swallowed hard and covered her belly with her hands. "You're a bastard."

"Maybe so," he said casually.

"You're also mighty brave with guns to back you up," she informed him.

"I get what I want. No matter what I must do to make it happen," he said coldly, then thought for a moment. "I believe Molly knows the truth about you as well." He gave her a malicious grin. "You wouldn't want anything to happen to her, now would you?"

True felt her face pale. Steven was cruel enough to do just that. Damn him. She would have to bide her time and go along with Steven's insane plan, for now – until Sam came for her.

True closed her eyes and kept her hands over her tummy. *Please hurry, Sam.*

"You'll do as I tell you, if you want to keep Molly alive," Steven told her flatly. "You'll be my wife and nobody will ever know the truth."

True looked at him and tears fill her eyes. He was right. If she wanted to keep Molly and her baby

alive, she would have to go along with this charade.
Her baby. What would happen after the baby was
born? She knew Steven wouldn't let her keep the
baby. True fought hard not to cry as she desperately
tried to think of a way out of her situation.

"We're here," Chuck said and pulled his horse
to a stop. "There." He pointed to a cluster of
buildings in the distance.

"About time," Steven grumbled as he shifted in
the saddle.

True looked at Ft. William and her heart sank.
From here they would head east and be back in
Charlotte in a few weeks. Her life was going to be
complete hell with Steven, but she would find a way
to get away from him and back to Sam.

***

Sam stood with Jack and Heck on the bluff
overlooking Ft. William, a bustling little settlement
thriving on the fur trade, and waited for Travis to
return. He had ridden in to look around and find out
if True was in fact there. They had trailed Steven
and his cohorts here. Sam was anxious to get True
back, but he couldn't chance being careless.

"Here he comes," Heck said, his eye focused
on a rider leaving the settlement.

Sam watched as Travis's horse loped down the
road before branching off at the edge of the bluff.
His horse took the steep trail easily and Travis
pulled him to a halt before the group in moments.

"She's here," he told them.

"Is she all right?" Sam asked.

"I don't know," he said with a shrug. "Didn't
see her. But they're staying with a woman named

Ma Beasley."

Sam swore softly. "If they intend to leave town they'll have to go to the livery for their horses."

Jack thought. "We could catch them there. More cover, less people."

Sam nodded in agreement. "Travis and I'll go inside the livery, Jack you stay close and keep your rifle ready. Heck find her, follow her, and don't let her out of your sight."

"Sure thing," Heck said with a nod.

"Wait," Travis protested. "You're sending the fella with one eye to watch things." He grinned at Heck. "Can you handle it, Winkey?"

"Better than you could," Heck informed him. "You'd get distracted by the first pretty girl you see and mess everything up."

Travis looked at him for a moment. "You're right."

Sam couldn't help but chuckle. "Travis, since when did you turn into a lady's man?"

"I haven't – yet." He grinned. "But I'm still gonna try."

Sam shook his head. "Let's go."

The men mounted and went to their positions. Sam and Travis skirted the settlement and came up on the back side of the livery. He sent up a silent prayer that this worked.

***

True followed Steven into the small log building that served as a café and sat down at the table with him and the other two men. It had taken everything she had to leave Ma Beasley's this morning with Steven. She wanted to stay with the woman, but she didn't want to risk Ma Beasley getting hurt. She was thankful that the woman hadn't let Steven sleep with her, knowing that they weren't married yet. Unfortunately, True had slept in a room without a window and Richard was across the hall watching her door. There was no chance of escape.

Looking around the tiny café, True saw that the other patrons having breakfast were mostly trappers. It was still too early in the year for the wagon trains and settlers.

"Good morning," a woman said as she approached with four cups and a pot of coffee. She set the cups down and filled them. "You all want a breakfast plate?"

"Yes, please," Steven told her.

She nodded and walked away with the pot.

True sat patiently and said nothing as they waited for their food to arrive. She wasn't hungry but she knew she had to eat to keep up her strength. When the plate of eggs, salt pork, and biscuits arrived, she began to eat.

She ignored Steven and the other two men as they talked about their travel plans for the day. She focused on her food and occasionally looked up to observe the people in the café. Milly's café was far nicer, but at least this was a place to get good food. She supposed frontier people weren't too picky.

The door opened and she looked up and her eyes widened as she stared at who had entered.

Heck! He gave his head a slight shake and sat at a table facing them.

Steven frowned. "What is it?" He looked

behind him.

"Nothing," she managed to say. "That man had a patch on his eye. It just startled me for a moment. He looks dangerous." That was a lie, Heck looked anything but dangerous.

Steven grunted and went back to his meal. "Eat up, I want to head out as soon as possible. The sooner I get home the better off we'll all be."

Richard gave him a stern look. "Don't forget you promised more money when we get to St. Joe."

"And you'll get your money," Steven snapped.

"Good," Richard said coldly.

"Hurry up," Steven ordered her. "We need to get going."

True focused on finishing her meal, doing her very best to keep from looking at Heck. The last thing she wanted was for Steven to get suspicious. If the man had any idea she knew Heck, it could put her friend in danger.

Steven paid for their meal before grabbing her by the arm and pulling her to her feet. She had no choice but to follow. He kept a tight hold on her and headed for the door. She cast a look at Heck, but he was talking to the waitress as she poured him a cup of coffee.

True braced herself for the cold as they left the café. Much to her surprise the day was tolerable. Riding today wouldn't be as miserable as yesterday, because she knew she would be riding home with Sam.

As they made their way to the livery, she saw Heck leave the café and cross the street. Her heart pounded with anticipation.

Steven entered the livery and lead the way down the row of stalls. She saw the grey that belonged to Travis in a stall and hope leaped inside her. There was no doubt she would be rescued.

Then came the ominous sound of guns being cocked.

The men froze.

"Hands away from your guns, gentlemen," Travis said as he stepped from a stall, his rifle up and pointed at Richard.

"True move away from them," Sam said from behind her.

"He said hands up," Heck snapped as he entered the livery behind them, gun in hand as he moved to stand close to Travis.

True stared at the two young men in total shock, the two playful friends were gone, replaced with cold-eyed gunmen.

Shyfawn had told her about when she was rescued from the saloon and True now fully believed her sister. Heck and Travis had done a lot of killing to save Shyfawn and True had no doubt they were about to do the same to rescue her right now.

"Nobody try to run," Sam ordered as he moved to the side where Steven stood. "There's a rifle on the door, you won't make it far."

True saw Sam and tears of relief filled her eyes as she stepped away from Steven, but then she cried out as his arm snaked around her neck and he pulled her against him. He backed away keeping the three men in front of him. At the same time, Richard and Chuck went for their guns. They had barely cleared leather when Heck and Travis took them down. Each with a single shot.

"Let her go, you son of a bitch," Sam growled, lowering his gun slightly, not wanting to chance hitting True. He was a decent shot but didn't have enough confidence in his aim to try and shoot Steven as he held True in front of him.

"She's my ticket out of here," Steven told him, his voice full of anxiety. "Put your guns down and back away."

"No," Sam told him flatly.

True gasped for breath as Steven's arm tightened on her throat and he began to choke her. She was sure it wasn't intentional, but his fear of Sam was causing him to panic.

"Let her go!" Sam ordered.

"Throw your pistol down and back away!" Steven's voice was bordering a shriek.

Sam tossed his pistol down but held his ground. Steven took a step back toward the open livery door and True brought the heel of her boot into his knee. He howled with pain and his hold on her loosened enough for her to twist away.

True watched in shock as Sam closed the distance to Steven in an instant, sending a hard punch to the man's face that sent him to the ground with a thud. Dropping to a knee beside Steven, Sam grabbed the front of his coat to haul him up to send several more blows to his face.

"Sam, that's enough!" Travis shouted and rushed forward to slide his arm through Sam's on a downward swing, at the same time slamming a knee into his chest.

Sam fell back and rolled, a hand reaching for his pistol as it lay on the ground. He came up on his feet and pointed the pistol at Steven. The man lay on his back, bleeding and barely conscious.

Travis stepped up and put himself between Sam and Steven, though not foolish enough to step into the line of fire. "Back off, Sam."

"I'll kill this son of a bitch," Sam growled.

"You've never killed anyone, and I'll be damned if I let you start now," Travis snapped as he shifted his rifle slightly.

"You going to shoot me to save this piece of shit?" Sam growled.

"Just the outside of your calf. No major damage but you might have a limp," he said casually.

"Travis, no," True begged.

He ignored her. "Drop your gun."

"No!"

"He's unarmed, and it would be murder."

"I don't care!"

"You better," Travis said harshly. "Think of Marie, of True and that baby."

Sam blinked as he looked at Travis. "How did you know?"

Travis grinned. "She's starting to show, so you better hurry up and marry her."

Heck stepped up to Steven and pulled him to his feet. "Come on. You're going to jail."

Steven groaned and swayed for a moment, blood pouring from his nose and mouth. He glared at True as he spit blood onto the ground.

True let out a breath of relief and went to Sam, who holstered his pistol and opened his arms to her.

She was almost to him when Steven lunged, knocking Heck aside. There was a flash of a knife as he came at True. Sam grabbed her, shielding her with his body as he turned his back to Steven. Two guns thundered in the room then all was silent.

"Nice shot," Travis said.

True looked around Sam to see Steven sprawled back on the ground, a hole in his chest and one in his head. She swallowed bile that threatened and clung to Sam. His breath hissed out and she felt hot liquid on her hand. She lifted her hand to see blood and her heart nearly stopped.

"Sam!" True cried and pushed back to find the wound.

"I'm fine," he assured her.

"You're bleeding," she gasped as she moved his coat aside and saw blood soaking his side.

Travis stepped up and looked over the wound. "Just a scratch," he said casually, though he handed his rifle to Heck as he removed Sam's coat and pulled off his neckerchief. "Heck, help True cut strips from her petticoat."

Without a word Heck moved to True. He leaned the rifle against a stall and pulled out his knife. She squawked as he lifted her dress and cut away a section of petticoat.

"Heck don't you be getting that familiar with my woman," Sam teased, biting back a groan as Travis pressed the neckerchief hard on the wound. "Easy, Travis," he hissed.

"You're bleeding like a stuck hog," he grumbled. "You'll need stitches." He grinned at Sam. "That's gonna be fun."

"You aren't going to stitch me up," Sam informed him.

"I'm just returning the favor. Remember all the stitches you put in me?" He took the petticoat from Heck and said, "Get another section."

"It was your own fault," Sam grumbled. "You shouldn't have been playing with that mountain lion."

True lifted her dress to allow Heck to cut another section. "What're you going to do?" she asked.

Travis removed his blood-soaked neckerchief and folded the petticoat to place over the wound. "Gotta bind it until we can get him stitched up."

Heck wound the strip of petticoat around Sam's waist and tied it off. He stepped back and admired their work. "We may not be doctors, but it will do."

Sam chuckled and winced in pain. "I don't know what's worse, the cut or the two of you trying to help me."

True stood and watched the friends banter. They were making light of the situation, but she was worried. The blood quickly soaked the white cloth of the petticoat. They had to get him somewhere they could care for the wound.

"What about him?" Heck asked and jerked his head to Steven's body.

Travis studied Steven for a moment. "I don't think a bandage will help him any." He gave Heck a grin. "Leave him lay, he ain't going anyplace."

"Guess not," Heck agreed.

Jack appeared in the doorway, he looked around at the bodies. "Looks like you two handled everything the usual way."

Travis and Heck grinned, and then shrugged simultaneously.

Chapter Twenty-Seven

True stood with Sam as they watched their friends and family laugh and dance. She watched as Jack twirled Jo around the dancefloor with a smile on her face of pure happiness. True slid her arm around Sam's waist and leaned into him. He pressed a kiss on the top of her head and she smiled. The entire town had turned out to celebrate their wedding and the day couldn't have been more perfect.

"What are you thinking?" he asked softly.

She smiled and looked up at him. "That I've never been happier in my entire life."

He returned her smile and lowered his head to kiss her. "I feel the same."

"Hey, you two, save that for later," Matthew teased as he approached with Shyfawn, Tim cradled in her arms.

Sam laughed. True felt herself blush and turned her focus to the dancers. Milly and Gussy May, as well as many other women in town, had provided food for their party. Clu had cleaned out his freight warehouse to hold the event. Aleena rushed around helping Milly with the food.

True had been so relieved to know that Aleena and Gussy May were all right after their incident with the bandits.

"Hell of a party," Travis said.

"That it is," Heck agreed as he moved to stand beside Travis.

"Folks need to get married more often," Travis pointed out. "It's fun."

True laughed and looked at him. "Maybe you're next."

Heck snorted and laughed uproariously at that. Travis scowled and elbowed him in the ribs. Heck grunted and staggered back a little, his laugh turning into a breathless chuckle.

"What are you laughing at? You'll probably get married first," Travis informed him.

Heck's laughter stopped. "No, I'm too young to get married."

"I've seen you eye-balling Melissa Perkins," Travis teased.

Heck glared at him. "I've seen you looking at Aleena."

Travis shook his head. "She has her heart set on someone in particular and it's not me."

Heck stared at him in confusion. "Who is it?"

"None of your business."

"That's enough you two," Shyfawn intervened with a laugh.

"There you are," a man said, and they turned to see Clu Bodine walking toward them. "Congratulations again," he said as he shook Sam's hand. "I hope everything is to your liking." He gestured around the large room.

True smiled at him. "It's perfect, thank you."

His eyes moved to Heck and Travis. "I'd like to have a few words with you."

"He did it," they said in unison, each pointing to the other.

Clu laughed and shook his head. "No, I have a job offer for the two of you."

"Job?" they said and grinned.

"I'd like to offer you the job of Sheriff and Deputy."

Travis and Heck exchanged looks. Travis turned to Clu. "We already have a job."

He nodded. "I know… and Matt will be mad as hell at me for taking you away. This town needs some honest, sober, and dependable law. In all honesty, the two of you are the only men around here that can get the job done."

"Ain't we kinda young for that job?" Heck asked. "We don't really know our age but it's probably in the neighborhood of twenty."

"Doesn't matter to the town," Clu stated.

"I don't know…" Travis looked at Matthew for a little guidance.

Matthew smiled. "I'd hate to lose my right and left hands, but the decision is yours. I think you'd be damn good at it."

Travis shook his head. "But we can't—"

"The two of you have helped more people out of scrapes than anyone else I know," Matthew said.

Clu chimed in, saying, "You guys are the first ones we go to when we need help. You're each dead shots and the best trackers I know. Like it or not the town needs you."

They were quiet for a long time before Heck turned to look at Travis. "What do you think?"

He thought about it for a moment. "We might

as well. We've been doing the Sheriff's job for years already."

"That may be so," Heck agreed.

"But you get the Deputy badge." Travis playfully punched Heck on the shoulder. "I get to be the Sheriff." He looked at Matthew. "You would be all right with this?"

Matthew nodded. "Yes, I agree with Clu."

Shyfawn sniffed and had tears in her eyes. "You boys be careful."

Heck grinned at her. "You know us."

"Yes, I do. Be careful," she teased even as tears trailed down her cheeks.

True knew her sister would miss the two young men, but from what she had seen, they could easily handle the job Clu offered. She also knew they were good, honest men. Travis had kept Sam from killing Steven, because he knew it would have been murder, and Travis and Heck had only killed Steven when he intended to use the knife. True knew she would feel safe with them looking after the town.

"Our town's growing and we need honest law and order," Clu told them.

"We'll do it," Travis offered his hand to Clu, who shook it firmly.

"Glad to hear it," he said, shaking Heck's hand. "Now enough business talk, let's enjoy the party."

Travis frowned as he thought. "I suppose we'll have to live in town now."

Clu laughed. "Yes, I'm sure you'll survive." He turned and made his way through the crowd of people.

"I'm sure Gussy May would love to have you,"

True teased, thinking of the cranky woman.

Heck cringed. "I hope it won't be a long-term thing."

Travis laughed and patted him on the back. "You'll survive."

"Maybe you could stay with us for a little while," True suggested and looked at Sam.

He shrugged. "As long as it's not a long-term thing, we don't need four kids to look after," he teased.

Travis shook his head. "Naw, I wouldn't want to intrude on the newlyweds. I'm sure there won't be a lot of sleeping going on and I'd hate to be kept awake all night from the noise." He winked at Sam and hurried away before Sam could retaliate.

True felt herself blush as Heck laughed and followed Travis. She had a feeling Travis was right, now that they were married there was nothing to keep them apart at night.

Sam chuckled and pressed a kiss to her temple. "He's right. Think we'd be missed if we left now?"

She smiled and looked up at him. "Probably."

"Go on," Shyfawn told them. "We'll look after Marie for a few days to give you privacy."

True liked the idea but wasn't sure how Marie would feel about it. "I'm not sure Marie will go for that. She's anxious for us to be a family and will probably want to stay at home."

"I'll just tell her that Travis and Heck are moving to town and she needs to help them pack," Shyfawn said simply. "She'll go for that."

Sam laughed. "She's right."

True bit her lip as excitement raced through her

and looked at Sam. "Let's go."

He didn't argue, but she knew he wouldn't. She took his hand and they hurried toward the door. They left the warehouse without being spotted and rushed down the street to Sam's house. Their house. The house they were going to raise their family in.

When they reached the porch Sam opened the door, but before she could go in, he scooped her up in his arms. She laughed as he carried her inside and kicked the door closed behind them. She reached down and slid the lock into place before he carried her up the stairs to his room. Their room. She laughed as he deposited her on the bed and moved over her.

"Today was perfect," Sam told her as he smiled down at her. "And now I get to spend forever with you – without fear of Jo wanting to kill me for having my way with you."

True laughed. "Yes, you're safe now."

Sam lowered his head to kiss her gently, but the kiss soon turned urgent and passionate. True's heart was filled with love and happiness knowing that she and Sam would spend many years together making passionate love.

"I love you, True," he whispered against her mouth.

"And I love you," she said as she caressed his face. "I knew when we were together in the cabin that we were meant for each other, even though I was afraid of how much it would change my life."

He looked steadily into her eyes. "I'm glad you felt that way about me, because I wasn't going to let you leave. I need you and Marie needs you."

She blinked back tears. "And I need you and Marie."

He smiled at her and kissed her again before grabbing her and rolling to his back, pulling her on top of him. She braced herself over him and kissed him as his fingers worked with the buttons on her bodice. She knew that tonight was going to be filled with endless passion, just like many nights to come.

***

True stood on the hill behind the small town she had come to call home and smiled as she watched Marie and Cody play in the spring flowers. She placed a hand on her pregnant belly and felt Sam move up behind her to slide his arms around her and rest his hands on their baby.

"Are you feeling all right?" he asked as he nuzzled her neck.

She leaned back into him and felt her chest swell with love. "I feel great," she told him honestly. "I'm huge, hungry, moody, and uncomfortable, but I've never been better."

He laughed softly and turned her in his arms. "You forgot beautiful, amazing, and in love with a dashing doctor."

She smiled brightly. "I could never forget that I love you."

He lowered his mouth to hers and gave her a long sensual kiss. She moaned and leaned into him as her arms went around him. At that moment the baby decided to kick and her moan turned into a grumble. She drew back and placed a hand over her restless child.

Sam laughed and put a big hand on her tummy.

"This one is going to be a handful."

She nodded and let out a long breath. "Yes, he is."

"He?" Sam lifted his free hand to brush her hair back. "Are you so sure?" He looked at Marie. "I don't think another daughter would be too bad."

"Don't worry, you'll get a couple more girls, too," she said, then bit her lip. Damn, she never intended to tell him.

He looked at her and his brows drew together. "Let's not get ahead of ourselves. Let's start with this one and…" His voice trailed off as he took in her expression. "What is it?"

She debated whether to tell him for a moment, but she wanted no secrets between them. "I-I had a vision a while ago. This baby will be a boy."

He smiled and the breath left him in a rush. "Are you sure it was a vision and not a dream?"

She shrugged. "I'm pretty sure it was a vision."

"Will he be able to have visions as well?" he asked, as he caressed her cheek.

She shook her head slightly. "I don't think so. The gifts we have pass from mother to daughter." She bit her lip for a moment. "So, our two daughters will more than likely have visions."

He stared at her. "We're going to have a son and two daughters?"

She shook her head. "We're going to have three sons."

He appeared to have trouble breathing for a moment before he took her face in his hands and kissed her soundly. She was pretty sure he was feeling relieved in knowing she'd give him the children he longed for and would come through the births alive and well. She had no doubt that his fear of losing her in childbirth had been gnawing at him for many months.

"I love you, True," he whispered before he kissed her again.

"Daddy," Marie said excitedly and ran to them.

He drew away from True and looked at Marie. "What is it?"

"Look," she said happily as she raised her hand to show a fist full of flowers.

Sam released True and lifted Marie to settle her on his hip as he easily held her in one arm. "They're pretty."

"Look, True." She held the flowers out for her to see.

The flowers nearly hit her in the nose and she took a moment to smell them. "They're lovely and smell nice."

Sam put his free arm around True and pulled her close. "We'll put them on the table when we get home."

"They'll be pretty. Whatcha talking about?" Marie asked casually while sniffing the flowers.

Sam looked at True and smiled. "We're trying to decide what to name your brother."

She looked at Sam and her top lip crinkled up on one side. "Huh? My brother?"

True laughed. "Yes, brother."

She shrugged. "I guess that will be fine. We should name him Adam."

"Adam." Sam nodded. "I like that."

True smiled at them. "Adam it is then."

"Good. I think I'll like having a brother," Marie told Sam. "I bet you'll like having one, too."

Sam laughed and kissed her cheek. "I think I'll like it a lot."

True watched Sam and Marie as they talked about her future brother and felt as if she might explode from happiness. All her life she had been longing for something more than she had in Charlotte. There she had been surrounded by every luxury she could possibly want, and she had been showered with attention from suitors, but she had always felt out of place.

In Rimrock she had found everything she'd been missing. She was with her sisters and surrounded by people who truly cared about her. She had a family in Sam and Marie, and that family would grow. Her life had become complete and perfect.

Sam kissed Marie on the cheek and reached for True's hand, which she took and held tightly as they walked down the hill to town. She had finally found exactly where she belonged.

To my readers,
If you enjoyed this book, please consider leaving
a review at your favorite book store.
All reviews are much appreciated.
Thank you.
T.K. Conklin

Books by T.K. Conklin

Promise of Tomorrow
Promise of Spring
Threads of Passion

Made in the USA
San Bernardino, CA
19 March 2020